George Spencer Bower

Hartley and James Mill

George Spencer Bower

Hartley and James Mill

ISBN/EAN: 9783744664431

Printed in Europe, USA, Canada, Australia, Japan

Cover: Foto ©Raphael Reischuk / pixelio.de

More available books at **www.hansebooks.com**

ENGLISH PHILOSOPHERS

HARTLEY

AND

JAMES MILL

BY

GEORGE SPENCER BOWER, B.A.

OF THE INNER TEMPLE, BARRISTER-AT-LAW; LATE SCHOLAR OF NEW
COLLEGE, OXFORD

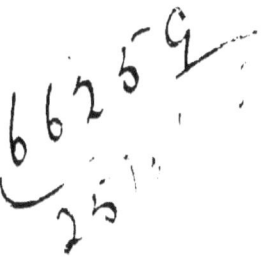

London

SAMPSON LOW, MARSTON, SEARLE, & RIVINGTON

CROWN BUILDINGS, 188, FLEET STREET

1881

LONDON:

GILBERT AND RIVINGTON, PRINTERS,

ST. JOHN'S SQUARE.

CONTENTS.

HARTLEY & JAMES MILL.

Part I.

THEIR LIVES.

CHAPTER I.

DAVID HARTLEY.

DAVID HARTLEY, the son of a clergyman residing at Armley in Yorkshire, was born on the 30th of August, 1705. He was educated at a private school, and, in 1720, entered at Jesus College, Cambridge, of which society he subsequently became a fellow. Owing to conscientious scruples with reference to the Thirty-nine Articles, he abandoned his preparation for the clerical profession, for which he was originally intended; and thenceforth applied himself to the study of medicine. Commencing practice at Newark, he afterwards removed to Bury St. Edmund's, and thence to London. In the later years of his life, he took up his residence at Bath. In the exercise of his functions as a physician, he was sympathetic, assiduous, and skilful. He especially devoted himself to the study and cure of the stone, and was the author of several medical pamphlets on Mrs. Stephens' medicine for that disease,[1] besides

---

[1] "Observations made on the persons who have taken the medicament of Mrs. Stephens," 1738. "View of the present evidence for and against Mrs. Stephens' medicine as a solvent for the stone, containing 155 cases"

B

being the instrument of finally procuring for her the reward of 5000*l.* offered by Parliament.[2] He is said to have written against Dr. Warren in defence of inoculation for smallpox; and several other of his medical disquisitions are to be found in the *Philosophical Transactions* of the time. He was twice married, and had issue by both marriages. He died on the 28th of August, 1757, at Bath, of the disease which he had so patiently investigated in his lifetime.

Both the philosophical and the moral character of Hartley were no less conspicuous in his life than in his writings. Philosophically, he was remarkable for patience of research, variety of study, thorough scientific candour, and a constant readiness to receive new impressions and ideas. Morally, he was distinguished by modesty, unaffected openness, and benevolence. In the one case, his inquisitiveness of intellect well qualified him for a writer on the connexion between body and mind, and their reciprocal influence on one another,—a kind of inquiry where alertness in the seizing of analogies is above all things requisite; in the other, his sympathy of heart was of eminent service to him in the observation and appreciation of moral phenomena.

His great work *On Man* occupied sixteen years of slow thought and toil in maturing (1730—1746); and even for some years before 1730, " the seeds of this work were lying in latent germination," as he himself used to tell his friends. One cannot fail to notice the results of this steady and persistent investigation, (extending over so long a period, and

[of which his own was one], " with some experiments and observations," 1739. " Directions for preparing and administering Mrs. Stephens' medicine in a solid form," 1746 (in the *Gentleman's Magazine*). A large ingredient in this medicine was soap, of which the unfortunate Hartley was said to have himself consumed 200 lbs. before he eventually died of the disease.

[2] *Gazette,* June, 1739.

into so many different fields), in the astonishing wealth of illustrative matter by which the principles laid down in his book are confirmed. It was first published in two volumes in 1749. Another edition by Dr. Priestley with elucidatory dissertations appeared in 1775. In this the vibration theory, and most of the Second Part on theological questions, were omitted. But the book was, notwithstanding, practically almost ignored till 1791. In 1801, Hartley's son published the entire work, in three volumes, from the German of the Rev. Dr. Herman Andrew Pistorius, rector of Poseritz, in the island of Rügen, accompanied with the latter's notes and essays.[3] Hartley himself was not at all sanguine as to the chances of the immediate acceptance of his novel theory. " He did not expect that it would meet with any general or immediate reception in the philosophical world, or even that it would be much read or understood; neither did it happen otherwise than as he had expected. But at the same time he did entertain an expectation that, at some distant period, it would become the adopted system of future philosophers. That period " [writes his son in 1801] " seems now to be approaching,"—and by this time it has arrived, and a formidable and industrious school of philosophy, known as the Association Psychology, has been constituted on the lines sketched out by him.

From a very early age, Hartley had a fancy for natural science, experimental philosophy, and mathematics, which he studied under the tuition of a celebrated man in his day, Professor Saunderson. To optics, statics, and other special departments of science, he devoted himself in company with Dr. Hales, Dr. Smith (then Master of Trinity College, Cambridge), and some other members of the Royal Society. He

---

[3] This is the edition to which the references throughout this work are made.

was a keen observer, in the exercise of his professional duties, of physical peculiarities and habits, and mental diseases and defects; and acquired early the habit of sound and rapid generalization, which proved so useful to him in the construction of his philosophical system. Historical and chronological researches also claimed a large portion of his spare time; and he was on intimate terms with N. Hooke, the Roman historian. In chronology, so far as physical science could be brought to bear on its numerous problems, as indeed in all kinds of natural science, he was an ardent admirer and disciple of Newton, whose *Principia* and other works first suggested to him the theory of vibrations. He was much interested in all schemes for the reformation of language, either as written, (e.g. methods of short-hand), or as written and spoken both; and welcomed proposals of universal and philosophical languages and dictionaries, and similar fresh ideas.

But it was to mental science, ethics, and theology that Hartley's tastes were principally drawn. In regard to these subjects, the intellectual atmosphere in which he lived was that of Edmund Law, Warburton, Butler, and Jortin, who were his intimate associates and fellow-labourers both in these fields and in that of ecclesiastical history. It was, however— as he himself acknowledges, with his usual candour—from one Mr. Gay that he derived the germ of his association theory—at all events, as applied to morals. It was only the germ, however, that he obtained; and how fruitful Gay's two short treatises became in Hartley's hands it only needs a comparison of them with the latter philosopher's second volume to show. In the latter part of his life he corresponded very much with Dr. Priestley on their common subject.

Nor did Hartley neglect the more distinctly humanizing studies of history, poetry, and art. Of the first of these means of cultivation he was especially fond. He was a great admirer of some of the poets of his own country, such as Pope, whom he respected not only as a man of genius, but also, and chiefly, because he was a poet who " moralized his song," and pursued by a different road the same goal as himself. On similar grounds he was interested in Dr. Young, and also in Hawkins Browne, the author of a Latin poem, *De Animi Immortalitate.* It must be confessed, however, that Hartley does not seem to have been a very enthusiastic lover of poetry,-except as a veil for philosophy, and that he was disposed to regard the exercise of the imagination too much in a didactical light. Owing to this latter attitude of mind, he even took offence at the *Essay on Man,* which he thought inspired by Bolingbroke, and calculated to weaken the force and inviolability of the moral law, of which—though characteristically charitable in judging individual instances of its perversion in practice—he was extremely jealous. To the " lewd" poets, who discoursed of love and beauty, entirely unmoved by the puzzles of metaphysics and morals, he felt—and frequently displayed in his works—a hearty aversion. In music he took a passionate delight.

He was also a fair classical scholar; and the first preliminary sketch of his system—a little treatise, *De Sensu, Motu, et Idearum Generatione,* which he published in the form of an appendix to a medical tractate on the stone—was written in elegant Latin. With Hebrew he seems to have been at all events moderately well acquainted.

All these varied tastes were reflected in the pages of his work, as we shall have occasion to remark below.[4] So, also,

---

[4] See Part. III. Cp. the *Life* by Hartley's son, *Observations on Man,* vol. ii. p. ix. " It was from the union of talents in the moral sciences with natural philosophy, and particularly from the professional knowledge of the human frame, that Dr. Hartley was enabled to bring into one view

was his personal character. His amiability,—no pen was ever freer from gall than his, and in the whole of his work we do not find a single harsh criticism of a personal nature, while his kindly appreciation and recognition of the labours of his precursors is abundant and marked—his openness, and his easy-going *laissez-faire* tendencies,—all these are manifest in the tone of his recorded opinions, and the style of his · writing. As his son says, "it may with peculiar propriety be said of him, that the mind was the man." His philosophical character was only his personal character in one of its aspects.

Hartley's was a quiet, useful, unromantic life,—unromantic in all respects, except in that steady devotion to truth and fact which tinges the most uneventful life with a hue of romance,—too often of pathos. Eminently typical of the century in which he lived,—comfortable, and ready to comfort others,—disposed to ponder and wait, not very prone to action, unambitious,—he was always in a mood to make allowances for the frailty of others, and to take things as they came, while he was utterly destitute of the "passion for reforming the world," which possessed James Mill. On the other hand, if his life was not lit up by such noble aims as that of his great successor, he had all the compensating advantages incidental to a lack of enthusiasm. While he was not to the same extent as Mill the cause of good to unseen masses of men, he made far more friends and intimates out of those whom he did know. The bitterness and violence, which in Mill's case were engendered by consuming earnestness, were unknown to him. No zeal could eat him up. His philosophical system was not converted by him into a dogma or

the various arguments for his extensive system, from the first rudiments of sensation through the maze of complex affections and passions in the path of life, to the final, moral end of man."

discipline; by thus having no practical reference, while it won him no partisans, it made him no enemies.

Though accurate and precise in his reasoning, and methodical in his daily habits, Hartley was far removed alike from pedantry and fussiness. He was polished and gay in society, and eloquent in conversation, without becoming importunate or a bore; and he was entirely without the vices of pride, selfishness, sensuality, or disingenuousness. In the endeavour to suggest the proper associations of ideas to the minds of others, and to form their habits on the lines, and with the help, of their position and previous circumstances, he was "the faithful disciple of his own theory." He did what some one has said should always be done by every man, whether Libertarian or, like Hartley, an advocate of the doctrines of Necessity: in actual life he regarded himself alone as free, and all other men as determined.

"His person was of the middle size and well proportioned: his complexion fair, his features regular and handsome; his countenance open, ingenuous, and animated. He was peculiarly neat in his person and attire. He was an early riser, and punctual in the employments of the day; methodical in the order and disposition of his library, papers, and writings, as the companions of his thought." [*Observations on Man* (*Life*), vol. ii., pp. xvii, xviii].

During the nine years that elapsed between the completion of his book and his death, Hartley, though reposing from active work and collection of materials in reference to it, continued to keep his mind open to any further suggestions or discoveries that might have the effect of destroying or modifying any of his doctrines. None such, however, were made of any materiality sufficient to render an alteration of his *Observations* necessary.

CHAPTER II.

JAMES MILL was born at Northwater Bridge, in the parish of Logie Pert, in the county of Angus, on the 6th of April, 1773. His father, a shoemaker, lived in one of the little two-roomed clay-built cottages, some dozen of which made up a hamlet of the parish. Industry, soberness, and piety, without any remarkable gifts of intellect, distinguished the elder James Mill in his life and vocation. The mother, Isabel Fenton, was a woman of a somewhat different stamp. She was proud—(being the daughter of a substantial farmer, who had been in very good circumstances before he joined in the Stuart rising of 1745, she probably felt her marriage to have been something of a descent, and was not slow in manifesting her feelings to her neighbours, and in domineering over their wives)—but, together with her pride, possessed some of the good qualities which usually spring out of it. She was most ambitious for her eldest son James, and soon determined to rear him to some destiny higher than his father's workshop. Her influence over her husband was successfully exerted for this purpose, for we find no record of James having ever been required by his parents to assist in his father's trade, or indeed, engage in any manual labour; while there are "emphatic assurances," as Professor Bain[1] tells us, to the

[1] *Life of James Mill, Mind,* vol. i. p. 101.

contrary. William,[2] the second son, took to the family business, but the tender hand of his mother reserved James exclusively for study. So that it must be remembered that to her pride and motherly interest we, in some degree, owe the *Analysis* and the *History of British India*.

At Montrose Academy, one of the Scotch grammar-schools, James acquired the rudiments of a good classical education, and meanwhile received kindly and constant encouragement in his studies and aspirations from the minister of his parish, Mr. Peters. At about the age of eighteen he came under the notice of Sir John Stuart, of Fettercairn, one of the Barons of the Exchequer in Scotland, a man who, though reputed in the neighbourhood to have been haughty and morose, must always command our respect for his fidelity to his young friend. By Sir John and Lady Jane Stuart's influence James Mill was sent, in the year 1790, to the University of Edinburgh, under the following circumstances :—" Some pious ladies," writes Mr. Bisset,[3] "amongst whom was Lady Jane Stuart (she was then ' Belsches'), "having established a fund for educating one or two young men for the Church, Lady Jane applied to the Rev. Mr. Foote, minister of Fettercairn, to recommend some one. Mr. Foote applied to Mr. Peters of Logie Pert, who recommended James Mill; both on account of his own abilities, and the known good character of the parents." It was a great advantage to Mill to be able to go to Edinburgh at a mature age (for a Scotch university), instead of receiving his education as a boy at Aberdeen, as, without the intervention of the Stuarts, he would in the ordinary course have been compelled to do. Being at this period destined for the Church, he was bound to frame his

---

[2] Besides the two sons there was a daughter, Mary, who was the youngest child.

[3] In the article on James Mill, in the *Encyclopædia Britannica*.

course of study accordingly. Moral philosophy in the first place was required; nor, had it not been, can we imagine Mill neglecting it, more especially as the professor and lecturer was Stewart, of whose discourses on this subject he ever afterwards spoke with the greatest enthusiasm, even declaring that their eloquence was superior to that of the most admired speeches of Pitt and Fox. He is recorded in the registers of the university as having attended the Greek, Latin, natural philosophy, and logic classes, between 1790 and 1792. There is no mention of mathematics, but it is probable that he attended this class, because of Playfair's reputation, and also because he could scarcely have otherwise begun natural philosophy and Newton's *Principia* under Robison. John Stuart Mill (*Autobiography*) supposes that he may have also studied in the medical classes at this time.

During his residence at Edinburgh James Mill became acquainted with a variety of men, who subsequently became distinguished in their different walks of life, and some of whom kept up their intimacy with him to the last. Among these were Brougham, who probably then commenced a friendship which did not terminate with his Chancellorship, Professor Wallace, Thomas M'Crie, John Leyden, Jeffrey, and Mountstuart Elphinstone.

Mill's divinity studies proper began in 1794, and lasted for four winters. Professor Bain gives a curious list of the works which he took out from the Theological Library at this period, which shows very fairly the bent of his mind. A large proportion of these are philosophical, such as Alison on *Taste*, of which he afterwards made considerable use in the *Analysis*, Cudworth's *Morality*, Smith's *Theory of Moral Sentiments* (to which he also refers in the *Analysis*), Locke, Reid, Hume, Rousseau, Bolingbroke, Ferguson, Jortin (a friend of Hartley's), and especially Plato, of whose influence (strange as it may seem) many traces are to be found in the method, and even sometimes in the tone, of his philosophy. In other departments of literature, we find him reading Rousseau's *Emile* and *Discours*, Massillon's *Sermons*, Kames's *Sketches*, Hakewell's *Apology*, Campbell on *Rhetoric*, Œuvres de Fénélon, Maupertuis, Abernethie's *Sermons*, Whitby on the *Five Points*, &c. He must, therefore, have become by this time a very fair French scholar. But one sees that divinity was not occupying a very large share of his time. However, on the 1st of February, 1797, he is introduced by Mr. Peters to the Presbytery of Brechin, with his proper certificates, to be licensed as a preacher. After the due amount of "questionary trials," probationary sermons, lectures, homilies, and the like, he is formally licensed on the 4th of October, 1798. He began to preach in the church of Logie Pert. Those who heard him said that his voice was "loud and clear," but we are told that " the generality of the hearers complained of not being able to understand him;" and we may easily imagine that his discourses were somewhat over the heads of the good people of Logie Pert. He also preached in Edinburgh, where Sir David Brewster heard him. From 1790 to 1802, Mill acted as private tutor in the Fettercairn family, (where, during the vacations of his Edinburgh course, he instructed Miss Stuart,[4] for whom he always preserved the warmest affection), and also in the family of Mr. Burnet at Aberdeen, (this tutorship he is reported to have given up, owing to an insult put upon him at a dinner-party), and in some others. The tradition as to his having been tutor to the Marquis of Tweeddale does not appear to be substantiated. These tutor-

---

[4] This was the lady who married the son of the banker, Sir William Forbes, and was the mother of a distinguished Edinburgh Professor of Natural Philosophy, James David Forbes. Sir Walter Scott was vehemently, but fruitlessly, devoted to her before her marriage.

ships were his first source of income. Meanwhile his parents were becoming somewhat reduced in circumstances. James Mill generally spent what time was spared him from his university studies and tutorial engagements at his home, of which we have the following picture by Professor Bain: "The best room of the house contained two beds along the right hand wall; in that room the mother hung up a canvas curtain ('cannas' it was called, being what is laid on the threshing-floor to keep the corn together); thus cutting off from the draught and from the gaze, the further end of the room, including James's bed, the fire, and the gable window. This was his study. . . . Here he had his book-shelves, his little round table and chair, and the gable window-sill for a temporary shelf. He had his regular pedestrian stretches; one secluded narrow glen is called 'James Mill's walk.' He avoided people on the road; and was called haughty, shy, or reserved, according to the point of view of the critic. . . . His meals were taken alone in his screened study; and were provided by his mother, expressly for his supposed needs." Certainly it cannot be said that James Mill was not appreciated by his parents, at all events by his mother. Nor did he lack sympathetic friends in David Barclay, Peters, and others, at Logie Pert, besides his little knot of associates in Edinburgh.

In the beginning of 1802 all preaching and tutorial work was given up, and James Mill went up to London in company with Sir John Stuart. Now commenced his journalistic career, into which he entered with zeal and energy. Immediately on his arrival in London we find him recounting in a letter to his Edinburgh friend, Thomas Thomson (a well-known devotee of science, and especially chemistry), his literary adventures and prospects. He was delighted with the large scope which London life afforded to an ambitious spirit, as compared with the life of his "over-cautious country-men at home," where "everybody represses you, if you but propose to step out of the beaten track." He obtained intro-ductions from Thomas Thomson to Dr. Robert Bisset, and Dr. Gifford, editor of the *Anti-Jacobin Review*. Besides this, he takes the greatest interest in politics, and often goes to the House of Commons to hear the speeches of Pitt, Fox, and Sheridan. Of the eloquence of the other members whom he heard he had the lowest possible opinion. He has an idea of starting a class of jurisprudence, and of entering one of the Inns of Court, for that purpose, but subsequently abandons it. It may be inferred that he had studied law, or at all events the philosophy of law, at Edinburgh, and had perhaps begun to study Bentham in Dumont's translation. His first few weeks in London were thus full of hopes and schemes and enthusiasm.

He soon gets into harness as a journalist. Dr. Bisset first of all tried him as an occasional writer on politics. For Dr. Gifford's *Anti-Jacobin Review* he writes his first philosophical production, a review of Belsham's *Elements of Logic and Mental Philosophy*, which is very interesting as containing an attack on Hartley's theory of vibrations, and also on the selfish theory of morals, which "imposes an obligation to be vicious, removes the moral character of the Deity, and renders it im-possible to prove a future state." An argument appears in this connexion, which seems to reflect a turning-point in the history of his religious belief. He contends that till the moral attributes of God are proved, it is useless to offer proofs of revelation. "Unless I know that God is true, how do I know that His Word is true?" Another article from his pen followed shortly after this in the same *Review*—on his friend Thomson's *System of Chemistry*.

Besides reviewing for Dr. Gifford, he is now writing articles

for the *Encyclopædia Britannica*, on which he hopes to be able
to support himself at least for a year. "I am willing to
labour hard and live penuriously," he writes to Thomson in
May, "and it will be devilish hard, if a man, good for anything, cannot keep himself alive here on these terms." The
rewriting and rearrangement for Dr. Hunter of a work called
Nature Delineated, brought him in some more money, besides
making him known to the booksellers; so that at the end of
May he was able to take rooms by the year in Surrey Street,
with an old pupil of Thomson's. Meanwhile he was attending
the debates in the House of Commons with the keenest
interest. In November Mill had an opportunity of showing
his powers not only as a contributor, but as an editor as well.
Together with Baldwin he projected a new periodical, to be
"devoted to the dissemination of liberal and useful knowledge," called the *Literary Journal*. It was to embrace
Physics, Literature, Manners, Politics, to commence in
January, 1803, and to be issued weekly in shilling numbers.
Mill was to be editor and contributor for four years. He
corresponded extensively with all his friends, in order to get
assistance in the various departments, and especially took
counsel with Thomson, whose brother James was to undertake
the Literature and Philosophy of the Mind. Thomas Brown,
the metaphysician, was also thought of; but, whether he
accepted the offer or not, we are not told. Most of the Edinburgh contributions were very good, but those from London
quite the reverse. "His energies and his hopes," Professor
Bain tells us, "were concentrated in the success of his bold
design. It was no small achievement for a young man to
have induced a publisher to make the venture. But he had
the power of getting people to believe in him. He was also
cut out for a man of business, and shows it now as an editor."
The first year of the *Literary Journal* contains some curious

articles either written or inspired by Mill, such as an essay on the structure of the Platonic dialogue (he always maintained his admiration for the Platonic mode of philosophical produre), another (curiously enough) to prove that Utility is not the foundation of virtue, and another on Stewart's *Life of Reid*, wherein some of his well-known opinions on the necessity of bringing early influences systematically to bear on children are for the first time expressed. In the year 1804 were produced (amongst others) a thoroughly characteristic paper on religious *feeling* as distinguished from action,[5] and several reviews of apologetic treatises in theology, most of which he is inclined to discourage. In 1805 Mill continues the *Journal*, and also publishes his translation of Villers' work on the *Reformation*, adding very copious notes of his own, in which he quotes largely from, and refers to, Dugald Stewart, Robertson, George Campbell, &c., expresses here and there his poor opinion of Voltaire, who "used not only lawful but poisoned arms against religion and liberty," and warmly defends the books of the Bible as comprising " the extraordinary code of laws communicated by a benevolent divinity to man." Villers' Kantism is also thrown in his teeth : consequently, since Mill was a conscientious man, we must presume that he had made himself acquainted with the writings and arguments of Kant (probably in some French translation) : also that he was as yet far from having reached the purely negative standpoint in religion. In this year Mill further commenced his editorship of the *St. James's Chronicle*, about which unfortunately little is known. The proprietor was Baldwin, his co-adventurer in the *Journal*. The paper lasted for at least two or three years, possibly more. In 1806 the

---

[5] "Religion," he says in it, " without reason may be feeling, it may be the tremors of the religious nerve, but it cannot be piety towards God, or love towards man."

form of the *Literary Journal* was altered. Henceforth it was
announced that a Second Series would come out monthly, and
that the plan of the contents would be somewhat varied. This
year contains an article on Tooke's *Diversions of Purley*, which
is a book well-known in connexion with the obsolete philology
of the *Analysis*, a severe one on Payne Knight's *Principles of
Taste*, and some reviews on works of Political Economy. In
one of the articles a reviewer, whether with or without the
editor's sanction, takes the side of the clergy against Dugald
Stewart and Leslie.

Soon after its transformation, however, the *Literary Journal*
had to be given up. Apparently, it had not succeeded. The
Chronicle, as we have said, was also abandoned not very long
after this date. By these steps a large portion of Mill's income
was withdrawn. His burdens, moreover, were increasing,
since his marriage had taken place in the preceding year to
Harriet Burrow, a lady of considerable beauty and grace, but
to whose lack of the necessary intellectual requirements he
was at the time quite blind. She, on her side, was soon dis-
appointed with the union, which she expected to be productive
of more material benefit to herself than it turned out to be.
Consequently Mill in this year, to meet the growing demands
of his situation, commenced his famous *History of British
India*, which he fondly anticipated would only take three years
in the writing. It eventually took twelve! His steady
friend Sir John Stuart ceased in 1807 to come up to London
regularly for the Parliamentary sessions, and one more support
in his uphill career was, not indeed withdrawn, but necessarily
rendered less available. Mill's connexion with the *Edinburgh Review* (1808—1813) had not yet commenced. A
variety of circumstances therefore combined to render the
year 1807 one of the gloomiest in his life. After such a
brilliant start, everything now seemed to be working against

him. In strong contrast with his early letters to David Barclay, we find this of the 7th of February, 1807, written in a very doleful and desponding strain :—" I had a letter about the beginning of the winter from Mr. Peters, which informed me that you were all well, and managing your affairs with your usual prosperity, which, you may believe, gave me no little pleasure to hear. I should be happy to see it too. Have you no good kirk yet in your neighbourhood, which you could give me and free me from this life of toil and anxiety which I lead here? This London is a place in which it is easier to spend a fortune than to make one. I know not how it is; but I toil hard, spend little, and yet am never the more forward." At this time also his father's complicated affairs were the cause of a demand being made upon him for 50*l.*, which not a little distressed him; and altogether the future looked decidedly dark. During all this period he is recorded to have enjoyed the society of an extensive literary circle, but not to have made many friendships in London, owing to the strong dislikes which he used with great rapidity to conceive, and his unpopularity on other grounds.[6]

But in 1808 came better things. In this year, which was a notable one in Mill's career, commenced his friendships with Bentham, with Ricardo, with General Miranda, and with William Allen, the Quaker and chemist of Plough Court. In this year also his intimacy with Brougham—he had been acquainted with him previously in Edinburgh—was formed, as also his connexion with the *Edinburgh Review*, under the editorship of Jeffrey. Each of these friendships and con-

---

[6] From this point we may pass much more rapidly over the remaining ground, both because Mill's subsequent career was of a more public nature, and the works which record it (such as J. S. Mill's *Autobiography*) are more generally known; and also because Part III. in some measure deals with it.

nexions gave its separate and distinguishable colour to Mill's habits of thinking, and aims in life, at least during the years 1808—1819, while some of them influenced him much longer. During all this time the *History of British India* was slowly progressing. And in the earlier part of this period his views on religion were becoming fixed, and approaching more and more nearly to absolute negation.

The connexion with Bentham was of course the predominating influence of his life. Mill used to stay with Bentham for short periods at his house (called Barrow Green) at Oxted, in the Surrey hills, during the years 1807—1814; and afterwards, during much longer portions of the year, at Bentham's new house, Ford Abbey, in Devonshire, during the years 1814—1817. When in London, Bentham lived in Queen's Square, which was some distance from Mill's house at Pentonville. Being anxious that Mill should live nearer himself, in 1810 he gave him Milton's house, which was almost adjoining his own. After a few months, however, Mill removed to Newington Green, where he stayed for four years. But in 1814 Bentham leased a house in Queen's Square to Mill, who thus finally became his neighbour in London.

The intimacy between the two philosophers was not without those little breaks and pauses—those unphilosophical squabbles—which are familiar to us from such well-known histories as that of the intellectual communion of Voltaire and Frederick the Great. In later life Bentham used to apply harsh expressions to his old admirer and disciple, such as "selfishness, coldness," &c. One day in 1814 we read that Bentham was offended because James Mill had left off taking his walk with him for a time, and the latter writes to suggest that they are in the habit of seeing too much of one another. On a later occasion Bentham surreptitiously sent over to Mill's house, while the latter was engaged in the India Office, to take away from it all the books out of his library which he had allowed him to keep there and use, solely owing to some offence which he had taken at his friend's neglect. On the whole, however, their sympathy—personal and intellectual—was most cordial.

Ricardo's friendship of course to some extent determined Mill's interest in political economy. Miranda's influence is important, since it is said to have contributed to the formation of Mill's religious scepticism, in conjunction with the authority of Bentham, of whom Miranda was an enthusiastic admirer even to the point of desiring to introduce into his native country, Spain, a Benthamic code. Mill's connexion with Allen, and the joint efforts of the philosopher on the one side, and the practical philanthropist and man of science, on the other, to ameliorate the education of the poor, are worthy of some notice, as they help to explain the former's views on education, about which it is evident from all his works, and from his son's *Autobiography*, that he felt very strongly indeed. Mill co-operated with Allen in the quarterly journal called the *Philanthropist*, and with Allen, Zachary Macaulay, and others, in agitating their various educational projects. Among the proposed methods of educating the poor discussed in the pages of the *Philanthropist* were the rival systems of Dr. Bell and Mr. Lancaster (a Quaker). Mill, together with Allen, espoused the cause of the latter. The battle between the Bellites and the Lancastrians, as they called themselves, waged long and fiercely in the columns of this journal; and in the course of the controversy a great many interesting educational questions were threshed out. The best means of civilizing barbarous tribes were also largely considered, as well as the systems in use at home for the reformation of criminals by means of penitentiary houses, and the like, in connexion with which Bentham's *Panopticon* was examined and approved. These and similar subjects, connected with the improvement of the condition of the poor in body or in mind all over the world, justified the description of the *Philanthropist* by its editor as "a repository for hints and suggestions calculated to promote the comfort and happiness of man."

In connexion with Brougham, we may presume that Mill became interested in questions of legal reform. The defects of the English penal system are pointed out even in the *Philanthropist*, while the *Edinburgh Review* for these years contains several articles from Mill's pen on subjects connected with law and codification, English and foreign, mainly in relation to speculations and proposed improvements issuing from Bentham. The younger Mill always thought that Brougham exercised a much stronger fascination on his father than was just, and that certain defects of character—such as disingenuousness—were far from being compensated for by his attractive manner.

James Mill's contributions to the *Edinburgh Review*, under Jeffrey's editorship, extended over some years (1808—1815). Jeffrey used to hack his articles about remorselessly; and Mill often, like other contributors, complained bitterly of this treatment, but was met with apologies, accompanied, however, by steady persistence in the line of conduct reprobated. Jeffrey was continually urging Mill to soften his tone of writing, and on comparing the *Fragment on Mackintosh*, for instance, with some of the articles by Mill in the *Edinburgh Review*, as altered by Jeffrey, we cannot help feeling that Jeffrey may have been in the right. The contributions of Mill during the above-mentioned years embraced the following subjects: Political Economy [article on Money and Exchange, Oct. 1808], Law and Codification [Review of Bexon's *Code de la Législation Pénale* —the first of his articles on Bentham's theories—Oct. 1809;

article on the part of the Code Napoléon referring to criminal procedure, Nov. 1810], Education [the Lancastrian system is discussed in the Feb. number of 1813], Indian Affairs [April 1810, article on the government of the East India Company; July 1812, review of Malcolm's *Sketch of the Political History of India*; Nov. 1812, article attacking the commercial monopoly of the Company; July 1813, review of Malcolm's *Sketch of the Sikhs*], Religious Toleration [August 1810] ; Politics [review of a French treatise, *Sur la Souveraineté*, by M. Chas, Feb. 1811], the Liberty of the Press [May, 1811] ; and the Emancipation and Condition of Spanish America [two articles in Jan. and July, 1809, evidently inspired by General Miranda].

During the years 1815 to 1824, Mill furnished the articles to the *Encyclopædia Britannica* which were afterwards reprinted in a separate volume, and have now attained some celebrity. In 1817 the *History of British India* went through the press, and on its appearance, at the beginning of 1818, met with a rapid success. A second edition was demanded in 1819. Meanwhile Mill was gradually rising in the India House, and in 1820 he was drawing a salary of 800*l.* a year from the Company, with promotion in store. At this time his old friend, Dr. Thomson, the professor of chemistry in Glasgow, wrote to inform him of a vacancy in the Greek chair at that university. Mill is said to have seriously thought of entering himself as a candidate; but was prevented by considerations of the probable opposition of the Tories at the election, the necessity of signing the Confession of Faith, his possible advancement to the India Office, and the pecuniary loss which such a change in his circumstances, even if successfully brought about, would entail.

By gradual advancements, Mill rose in the India House till he became chief examiner, in 1830, at a salary of 1200*l.*,

which was finally fixed at 2000*l.* in 1836, a few months before
his death. From 1819 to 1830 he was in the revenue department of the Company, and (as J. S. Mill tells us) introduced
several important reforms into the administration of India,
more through his large unofficial influence with the directors.
than by the use of any immediate opportunities afforded him
by his position.

The remaining points of interest during this last stage of
Mill's life [1819—1836] are his connexion with the *Westminster Review* (beginning in 1823), his composition of the
Analysis during six summer holidays at his country house in
Dorking (1822—1829), the production in 1821 of the
Elements of Political Economy, his electioneering efforts in
Westminster on behalf of philosophical radicalism, his part in
the institution of the London University (afterwards University College) for unsectarian education, and his quarrel[7] and
subsequent reconciliation with Macaulay, whose appointment
to India he afterwards strongly supported with the directors of
the Company.[8] One of the most extraordinary educations of
modern times, familiar to all from the pages of J. S. Mill's
Autobiography, was being concluded during the first two or
three years of this period. Meanwhile Mill kept up some of his
old intimacies, as those with Brougham, Dr. Thomson, and
Allen, and formed some fresh friendships, as those with Grote,
the historian, Mrs. Grote, Henry Bickersteth (afterwards
Lord Langdale and Master of the Rolls, who advised him as
to the toning down of the *Fragment on Mackintosh*), John
Romilly, and Charles Buller. In 1830 Mill left his house in
Queen's Square and took one in Church Street, Kensington,
where, as well as at his summer residence in Surrey, he spent

[7] Re Macaulay's *Review of the Essay on Government.*

[8] Before setting out for India, Macaulay was earnestly counselled by
Mill (as J. S. Mill tells us) to keep to the line of an " honest politician."

the remaining six years of his life in comfort and prosperity. He had now become chief of the India Office. His nine children were all gathered round him in his house, and were one after the other being educated in the same way as J. S. Mill, the eldest, then twenty-four years old, had been trained. "For twenty years," says Professor Bain, "the house had been a school, and it continued so while he lived." In the latter years of his life he was troubled with disease of the chest, which began to affect him seriously in April, 1836. He gradually became worse, and expired on the 23rd of June.

Mill's character was in some aspects grand, but scarcely in any lovable. His absolute honesty, his unswerving devotion to the cause or opinion which he considered right, however unpopular it might be, his indomitable energy in overcoming apparently insuperable difficulties, his philanthropy—all these are beyond praise; but his narrowness, his impatience, his want of tenderness and sympathy for minds differently constituted from his own—these defects were unfortunately equally conspicuous, and should qualify our judgment on his merits.

Part II.

THEIR PHILOSOPHICAL SYSTEMS AND OPINIONS.

CHAPTER I.

PRELIMINARY REMARKS ON THE THEORY OF ASSOCIATION OF IDEAS
—THE PHYSICAL GROUNDWORK OF THE THEORY—HARTLEY'S
VIBRATIONS—JAMES MILL AND HARTLEY ON SENSATIONS—
IDEAS AS COPIES OF SENSATIONS.

THE theory of Association of Ideas, now so familiar to us as
applied to the different practical fields of language, law, morals,
politics, education, religion, and sociology, was first formulated
as a philosophical system, and made the serious study of a lifetime, by Hartley. Obvious enough it seems when stated, and it
is only when the question of the extent of its application comes
in, that the widest divergency of opinion is manifested. Some
sort of belief in it has always been tacitly recognized as the
ground of prediction in the common affairs of life, and has
been at the root of most of the proverbial philosophy and folk-
lore of ages. Nor were more formal, though isolated, admis-
sions of its validity wanting in the works of pre-Hartleian
philosophers in different countries. Aristotle and Hobbes had
noticed the principle (the latter under the name of Mental

Discourse). In France, Condillac (Hartley's contemporary) worked out similar results. The name had been invented by Locke.[1] One Gay had very briefly, but in a lucid and agreeable manner, sketched out his ideas on the subject, and applied the doctrine chiefly to moral phenomena, both in a dissertation prefixed to Edmund Law's translation and edition of Archbishop King's "Origin of Evil," and (probably) in an anonymous "Enquiry into the Origin of the Human Appetites and Affections" (1747), printed in Dr. Parr's "Metaphysical Tracts of the 18th Century" [pp. 48—170]. Edmund Law, in his prefatory observations to King's work [pp. lvi, lvii], dwells with enthusiasm on "the power of Association which was first hinted at by Mr. Locke, but applied to the present purpose more directly by the author of the foregoing ·Dissertation" [the Rev. Mr. Gay], "and from him taken up and considered in a much more general way by Dr. Hartley, who has from thence solved many of the principle appearances in Human Nature, the sensitive part of which, since Mr. Locke's essay, has been very little cultivated, and is perhaps yet to the generality a *terra incognita*, how interesting soever and entertaining such inquiries must be found to be : on which account it is much to be lamented that no more thoughtful persons are induced to turn their minds that way, since so very noble a foundation for improvements has been laid by both these excellent writers, especially the last, whose work is, I beg leave to say, in the main, notwithstanding all its abstruseness, well worth studying, and would have been sufficiently clear and convincing had he but confined his observations to the plain facts and experiments, without ever entering minutely into the Physical Cause of such Phenomena." He speaks, too, with some impatience of the principle of Association being

---

[1] Locke's Essay,—Conduct of the Understanding, § 40, 4th ed., 1690. See J. S. Mill's note on p. 377 of vol. i. of the Analysis of James Mill.

often slighted as vague and confused by later writers, particularly Dr. Hutcheson,[2] and expresses [p. lvii] his own conviction that " it will not appear of less extent or influence in the
Intellectual World than that of Gravity is found to be in the
Natural."[3]

This theory, then, of the Association of Ideas, propounded
by Gay, ushered in by Edmund Law with the exuberant
hopefulness which has always characterized the Columbuses of
philosophy, elaborated by Hartley, and kept alive by Priestley,
the elder Darwin, and Brown, was that which subsequently
attracted the attention of James Mill, who added to it from
the richer scientific stores then at his disposal, while stripping
it of certain excrescences not necessary to the vindication and
establishment of its truth, and solely due to the physical tastes
of Hartley.

Let us first find a statement of the doctrine in its very
simplest terms.   So far Hartley and James Mill are perfectly
at one ; we will take the definition given by the latter. "Our
ideas," he says [Analysis, vol. i. p. 78],[4] "spring up, or exist,
in the order in which the sensations existed, of which they are
copies.   This is the general law of the Association of Ideas,
by which term, let it be remembered, nothing is here meant to
be expressed but the order of occurrence."

Next, what was that physical hypothesis with which, to
Edmund Law's regret, Hartley encumbered his theory, and
which James Mill, as we shall see, cast aside ?

Hartley, like many another theorist, strained every nerve
to evolve some grand and comprehensive law which should

[2] *Science of Morals*, p. 55, sqq.

[3] J. S. Mill uses the same comparison in speaking of the theory. "That
which the Law of Gravitation is to Astronomy . . . . the Law of the
Association of Ideas is to Psychology." *Comte and Positivism*, p. 53.

[4] Throughout this work the references are to J. S. Mill's edition of
The Analysis of the Phenomena of the Human Mind, 1869.

interpret all the phenomena. His bias towards simplification was excessive; and the consequence was that his foundations were not wide enough to support the superstructure. Not content with showing how large a variety of our mental processes are merely instances of the general law of Association as stated above, and how many of our complex ideas are, on analysis, reducible to simple ideas (the copies, in his language, of sensations), he endeavoured to prove that the primary law itself was nothing but the experience of a physical change in first, the nerves, and then the brain, produced in the first instance by the impression on the senses of external objects. For this purpose he assumed, on certain (chiefly pathological and medical) analogies, that, when sensations are experienced, vibrations in the infinitesimal particles of the medullary substance of the brain are set going by external objects; and surmised that, on the removal of these objects, the vibrations survive in the form of miniature vibrations or vibratiuncules which represent or cause what, from the subjective point of view, we call ideas. The ideas (or diminutive vibrations) would necessarily be of the same nature and constitution, and have the same arrangement and sequence of their elements as the original vibrations (or sensations) themselves.

The vibration theory was suggested, as Hartley tell us, by Newton's hints as to the relation between motion and sensation, just as, on the intellectual side, the association theory was suggested by Locke and Gay; and, as a medical man and student of physical science, Hartley saw no reason why an ingenious combination of the two should not be effected. It is easy now to see why such a hypothesis in his time could be nothing but the merest guesswork, since, even at the present day, its lineal successor, the doctrine of "neural tremors" and groupings, under the auspices of such able exponents as G. H.

Lewes and Dr. Maudsley, does not advance the Association theory much, which is far better left to stand on its own legs as the expression of an ultimate psychological law. In his system of vibrations Hartley had to assume both the causal nexus and the existence of the alleged cause. The theory was doubly hypothetical. Granting the existence of vibrations at all, and, further, their activity to the extent and under the conditions postulated by him, there still remains unproved their operation in giving birth to sensations and ideas : he at most shows the probability of the concomitance of the physical and mental conditions in a large number of cases. His vibrations are like the French chemists' substance X, in being undiscovered and unproved, though unlike it in the fact that, even if their existence were proved, it could not be shown that they caused the phenomena to be accounted for and interpreted.

Hartley, at the outset, anticipates that his readers may see little connexion between vibrations and the association of ideas, and modestly expresses his fear that he will be able to do but little in the way of combining the two theories, "on account of the great intricacies, extensiveness, and novelty of the subject." [*Observations on Man*, vol. i. p. 6.[5]] " However," he says—and in these words he betrays the weak point in his attempt—" if these doctrines be found in fact to contain the laws of the bodily and mental powers respectively, they must be related to each other, since the body and mind are." In the reason thus naively assigned the whole question is begged.

Starting from Newtonian principles, he first lays down that the immediate instrument of sensation and motion is to be found in the medullary substance of the brain, spinal marrow, and nerves ; and, furthermore, that the medullary substance of

---

[5] Our references throughout are to the edition of Hartley's works, in 3 vols.) by his son [1801].

the brain is the immediate instrument of ideas, so that a change in the former works a corresponding change in the latter. But sensations notoriously persist after the removal or disappearance of the external phenomena which occasioned them. Now, no motion can persist of itself in any space or part of a physical body, except a vibratory one. Therefore, he argues, these surviving sensations must be the result of vibratory motions communicated first to the nerves, and then to the brain, by sensible objects. Then, as if not quite sure of the efficacy of his reasoning, he adds, that if the vibrations could be proved independently by physical arguments, the persistence of sensation after disappearance of the object might be proved from vibrations, instead of *vice versâ*. This latter task he then sets himself to do, and assumes (without proving) certain probable exciting causes, conditions, and media of the vibrations, such, for instance, as a very subtle and elastic fluid or æther, which he holds to be " of great use in performing sensation, thought, or motion." [Vol. i. p. 32.] He speaks also of the infinitesimal character of the particles of the medullary substance operated upon, and their uniformity, continuity, softness, and active powers, as favouring his hypothesis. Here again he is taking hints from Sir Isaac Newton. He also brings forward analogies and illustrations derived from the exercise of his own profession,[6] and attempts to show how the phenomena of pleasure and pain, of sleep, and of light, are agreeable to his theory, and how muscular contractions and motions (automatic, semi-voluntary, and voluntary, according to his division) are all satistorily explained by it. The general conclusion is, that vibrations and association mutually support one another.

[6] .He has a section (vol. i. pp. 264—268) on the Relation of the Art of Physic to, and the improvements which it is capable of receiving from, the Vibration Theory, judiciously applied.

"One may expect that vibrations should infer association as their effect, and association point to vibrations as its cause." Ultimately, however, he leaves us somewhat in the dark as to which is to be held the cause of the other, and seems to content himself with placing the two laws in juxtaposition, expounding their correspondence and parallelism, and drawing the inference that the agreement of the doctrines, "both with each other and with so great a variety of the phenomena of the body and mind, may be reckoned a strong argument of their truth." [Vol. i. p. 114.] He even appears to give up the idea of a definite causal relation in the assertion that " as in physics, we may make the quantity of the matter the exponent of the gravity, or the gravity the exponent of it," so, in inquiries into the human mind, "if that species of motion which we term vibrations can be shown by probable arguments to attend upon all sensations, ideas, and motions, and to be proportioned to them, then we are at liberty either to make vibrations the exponent of sensations, ideas, and motions, or these the exponents of vibrations, as best suits the inquiry, however impossible it may be to discover in what way vibrations cause, or are connected with, sensations or ideas." [*Observ. on Man*, vol. i. p. 32.] And he then abandons himself for a moment to a wild search for a cause behind the cause, for a hypothetical substance on which to rest a hypothetical kind of motion, and suggests an infinitesimal elementary one, intermediate between the soul and the body. As his work proceeds, however, we find him merely placing side by side with each law of Association successively enunciated the corresponding law of the vibration theory, by substituting vibration for sensation, vibratiuncules for simple ideas of sensation (that is, vestiges or images of sensations left behind in the brain), and complex miniature vibrations (compounded of simple miniature vibrations running into one another) for complex (or the more intellectual) ideas, compounded of simple ideas of sensation running into one another. These laws of the association, both of vibrations (on the physical or external side), and of sensations and ideas (on the subjective or psychical side), Hartley (as stated above) believed to apply also to the association of muscular contractions. Consequently, he expresses his vibration-association theory in its complete shape and threefold application in the following formula or theorem :—

1. If any	Sensation A.	be associated for a sufficient number of times with any other	Sensation D.	it will at last, when occurring alone, excite	d, the simple idea belonging to D.
2.	Idea B.		Idea E.		The very idea E.
3.	or Muscular Motion C.		Muscular Motion F.		The very Muscular Motion F.

By a comparison of the first branch of this law with the second, it will be seen to express the obvious fact that the recurrence of one of two originally associated sensations does not guarantee the recurrence of the other sensation itself, because such a result depends on the disposition of external phenomena, independent of subjective conditions, but only of the ideas corresponding to it : that is, in any case of association, as Mills puts it, the antecedent may be either a sensation or an idea, but the consequent must be always an idea. [*Anal.* i. 81.]

The elements or materials of all our mental states, according to both Hartley and James Mill, may be represented by the following scale or psychological spectrum :—

1. *Sensations* (impressed by external objects, in most cases, though not in all).
2. *Ideas of Sensations, or Simple Ideas* (Ideas surviving Sensations after the objects have been removed, or the Ideas most nearly allied to, and indistinguishable from, Sensations).

3. *Complex Ideas* (the more purely intellectual Ideas, compounded of the above).

It is natural, therefore, that both philosophers should commence with some account of the prime *data*, Sensations, of which they conceive all ideas to be either copies, or combinations (according to the laws of association) of such copies, and into which, by analysis, they may ultimately be resolved.

James Mill does not originate any startling physical theory of the senses: this, indeed, was not his object. He merely wished the student to accustom himself to reflect on the different classes of simple sensations, and learn to discriminate them not only from one another, but from all other feelings or states of mind with which, from their very familiarity, they were in danger of being confused. This was, in his opinion, a necessary step by way of preparing the ground for an examination of "the more mysterious phenomena." He accordingly gives a short account of the five senses of Smell, Taste, Hearing, Touch, and Sight, to which he adds two fresh classes of sensations, viz., those which accompany the muscular actions of the body, and those which have their seat in the alimentary canal, or the feelings associated with digestion.

In discussing each of these in order, Mill points out that three conditions are requisite to sensation,—first, its organ, next, the actual feeling itself, and, lastly, the antecedent of sensation, or the external object to which it is referred as effect to cause. With regard to the muscular sensibilities, he expresses his surprise at the extent to which this part of our consciousness had, up to his day, been neglected by all philosophical inquirers in this country except Hartley, Erasmus Darwin, and Brown (all of them, it is noticeable, physicians). He explains this neglect on the ground that they are feelings in the main leading up to more interesting states of mind, to which the attention is immediately called off, to the swallowing up of any interest in the former which might otherwise have been taken. In discussing the sensations of the alimentary canal, Mill justly (and somewhat dolefully) observes that " when they become acutely painful they are precise objects of attention to everybody," though, in their ordinary form, they too, as being merely productive of, or preliminary to, more interesting sensations, are lost sight of and forgotten as soon as the latter supervene.[7] Hartley's description of the classes of sensations [*Observ. on Man*, vol. i. pp. 115—268], as coming from a physician, is fuller and more elaborate; but, notwithstanding that it is replete with valuable and striking suggestions, its scope and aim is far more indefinite, and it forms a far less coherent and integral part of the general theory, than that given by Mill. In speaking of the various senses and sensations, he seems to have no very determinate object before him. Mill's purpose, on the contrary, was very plain and intelligible. His theory being that ideas are copies, or combinations of copies, of sensations, he begins with sensations, as being the primary element to which all intellectual operations are reducible, and the most simple and primitive of all our natural states, no less properly than Euclid begins with his definitions, and then proceeds to his postulates, axioms, and theorems. And he dwelt on them just long enough for purposes of definition, and no longer. Hartley, on the other hand, though he began with sensation, could not confine himself within proper limits.

In his long second chapter on " the application of the doc-

---

[7] Besides these, Mill notices the Sensations of Disorganization, or of the approach thereto in any part of the body (such as painful cuts, wounds, &c., and similar feelings) though here there is neither a specific organ nor external object of the sensation. Some of his remarks throw light on Kant's dictum that "pain is the sense of that which destroys life."

trines of vibration and association to each of the sensations and motions in particular," Hartley seems to have had at least three objects indistinctly before him at various times :—(1) a division and classification of the senses (though he brings forward no very satisfactory *fundamentum divisionis*, and often puts species on the same level as genera); (2) to show that the vibrations accompanying the *special* sensations propagated diminutive vibrations representing the simple ideas of those sensations; and (3) to explain how the special sensations contribute to form our intellectual pleasures and pains " *in the way of association;*" which latter qualification exhibits a certain confusion in his mind, since the inquiry into the tones of mind produced by sensations is properly a physical, almost a medical, inquiry, and has nothing to do with Association, which professes to interpret the sequences of ideas as dependent upon, or related to, the sequences of sensuous impressions.[8] On the whole, then, we may take Mill's classification of the senses and sensations to be quite sufficient as a necessary introduction to the theory of association; and the many interesting observations scattered up and down the corresponding part of Hartley's work need not detain us at present.

Ideas are, as we have seen (when simple), copies, or (when complex) combinations of copies, of sensations. We have noticed Mill's succinct account of sensations, the originals : let us now see what he has to tell us, by way of definition and explanation, about the copies, images, or ideas, the other material of consciousness.

Like Hartley, Mill first of all examines the idea in its simplest form : and, to both philosophers, the idea in its simplest form

---

[8] James Mill falls occasionally into the same mistake, as, for instance, where he talks of dismal ideas being associated with (instead of being, as they are, produced, through direct physical agency, by) intestinal sensations of discomfort [Anal. vol. i. pp. 101, 102].

is that vestige or trace of a sensation which remains in the mind after the external phenomenon which occasioned the sensation has been removed. Hartley, indeed, at times seems to be so taken up with this aspect of the simple idea that he apparently disregards the other and far more important points of view from which it may be looked at. He confuses, for instance, the images before the retina of the eye immediately after the disappearance of a bright-coloured object, with the thought of that object at any time after its disappearance—a purely physical with a purely intellectual state or operation. And even Mill does not distinguish quite sharply enough between the mere persistence of a sensuous impression *in* the mind immediately after the vanishing of the external object, and the reproduction or recollection *by* the mind of such an impression long afterwards. " When our sensations cease, by the absence of their objects, something remains. This something is a feeling which, though distinguishable from the sensation itself, is yet more like it than anything else, and therefore may not inaptly be called a copy, trace, or representation of the sensation." To this latter class of feelings—to every feeling, that is, other than a sensation in immediate relation to its exciting object—Mill gives the generic name, Ideas, as opposed to sensations in the above sense ; and as opposed to Sensation in its other sense of the mental process, of which each specific sensation is an example, he proposes with some hesitation a term, which has since been taken up by Dr. Maudsley and others, Ideation. In this way we may be said to have Ideas of Sight, Ideas of Hearing, Ideas of Touch, of Smell, of Muscular Contraction, of Disorganization, &c. In each of these classes, we experience " something which remains with us after the sensation " [of Sight, Hearing, Touch, &c., as the case may be] " is gone, and which, in the train of thought, we can use as its representative." The sound of thunder, for example, the sensation, is the primary state of consciousness; the thought of it, when it is gone, is the secondary state of consciousness.

> Music, when soft voices die,
> Vibrates in the memory:
> Violets when they die and sicken,
> Live still in the sense they quicken.

Here again we have cases of the secondary state of consciousness, as Mill calls it.

Up to this point the idea has been regarded solely in the light of a remnant of sensation, and ideation as a sort of dissolving view, in which the idea represents the fading outline of the figures which were just now distinct and vivid. But Mill soon begins to introduce the discriminative or retentive powers of the mind, though he expresses their operations in his own peculiar language. On tasting a wine, or observing a colour, we often have at the same time a secondary consciousness of other sensations of the same class as, but specifically unlike, the sensations of which we then have a primary consciousness; we distinguish the two feelings in a train of thought; and we say that the former sensations of which we have equivalents or images in our minds differ from those of which we have a present experience. Here we see the original conception of an idea as a mere remnant of sensation, a sort of weaker impression on the senses, considerably enlarged. And we shall notice, in the next two chapters, still further amplifications, when Mill comes to divide the ideas into classes corresponding in the main with those of Hartley.

CHAPTER II.

AFTER noticing the persistence of sensations (notably visible and audible sensations) in the sensorium, fancy, or mind—which he takes for his purpose to be equivalent expressions—after their exciting causes have been removed, and then apparently feeling conscious that this proposition does not carry us very far, since it merely represents a well-known physical law, Hartley in his eighth Proposition (vol. i. p. 56) begins to introduce us to the Association theory proper, and lays down that " sensations, *by being often repeated,* leave certain Types or Images of themselves which may be called Simple Ideas of Sensation " [of Sensation, because, as Mill too says, more like sensations than anything else; and simple, as contrasted with complex ideas, to be noticed presently]. He compares this proposition with the foregoing one [Prop. III.], and points out that, whereas, according to the latter law, the single impression produces " a perceptible effect, trace or vestige " for a short time, the repetition, in the former case, produces a more permanent effect, and generates an idea " which shall recur occasionally at long distances of time from the impression of the corresponding sensation." So, too, Mill remarks the constant interchange of sensations and ideas in our mental experience, sensations suggesting ideas; and those ideas suggesting still further ideas more and more remotely connected with the sensation which set the train of thought in motion, and more and more nearly allied to sensations long past, till the sequence of ideas is broken in upon by some sensation impressed by an external cause independent of us, and a fresh train is constituted. Then do our ideas follow one another at hazard, or according to law ? The latter assuredly ; and the law of their succession is determined by the order of succession or the order of co-existence of the corresponding sensations. Hartley and Mill agree that there are two orders of sensations—the successive order, or the order which answers usually, but not always, to a sequence in time of their objects ; and the synchronous order, or the order which answers to the relation of the corresponding objects to one another in space. When the sensations have been synchronous, the ideas of these sensations are synchronous; and when the sensations have been successive, the ideas of those sensations spring up successively, though not necessarily, of course, in exactly the same order of succession. From a stone, for example, several sensations are simultaneously derived—those of hardness, weight, roundness, colour, size, &c. When, therefore, the idea of any one of those sensations springs up in the mind afterwards, the ideas of all the others spring up, says Mill, simultaneously with it.[1] The sensation of hearing the thunder, on the contrary, follows the sensation of seeing the lightning-flash : when the idea, therefore, of one of these is recalled, the idea of the other follows in succession, and not simultaneously. The latter branch of the law is also most aptly exemplified by the case of committing passages to memory, where each word in succession suggests the following word. Of course a far

---

[1] This hypothesis is obviously crude and ill-founded, as Professor Bain points out [*Analysis*, vol. i. p. 79, note], since the same individual sensation has generally a place in many different groupings or clusters.

greater number of our sensations, and therefore also of our ideas, occur in the successive than in the synchronous order. Also nearly all the sensations occurring either simultaneously or successively occur very frequently in their respective orders, and the frequent repetition tends to rivet more firmly the corresponding sequences and associations of the ideas.

The above doctrines are expressed by Hartley in a somewhat different way, but to the same effect, in two of the propositions into which he delights to pack up his philosophy, namely, (1) the proposition, already noticed, that sensations, by being often repeated, leave types or images of themselves, called Simple Ideas of Sensation: this would include Mill's perpetuation of the synchronous order of sensations in subsequent ideation, e. g. in the case of the simultaneous sensations excited by a rose through its different sensible qualities: (2) any sensations, A, B, C. &c., by being associated with one another a sufficient number of times, get such a power over the corresponding ideas, a, b, c, &c., that any one sensation, A, when impressed alone, shall be able to excite in the mind, b, c, &c., the ideas of the rest. [Prop. X., vol. i., p. 65]. This association would include both the case of simultaneity and that of succession. Hartley gives us the physical counterpart of the latter of these two laws as follows: Any vibrations, A, B, C, &c., by being associated together often enough, get such a power over a, b, c, &c., the corresponding miniature vibrations, that any one vibration, A, when impressed alone, shall be able to excite b, c, &c., the miniatures of the rest. [Prop. XI.]. The former he translates into vibration language thus : Sensory vibrations, by being often repeated, beget in the medullary substance of the brain a disposition to diminutive vibrations, or vibratiuncules.

Having explained that sensations associated often enough tend to generate similarly associated ideas, Mill goes on to

show that there are degrees of strength in the associative link
itself, as there are degrees of clearness in the associated ideas.
The *symptoms or criteria* of the relative strength of such
links are, in the main, their relative permanence, and the
relative certainty and facility with which they are formed.
This may be seen by comparing the bond of association between names and ideas in a well-known language, science or
art, on the one hand, and an imperfectly known one on the
other. The *causes* of strength of association of ideas are two :
the vividness of the associated sensations, and the frequency
of their association. This Hartley expresses as usual in terms
of vibrations. [Vol. i., pp. 30, 31].

That vividness and frequency are two completely distinct
causes of strong and intimate associations is shown by the
fact that a single instance of a connexion of a highly
pleasurable or painful sensation with one which would otherwise have been indifferent, will often be sufficient to forge an
almost indissoluble link between the latter sensation, when
recurring, or the idea of it, when subsequently springing up
in the mind, and the idea of the pleasurable or painful sensation. The sight of a surgical operator, or of a place connected
with a delightful meeting, will respectively suggest painful
and pleasurable ideas long afterwards to the patient and to
the friend, although only once coupled with the sensations
corresponding to those ideas. So, too, recently-associated
sensations will, as compared with those associated at more
distant dates, generate a strong association between the
corresponding ideas, or between one of the sensations and
the idea of the other, by reason of the vividness and prominence in the memory of the original sensations, irrespective
of frequency. Conversely, a word frequently associated with
a sensation, or the sight of a particular class of citizen
frequently associated with the sight of a particular kind of

dress, will create an equally strong association between the corresponding ideas, though any one of the associations of the original sensations, taken by itself, would have left no impress on the mind at all.

The next primary law of the association theory is a very important one. It is that, when several simple ideas are frequently united together in the mind, they gradually merge into a complex whole, the several parts of which are practically indistinguishable, only distinguishable, that is, by a conscious effort of analysis : or, as Hartley puts it shortly, simple ideas will run into a complex idea by means of association, in which case, according to the vibration hypothesis, " we are to suppose " that simple miniature vibrations run into a complex miniature vibration. Mill compares the analogous physical effect of a rapidly revolving wheel, on seven parts of which the seven prismatic colours are painted, and which appears to a spectator white ; and Hartley characteristically instances the apparently simple flavour of a medicine where the tastes of the several ingredients cannot be distinguished. Such an apparently simple idea as that of gold is in reality a very complex idea,—one which the ideas (themselves not simple in every case), of hardness, colour, extension, weight, have by frequent union coalesced to form. The complexity of such abstract ideas as those of Humanity, Poetry, or Civilization, is more obvious. This law may be regarded as a case of the law of the generation of synchronous ideas by similarly synchronous sensations. Hartley draws attention to this, and, in his semi-mathematical language, puts the generalization thus :—A + B + C + D (sensations) often occurring together [or—though this does not seem so certain—A equally often occurring with B, C, or D alone, or with pairs of B + C, B + D, C + D alone] generate the synchronous simple ideas a + b + c + d, and these synchronous simple ideas, by their repeated union, coalesce into a cluster or complex idea, *abcd*. He regards the merging of the ideas of the letters of the alphabet into the ideas of syllables, and the ideas of syllables into the ideas of words,—in fact the whole process of learning a language,—as a conspicuous instance of this law ; and says that, similarly, the most abstract ideas are capable, with perseverance, of being analyzed into such simple ideas as are but copies or images of sensations; since, as simple ideas run into complex ones, so complex run into decomplex ideas; but the complex ideas which go to compose a decomplex idea adhere together less closely than the simple ideas which go to form a complex idea, just as letters adhere together more closely to form a syllable by association than syllables do to form a word, and these latter again than words to form a sentence. It is to be noticed that when a complex idea is made up of several simple ideas, one of which is a visible idea, the visible idea, being the most glaring, so to speak, will generally serve as a symbol to suggest and connect the rest, just as the first letter of a word, or the first word of a sentence, will often call up the entire word or the entire sentence.

In connexion with this part of the theory, Mill just mentions the principle (which will occupy our attention hereafter) of indissoluble association. Two or more simple ideas may be so constantly and invariably conjoined that they form what may, from one point of view, be called a complex idea, without a special name, the parts of which, though specially named, it is impossible to disconnect,—such pairs of simple ideas, for instance, as colour and extension, solidity and figure, two straight lines and unterminated space. The sensations of colour and figure are so firmly associated with the sensations from which we infer distance, solidity, &c., that we even imagine that we see distance and solidity, though in fact we see only the former, and the rest is inference of a somewhat complicated character. We here have an instance of a sensation and an idea being so closely and repeatedly united that they merge into a whole which appears to be a simple sensation.

Just as simple ideas thus associated cannot be disjoined, so neither of them can be conjoined by any effort of mind with the opposite of the other. Here we have the law of the inconceivability of the opposite, about which Mr. Herbert Spencer's views have of late given rise to so much controversy.

Mill further remarks that another instance of the law now under consideration is the case (already mentioned) of antecedent sensations or ideas leading up so rapidly to a train of more interesting consequent ideas, that a complex idea results in which the supervening ideas form the dominant element, and the antecedent sensations or ideas are almost entirely lost.

The main principles of association, as enounced by Mill, are compared by him to those which Hume put forward. The two theories, though expressed differently and worked out from a somewhat different starting-point, are found to be in substance much the same. Hume considers the elementary principles, according to which our ideas are associated, to be Contiguity in Time and in Place, Causation, and Resemblance. Causation, however, even according to Hume himself, and certainly according to Mill, is only a particular case of Contiguity in Time; and Contrast, which Hume mentions as another possible principle, he himself admits to be derivative, as being a compound case of Resemblance and Causation. James Mill, indeed, thinks this analysis unsatisfactory, and prefers to call Contrast either a case of Resemblance (as when a dwarf suggests a giant, the two resembling one another in the fact of both departing from a common standard), or a

combined case of Vividness and Frequency, as when the
sensation or idea of pain suggests the idea of relief from pain,
or of pleasure, because the sensation of pain has often been
followed by the sensation accompanying relief from pain, and
also, whenever it has been so followed, the associative link
has generally been of a vivid and forcible character. There
remains then Contiguity in Place and in Time, together with
Resemblance. The two former correspond to Mill's synchronous and successive orders; and we have seen that the
simultaneity or sequence of our ideas depends on the simultaneity or sequence of our sensations. As to Resemblance,
Mill, in a somewhat hasty generalization, infers that it is
merely a case of the law of Frequency, because when we
perceive an object by our senses we generally perceive other
objects of the same class together with it. This is a very
crude and unphilosophical explanation. We perceive, together
with any given object, quite as many objects of different
classes, at any given moment, as objects of the class to which
it belongs, and, therefore, might be expected to have formed
quite enough counter-associations to dispel the association
which is alleged to be created in this manner.

Reduced then to their simplest terms, Mill's primary laws
of Association come to this. I. Whenever a strong association
is formed between two or more sensations, the recurrence of
any one of these sensations, or of the idea of any one of these
sensations, will suggest the ideas of the remaining sensations
either simultaneously or successively, according as the sensations, of which the suggesting sensation was one, were connected together in a synchronous or successive order. II. The
strength of the association is caused by either (1) the frequency
of the association, or (2) the vividness of the sensations associated, or one of them, or (3) a combination of both. III. After
simple ideas have occurred together a great many times

simultaneously, or even successively, in an order corresponding to that of the associated sensations, they are apt to coalese into a single complex idea, which, from the close adherence and interfusion of the parts composing it, will *appear* to be a simple indecomposable idea; and when the association has been constant and invariable, those parts or elements will in fact, as well as appearance, be inseparable by any effort of imagination. IV. Complex ideas thus formed may, by a similar process, merge into decomplex ideas; and in this way are formed the most abstract ideas which the human mind can frame.

Thus, having, with Hartley's guidance, determined the constitution and construction of the *materials* of thought, viz. Sensations, Simple Ideas, Complex Ideas, and Trains of Ideas, Mill has paved the way for the consideration of the principal *operations* of the human mind in making use of these materials. And first he examines the process by which (through the formation of links of association between ideas and sensible symbols) thought is communicated from mind to mind. This subject demands a chapter to itself.

CHAPTER III.

HARTLEY attaches considerable importance to the process of associating impressions, made by written words and uttered sounds on the senses of sight and hearing respectively, with the corresponding ideas; and James Mill (always more precise and methodical than his predecessor) gives the theory of Naming a definite and a considerable place in his system. In all the more intricate and complicated states of human consciousness, to which, after the explanation of the simple and familiar states, we are now about to proceed, " something of the process of Naming is involved." This artifice, therefore, craves immediate attention.

In order to communicate the trains of our thoughts to others, as well as to record for our benefit and use our own past trains in the order in which the ideas composing them actually occurred, it was found absolutely necessary to employ sensible signs or marks. Mind cannot work upon mind directly. One person can only devise and use visible or audible signs, which shall impress themselves on the senses of another person, and, by means of predetermined associations, call up in his mind ideas in a certain order, and at the same time signify to him that those ideas are passing, or did at some previous time pass, in his (the first person's) mind. Nor can we at will recall any set of ideas we please, still less in the order in which on some past occasion they occurred to us. If we wish to recall an idea, that idea must be present to our minds in the very act of willing to recall it; and, of course, we cannot will to will to recall an idea. We have no power over the occasions of our ideas. But by our power over the occasions of our sensations, that is, natural objects, we can devise such an order of them as must necessarily, at any time we wish, raise up a corresponding order of sensible impressions. By making, therefore, certain sensible impressions stand for certain ideas, we can ensure the possibility of raising up in our minds at any future time both the connexion and the order of the ideas which have formed part of any of our past trains of thought.

For the first of the above-mentioned purposes of language, namely, the *immediate* communication of sensations or ideas to others, audible signs (owing to their rapidity and variety, and the flexibility of the human voice) are preferable to visible signs, or the language of action and pantomime, which savage tribes use to a considerable extent, and which, of course, is useless in the dark. For the latter purpose, the *permanent* recording of thought, the converse is the case: visible marks are preferable to audible, durable signs to evanescent. Mankind first of all invented, by way of visible marks, picture-writing or hieroglyphics, the association here being a direct one between a portrait-representation and the sensible object, the idea of which is intended to be presented to the mind. Gradually the hieroglyphics became less directly pictorial, and more technical; and began to depend more on the various combinations of certain fixed types or picture-symbols, than on the successive imitations in each case of separate sensible objects; till, finally, men arrived at a new method of pre-determining the associations requisite for the recording of thought, that, namely, whereby different arrangements of a few letters (which stand for certain simple sounds or motions

of the vocal organs preparatory to the emission of sound), are
associated with the various audible sounds which constitute
the evanescent signs by which ideas and their order are communicated to others. Thus the permanent signs have fixed
laws of association with the audible, and the audible again
with the ideas which they are intended to convey. The
former, therefore, are secondary marks of the ideas, the latter
are immediate and primary.

It was of the greatest importance to man, in the first
instance, to acquire the means of communicating to others the
sensations affecting him, in order to secure the co-operation
and assistance of his fellow-men in coping with the forces of
nature. He, therefore, first devised audible signs of these
sensations, such as hot, cold, black, white, pain, pleasure, sweet,
bitter, &c. It next became advisable, if only for purposes of
economy, instead of repeating on each occasion the marks of the
various separate sensations simultaneously affecting him in the
perception of a sensible object, to invent sounds which should
symbolize the entire cluster of sensations. Hence the names
of External Objects, (the sun, the sky, &c.,) or Clusters of Sensations, or, in the language of later philosophy, " permanent
possibilities " of clusters of sensations. Of these clusters some
included a greater, some a less, number of sensations. Men
advanced, no doubt, gradually from the latter to the former.
It was then further found necessary to make these marks of
sensations on the one hand, and of clusters of sensations on
the other, stand for *classes* of sensations, and *classes* of
clusters of sensations. Mill puts this again on the ground of
economy, though, as we shall see, this was not the only motive
which prompted the invention of class-names.

In the next place, marks for Ideas were required. Ideas,
as we have seen, are either Simple or Complex. And, for
purposes of Naming, the Complex Ideas are further divisible

into those as to which the mind has not exerted itself to form the combination, but the cluster of ideas has been copied directly from a cluster of sensations found ready made, so to speak, in the natural world; such ideas, that is, as those of external objects, rose, house, river, &c.; and, secondly, those ideas in respect of which the mind has exercised its active powers in putting together arbitrarily various copies of sensations, and has itself constructed the idea of a cluster of sensations, which cluster does not answer to any object in fact existing in the order of physical phenomena; such ideas, for instance, as centaur, mermaid, sea of glass, snark, &c., or again language, piety, nation, &c. The former of these may be called Sensible Complex Ideas, or *copies of clusters of sensations*, the latter Mental Complex Ideas (answering to Locke's Mixed Modes), or *clusters of copies of sensations*. The names of the Mental Complex Ideas as well as those of Simple Ideas and those of Sensible Complex Ideas stand for classes, as well as individuals, in order to be as extensively applicable as possible, and to economize the use of marks. But in the two latter cases, the name (according to Mill, though this seems decidedly doubtful) stands both for the sensation, and the idea of the sensation, for the cluster of sensations, and the idea of the cluster of sensations; whereas, in the case of Mental Complex Ideas, the name of course only stands for the idea, since there is in the order of nature no cluster of sensations corresponding to the idea. However, in escaping one sort of ambiguity (whether real or not), we are met by another; for, since the idea of the cluster is formed arbitrarily, each man frames his own idea of the cluster, and therefore cannot be sure when using the name corresponding to it that he is communicating to another the idea which he himself possesses, since there is no actual cluster of sensations experienced, or capable of being experienced, to

E

which reference may be made as a standard. One man's idea of religion or of patriotism is not another man's idea. Half the debates and controversies, political, religious, and philosophical, which have occupied the attention of the world, divided a house against itself, distracted humanity, and often culminated in bloodshed and war, have arisen in large measure from the impossibility of one man conveying to another by means of names the exact complex idea in possession of his own mind.

As soon as a name had been invented to stand for all the individuals of a class, it was found that, in the desire for economy, the name had been made to express too much. Men wished to distinguish between varieties of a class, and to signify sub-classes by signs. For this purpose adjectives were invented. This device, besides sufficiently effecting the ends of economy, had this further advantage, that cross-divisions were rendered possible, as well as (with the assistance of the copula) predication, which is a distinct means, or rather symbolizes a distinct means, of adding to the sum of our knowledge. (This latter feature in the use of adjectives Mill does not seem to properly appreciate.) Were names always to be invented for the smaller parcels into which the main genera are broken up, a language would become too copious for serviceable use; the appending of adjectives, however, to the names of the classes, when occasion demands, serves the same purpose, while the adjective is available for breaking up, not one class only, but several, into appropriate sub-classes. If substantives, consequently, are marks, adjectives are marks upon marks, as Mill says. Verbs are similar marks upon marks, and are essentially adjectives, but " receive a particular form, in order to render them at the same time subservient to other purposes." Mill's analysis of the moods and tenses of verbs corresponds with his analysis of the nature and use of

adjectives, and exhibits the same incompleteness. He conceives the verb to be merely a name qualifying its subject,
carving a sub-class out of the class represented by the name
of that subject, and stating that the particular phenomenon
adverted to belongs to that sub-class. He ignores the fact
that a proposition with a verb in it does more than merely
name; it involves a predication or affirmation, and is designed
to convey information from one person to another as to the
occurrence or order of sequence of certain sensations in the
mind of the person communicating the information, dependent
upon the occurrence or order of sequence of certain natural
phenomena. If I inform another that the sun rose at 5 a.m.
yesterday, I do not merely carve out of the class of rising
suns a sub-class of suns rising at 5 a.m., and name yesterday's
sun as belonging to that sub-class. I convey to him information as to the sequence of my sensations in a particular
order and manner. And, similarly, if I say that the rose
which I saw yesterday was a yellow one. To subdivide great
classes into smaller ones, and save labour and multiplication
of names, is not, as Mill seems to think, the sole or most
important object either of verb-framing or adjective-framing;
nor are verbs *merely* adjectives so fashioned as to imply "a
threefold distinction of agents, with a twofold distinction of
their number, a threefold distinction of the manner of the
action, and a threefold distinction of its time."

Besides the device of special marks to call attention to some
one prominent sensation in the midst of a cluster or bundle of
sensations, or to denote that a particular sensation or sequence
of sensations was experienced along with the cluster of all
those sensations usually comprised in its appropriate class-
name—the provinces of adjectives and ordinary verbs respectively—a symbol has been invented by means of which, when
coupled with a name denoting a sensation, or a cluster of

sensations, we signify the fact that the sensation, or cluster
of sensations so denoted, was at some past time in fact
experienced by some sentient being—or is now being so
experienced, or might then have been, or may now, or at any
future time, be experienced by any sentient being bringing
himself within the range of possibility of being affected by
them. This is the verb denoting Existence, the Verb Substantive as it is called. When we say that a thing exists, or
is, we mean that we may have sensations from it. This mark
is, therefore, the most comprehensive and generical of all the
secondary marks that have been invented.

But there is an unfortunate peculiarity attending the named
signifying Existence in most languages, namely, that this
same verb is also used for the copula in predication. Predication, according to Mill, serves two purposes; first, to mark
the order of the ideas in a train of thought which we wish to
communicate or record—(it will readily be seen that this
account is insufficient; we wish the order to be believed in as
having corresponded to fact);—secondly, to signify that a
certain name (the predicate) is the mark of the same idea of
which another name (the subject) is also the mark—(here
too, the essential element of information as to matter of fact
is omitted). A name merely brings an idea of a sensation,
or of a cluster of sensations, before the mind; a predication
denotes an order of sensations and ideas, and, supplementing
Mill, we may say, that it conveys information and contains
an assertion; it represents, in J. S. Mill's words, "some co-
existence, or succession of phenomena experienced, or supposed capable of being experienced." [*Anal.* vol. i. p. 162.
Editor's note.] Now, whenever we predicate, we employ the
word "is;" and we predicate quite as often of sensations
merely supposed, for the moment, capable of being experienced, as of sensations actually experienced, or *believed*

capable of being experienced. Yet, in the former case, where the subject of the predication does not, in fact, exist, nor ever has existed, the copula " is," from its association in other connexions with the idea of existence, induces the habit of belief in the existence, *in rerum naturâ*, of what is in fact, a nonentity. In this way endless confusion of thought has arisen. James Mill points this out very elaborately, and was, indeed, the first to do so in any detail. Still further evidences have, since his day, been forthcoming from the Positivists and others, to show the monstrous hypotheses, theories, and even systems, of philosophy for which this terrible little word is responsible. The Fallacy of the Copula was at the bottom of most of the false views of the ancient Greek, especially the Platonic, philosophy. It has induced the personification, even the deification of essences, qualities, attributes, &c. It has been the great king-maker of the metaphysical world: and from it alone such conceptions as Time, Space, Chance, Fate, Nature, hold their ontological dominion.

Mill's further remarks on predication by means of Genus, Species, Differentia, Proprium, Accidens, contain nothing new or remarkable. His account, however, of the different kinds of trains of thought, which are represented by predication, deserves notice. In communicating or recording we have occasion to mark either (1) the order of sensations experienced by us at any time, or (2) the order of ideas in a train of thought which has passed through our minds. In the former case the order which we desire to communicate or record, may either be the order of succession in time, or of position in space. In the latter, the ideas, the sequence of which we wish to represent. by predication, are generally related to one another, either as cause and effect, or in the way of resemblance, or lastly as included under the same name. When a man forbears to strike a match near a barrel of gun-

powder, Mill says that the train of ideas urging forbearance
is merely a sequence, or rather a set of sequences, of ideas :—
"I strike the match on a box"—"the stroke produces a
spark"—"the spark ignites the gunpowder"—"the ignition
of the gunpowder causes an explosion." This set of sequences
is all that is involved, according to Mill, in the predication,
"This gunpowder will explode if I strike the match against
the box." The analysis is here obviously, almost grotesquely,
deficient, from the omission once more of the element of
conviction. All the above ideas might successively pass
through the mind without giving rise to the *belief* which
would warrant a predication of the kind pointed out. [*Anal.*
i. 187. J. S. Mill's note.] Predication of Resemblance is
in the same way regarded as merely naming, and nothing
else. And just as propositions or predications are nothing
but naming, so also is the syllogism by which a third proposition is elicited from two of such predications as premises.
All idea of there being an inferential process, or of fresh
information being conveyed in syllogizing, is abandoned.
The successive predications : "every tree is a vegetable"—
"every oak is a tree"—"therefore, every oak is a vegetable," are, according to Mill, naming, and nothing but
naming, throughout. The same criticism which applies to
his account of predication will, of course, apply to his account
of syllogism, on which we may have something further to say
hereafter, and also to his corresponding view of arithmetical
and geometrical propositions, as being merely verbal. When
(according to Mill), we say that $7 + 5 = 12$, or that the three
angles of a triangle are equal to two right angles, we merely
call $7 + 5$, and the three angles of a triangle respectively, by
other names, the marking power of which is more precise and
well known to us than that of the names which we first assign
to them.

There is one other kind of predication to be noticed, namely, that in which the subject is a name, and the predicate the name of a name,—predications, for example, which contain descriptions or definitions of terms, such as " argument," " metaphor," " oration," &c. It is somewhat curious that, having specially called attention to this class of predications, Mill failed to see that it is only to this class, as distinct from the others, that his theory of Predication as a mere naming operation is applicable. In such cases as these, and in such only, we really do not mark any sequence of sensations or ideas as having been actually experienced, or even as having been the possible object of experience : we here import no element of belief into the predication, and we do, in fact, what Mill wrongly says that we do in all predications,—" signify that a certain name is the mark of an idea of which another name is also the mark."

Mill's further remarks on the other grammatical forms of language, such as Adverbs, &c., have no very necessary relation to his general system, besides being based on the obsolete, though ingenious speculations, of Horne Tooke, as contained in his *Diversions of Purley*. We pass on therefore to Hartley's account of the connexion between words or names and ideas.

Hartley does not treat the various classes of words after James Mill's fashion, or show how names are first given to sensations, then to clusters of sensations, then generalized into class-names, out of which sub-classes are carved by means of adjectives and verbs : he proceeds on a rather different tack, and prefers, in accordance with the more physical bent of his studies and observations, to give a sort of natural history of the process by which in the growing mind ideas are gradually associated with words, and thought wedded to language. For, as he says, words and phrases must excite ideas in us by association, and can excite them in no other way. Words may (physically) be considered from four points of view. They may be treated as impressions made upon the ear; or as the actions of the organs of speech; or, again, as impressions made upon the eye by written characters; or, lastly, as the actions of the hand in writing. And the above is the chronological order of the different ways in which children gradually become conversant with their use. The first of these relations in which words necessarily stand to the mind of a child, affords him some rough notion of their bare meaning, sufficient for the common purposes of life : the second makes the knowledge so acquired handy and serviceable : the third enlarges it, and renders it copious by association with other words in the way of definition and description : the last renders the mind " careful in distinguishing, quick in recollecting, and faithful in retaining, the new signi-fications of words " acquired by reading. Thus Hartley's very true account of the distinctive advantages of the methods by which a child learns a language, Hearing, Speaking, Reading, and Writing, corresponds exactly (as regards the last three of these) to Bacon's maxim : " Speaking maketh a ready man : reading maketh a full man : writing maketh an exact man."

When a child's attention is directed to a particular object, (say, his nurse) the name of that object will be pronounced to him. This will occur frequently, till a bond of association is formed between the sensation of hearing the sound of the name and the *sensation* of seeing the face and form of the nurse; and the child will then, whenever he hears the nurse's name pronounced (supposing him, that is, to have acquired sufficient voluntary power over his motions) turn his head in that direction; and thus the process of association of the name with the visible *idea* of the nurse will rapidly be accomplished. Later still, the converse process will take place, and the sensation of seeing the nurse will excite the audible idea of the sound of the name. He will next notice that the name of the nurse will still be repeated in her presence by those around her, notwithstanding change of dress and other accidental adjuncts, and that the name of fire, &c., will be pronounced notwithstanding that the cluster of sensations of heat, light, &c., may be accompanied on the different occasions of its being named, by different sensations impressed by adjacent objects. He will thus learn to distinguish between the strong associations of the names of nurse and fire with the constitutive elements of these objects respectively, and the less strong counter-associations of these names with the variable surroundings of the objects. In this he will be unconsciously performing the process (to which we shall come presently) of Abstraction. He will be creating, or rather re-cognizing for himself, one of those class-names of which Mill gives such a different account. The next stage in his mental progress will be that of associating abstract names, such as whiteness, with the ideas of the attributes common to several white objects, while by means of adjectives he will learn to make cross-divisions of clusters of sensations. He will, at the same time, be forming complex ideas out of simple by the process already mentioned : his idea of the nurse will comprise not only the simple visible idea of her face and form, but also the simple audible idea of the sound of her voice, and the simple idea of the taste of her milk, &c. The use and meaning of particles will be learnt mainly from their association with other names to which meanings have already been attached, they being, like the x, y, z of algebra, " determinable and decipherable, one may say, only by means of the known words with which they are joined " [*Hartley*, vol. i. p. 274]. The attempts made by the child himself to express his own wants, then reading, and lastly writing, complete the process of associating ideas with language.

Though Hartley modestly confesses himself [*Obs. on Man*, vol. i. p. 277] "a mere novice in these speculations," and thinks that he has rendered " by no means a full or satisfactory account of the ideas which adhere to words by association," because, as he says, " it is difficult to explain words to the bottom by words, perhaps impossible,"—yet it will be admitted that he must have studied the *growth* of association very carefully in children—a study of which evidence is afforded in several parts of his work—and that his lucid exposition proved of obvious service to James Mill in his more detailed theory of Naming.

Words are, according to Hartley, divisible into four classes :—

1. *Those that have ideas only :* (excluding of course the visible and audible ideas excited by the sight and hearing of the words themselves.)
2. *Those that have both ideas and definitions:* (including under " definitions," descriptions, and explanations by any but synonymous terms.)
3. *Those that have definitions only.*
4. *Those that have neither ideas nor definitions.*

In the first class are comprised the names of simple sensible qualities, of what Hartley calls Simple Ideas of Sensation and Mill Simple Ideas, such as " white," " soft," " hot," &c. These are felt : they cannot be defined. No more can the names of right-hand and left-hand, &c., in any terms that do not involve a definition in a circle.[1]   Most names of clusters of

---

[1] On this ground Kant argues against the possibility of spatial relations being abstracted from particular and individual spaces. That amusing gossip, Sir Thomas Browne, in his *Religio Medici* (p. 17, 7th edit.), says " whether Eve was framed out of the left side of Adam, I dispute not;

sensations (Mill's Sensible Complex Ideas), that is, of most objects of the natural world, vegetable, animal, and mineral, apprehended by science, belong to the second class; because, besides having ideas corresponding to them, they are capable of being defined by terms representing an analysis of those ideas into ideas of the sensations comprising the aggregates or clusters. To the third class belong what Mill calls Mental Complex Ideas, representing clusters of ideas of sensations connected together arbitrarily by the imagination (such as "centaur," "yahoo," &c.), abstract general terms, algebraical quantities (roots, powers, surds, &c.), the technical terms of science and art, and, generally, those names of names which Mill especially notices. Particles, which have a meaning or possibility of explanation only in connexion with other words, come under the fourth head. Hartley (in pursuance of a favourite analogy of his) compares rather neatly the above four classes to four corresponding kinds of mathematical relations, (language being, as he says, after all, only a kind of algebra). The first class would thus answer to purely geometrical propositions, such as do not admit of being expressed algebraically; the second to propositions which admit of being thrown into either form, geometrical or analytical; the third to propositions involving equations of the higher orders, chances, quadratures, &c., which cannot be demonstrated otherwise than algebraically; the fourth to the algebraical signs representing addition, subtraction, equality, &c., which have no meaning apart from their relation to other symbols. But as, even in the case of purely algebraical propositions, geometrical illustrations and analogies are advantageously employed to render intelligible what is otherwise

because I stand not yet assured which is the right side of a man; or whether there be any such distinction in Nature." There is not: hence the indefinibility.

exceedingly abstract and obscure; so fables, metaphors, allegories, parables, and myths, will often render vivid, comprehensible, and easily remembered, the most subtle and purely intellectual conceptions and modes of reasoning. In fact, it is doubtful whether, except for such helps, the deeper truths of religion would ever become intelligible to the masses whom they are designed to reach: and the most influential and penetrating philosophies have been those which have made use of figures, metaphors, and analogies the most; as, for instance, Plato's doctrines, as compared with those of Aristotle, and the Baconian system as compared with the Kantian. Indeed, in the case of words of almost all kinds, not those representing abstract ideas alone, men are continually mistaking one another, because they do not mean the same things by the same words, different ideas being associated with one and the same symbol according to the different surroundings and circumstances of the individual using it. Words, in the first place, may be associated by different speakers, with different sensible impressions; though this mistake is not common, and, when it does exist, is usually the result of a physical defect, such as colour-blindness, and is not, like the other misapprehensions of the meaning of words, an "idol of the tribe," or of "the theatre." Secondly, the ideas and definitions attached to a word in one man's mind may, owing to fuller, exacter, and more scientific knowledge, or richer artistic appreciation on his part, exceed in comprehensiveness the ideas and definition attached to it in another person's mind. A yellow primrose means, both to a botanist and to a poet, infinitely more than it did to Peter Bell. To a Max Müller the word "mill" means a chapter in the history of the Aryan race; to an ordinary miller it represents nothing but the means of his livelihood. It is easy to see how, in the communion of thought between scientific and non-scientific minds, artistic and non-artistic imaginations, confusion will inevitably arise, since both may use the same name, while each annexes to it his own meaning—a meaning which is really the result of, almost part of, his own life. But confusion and misinterpretation (as we have already seen) chiefly arise in the employment of names of the third class— names of Mental Complex Ideas—which have definitions, but no ideas directly answering to them ; though, of course, the terms of the definition are usually names (some of them, at least), of simple ideas of sensation.   Here not only is it the case that the uninstructed mind will have a different defini- tion from that of the scientific mind of the name used in common by both : and that even when the definition is identi- cal in words, the simple ideas represented by the explanatory terms are often so numerous, that the chances of mistake incidental to the use of the above-mentioned names of the second class are indefinitely multiplied :[2] but it is also true that two cultivated minds, but cultivated in different ways, brought up in different schools of thought, and possessed by opposing theories, are even more constantly misunderstanding one another, and arguing at cross purposes.   Neither takes the pains to get within the circle, and imbibe the atmosphere, so to speak, of the other's mental habits, and ways of looking at things.   To an Associationist and a disciple of Kant, for instance, the names, "Cause, Will, Motive, Self, Idea," would suggest even more widely different ideas than they would in the case of the philosophic and non-philosophic minds.   Can any one suppose that James Mill, for instance, or even J. S. Mill and Mr. Herbert Spencer, have ever really understood the

---

[2] Take the word " cause " for instance. To the philosopher and scientific man this term means something far more precise than to the untrained intellect. In the latter case it includes a variety of relations, rigidly excluded in the former, such as occasion, condition. etc.

Kantian or Hegelian stand-point? or that Coleridge and Mr. Stirling ever completely appreciated the *point d'appui* of the Associationist? In some few men, such as Goethe, and, in a less degree, G. H. Lewes, one sees some capacity of interpreting each view in terms of the other—a sort of "point of indifference," where true appreciation of both sides may be possible; but such men are very rare. Hartley pathetically expresses a hope, rather than an expectation, that "since children learn the use of words most evidently without having any data, any fixed point to go upon, philosophers and candid persons may learn at last to understand one another with facility and certainty." [*Obs. on Man*, vol. i. p. 285.] In the fourth class of names mistakes must obviously be of rare occurrence, rarer even than in the first, and "could not arise at all," says Hartley, "did we use moderate care and candour." Indeed in an even more hopeful, if not in a slightly ironical, strain he subsequently expresses his opinion, that "it seems possible and even not very difficult, for two truly candid and intelligent persons to understand each other *upon any subject.*"

In connexion with this part of his subject Hartley has some judicious observations on the difficulty of translating one's native into a foreign language, as compared with the ease with which the converse process is effected, which contrast he adduces as an illustration of that law of association by which, when two sensations or two ideas occur together in the order A, B, or *a, b,* respectively, the sensation B, or idea *b,* on recurring, will not excite the idea *a,* with the same facility or regularity as that with which the sensation A, or the idea *a,* will call up the idea *b.* He also has ingenious comments and suggestions on the subject of a philosophical and universal language—a kind of speculation which has engaged the attention of philologists and grammarians, since the building of Babel first elevated comparative philology into the dignity

of a science to the present day—and on the subject of a philosophical dictionary to assist "candid and intelligent" persons
in understanding one another; both of which schemes may
be noticed hereafter, together with other curious Hartleian
fancies.

We must not omit, before concluding this chapter, to notice
Hartley's remarks on analogies and figurative language. "A
figure," he defines as "a word which, first representing the
object or idea A is afterwards made to represent B, on account
of the relation which these bear to each other." But this is
clearly a process applicable to every formation of a class-name.
Indeed Hartley, though not very distinctly, admits as much,
and says that, when the analogy is very complete, the expression framed on it is considered a literal one (as in the case
of class-names); when not very complete the expression is
called a figurative one. If we suppose that the word " man "
has been applied to several individuals, A, B, C, &c., one
after the other, and that then the appearance of an individual X suggests the word " man," and he is denoted by it,
because of the analogy of X to A, B, C, &c., we have an intelligible law of association, and one which partly supplies the
deficiencies in Mill's account of the framing of class-names
with the single deliberate intention of economizing words. The
perception of analogy between the individuals comprising a
class is, it may be thought, one very necessary element in this
mental operation. Of course, as Hartley observes, when a
word appropriated ordinarily to the individuals of one genus
or species, is applied to an individual belonging to another;
the nearer the two genera or species are to one another in all
essential features, the nearer the use of the word as so applied
approaches literalness; and the less features the two genera
or species have in common, the nearer the use of the word
approaches analogy proper or metaphor, either of which, when

duly expanded and improved by means of art, may become a simile, a fable, a parable, or an allegory. Thus a name usually applied to the animal kingdom will with more literalness, and less metaphor, be applied to a member of the vegetable, than to a member of the mineral, kingdom. Expressions, it is to be remarked, in their original employment and application figurative become, from constant use, literal; and these expressions, literal, so to speak, by second nature, can by further and more extended applications, become analogical again. With his keen eye for the educational uses, which the principle of association of ideas may and should subserve, Hartley notices how in allegories, fables, parables, and other emblematic modes of speech, all the properties, whether beauties or defects of, and the feelings of desire or disgust excited by, the images are transferred by association to the things and conceptions imaged. " Hence," he concludes, with an almost Platonic sense of the importance of a judicious myth, or γενναῖον ψεῦδος, " the passions are nursed to good or evil, speculation is turned into practice, and either some important truth felt and realized, or some error and vice gilded over and recommended."

CHAPTER IV.

THE THEORY OF ASSOCIATION AS APPLIED TO EXPLAIN THE MORE IMPORTANT PROCESSES AND OPERATIONS OF THE MIND.

AMONG the different powers or faculties of the intellect (as a great many philosophers would call them), or the different mental operations and processes (to use the term which Mill would himself prefer), the most general and comprehensive, the one which—if we are to begin from the beginning, and work down from genus to species—immediately suggests itself, is Consciousness. Mill accordingly considers this in the first place. But "can it be called a special feeling, or mental process, at all?" he first asks. No: because "to be conscious of a feeling" is only another way of saying, "to feel a feeling," which again is a tautological, redundant, and cumbersome way of saying "to have a feeling." Similarly the feeling of an idea, and the consciousness, or the being conscious, of an idea are only different ways of expressing the same fact, namely, the having of the idea. Consequently to Mill Consciousness means nothing but Feeling in general. It is not a special feeling, operation, or state, distinct from other feelings, operations, or states; and to suppose (with Reid, for instance) that it is, only tends to introduce confusion and mystery into what is otherwise clear and intelligible. To feel, to remember, to reason, to believe, to judge, are severally identical with the processes described as "being conscious" of feeling, remembering, reasoning, believing, or

F

judging. The term Consciousness is merely a convenient generical mark. [*Anal.* vol. i. ch. v.]

Mill holds similar opinions as to the meaning of the term Reflection. [*Anal.* vol. ii. pp. 176—180.] He thinks that it, like Consciousness, is merely a class-name. Accepting Locke's definition of the word—" that notice which the mind takes of its own operations "—he again insists that the having a state of consciousness, and the knowing, or the observing, or the taking notice of, that state, are all one and the same thing. The notice is the consciousness, and the consciousness is the notice. Consequently Reflection = Consciousness. When we say that we attended to this sensation more than to that, we mean that we felt this sensation more than that—that this, in fact, was more a sensation than that. The so-called Idea of Reflection has, therefore, according to Mill, nothing mysterious about it. Its formation, as in the case of Consciousness and all other class-names, is merely the result of a previous process of generalization from particular instances,— in this case, particular instances of remembering, believing, judging, imagining, &c. The supposition that there is anything in the Idea of Reflection other than this has arisen from the unfortunate double use (already noticed) of the word Idea, to signify both a particular copy of a sensation, that is a fleeting state of consciousness entertained one moment and dismissed the next, and also the state of having ideas in general, which should more properly be called Ideation.

The identification of feeling (including under the term the having a sensation and the having an idea) with the act of attention to feeling, is a cardinal tenet of Mill's system, and is continually being reiterated by him. Most later Associationists dissent entirely from this position. Mill is on the whole consistent in his belief, though he does not appear to be conscious of all the objections which are capable of being

urged against it; at least he does not notice them all, or seem
to appreciate the importance of those which he does notice.
Take the case of reading from a book, or playing a musical
instrument; this supplies a ready objection, which does not,
however, seem to have occurred to Mill. It might reasonably
be urged that we must have had the sensations of seeing the
letters composing the several words, while reading, or of
touching the keys or strings of the instrument, while playing,
and yet we cannot be said to have attended to those sensations. Mill's statement is, notwithstanding, completely un-
qualified, to the effect that to talk of being conscious and at
the same time not attending to that consciousness, is to use
as contradictory an expression as if we were to talk of being
conscious and not being conscious at one and the same time.
The objection here noticed did present itself to Hartley, as
well as to the later psychologists, such as Mr. Herbert Spencer,
who takes the bull by the horns, and denies that we ever are
conscious of the sight of the letters, or of the sight and touch
of the keys, in the cases supposed; but he thinks that these so-
called sensations of sight and touch are really organic states,
which though not sufficient to excite corresponding sensations, are yet just sufficient to hold together the links in the
associative chain. [*Anal.* vol. i. p. 232. J. S. Mill's note.]

Conception, again, according to Mill, is a generical term,
but not so generical as Consciousness and Reflection. The
former marks a large class of feelings, but the latter terms
mark all classes of feelings. Which, then, is the particular
class of feelings (using Feeling always in Mill's large sense)
denoted by Conception? In brief—all kinds of complex
ideas. Conception, as the name imparts, is "the taking
together" of things : the term, therefore, is only applicable to
complex ideas, whether of External Objects (Sensible Complex Ideas), or of ideas of sensations arbitrarily put together

(Mental Complex Ideas). Here again Mill objects to the term, the use of which so strongly illustrates the irresistible force of association, as well when directed into wrong, as when directed into right, channels. The expression seems to attribute activity to the mind. Though to have a complex idea is in reality exactly the same state as to conceive, yet the use of the term " I conceive," being in form active, imports into the notion of Conception an element which does not belong to it, and leads us to fancy that the mind is taking a more originative part when this form of words is employed than when we say " I have a complex idea."

For Mill's views on the subject of Classification we shall have been somewhat prepared by his theory of Class-names, which has been already described. The misapprehension, which he conceives to have existed from the times of Plato and Aristotle to his own, of the nature, object, and significance of Classification, was merely in his opinion, the outcome of the equally prevalent misconception of the meaning of General Terms or Class-names. Hence it was that " the most eminent philosophers " were bewildered, and " the human mind enfeebled " [*Anal.* vol. i. p. 248]. Mill will have nothing to do with the Platonic ἰδέα, or the Aristotelian εἶδος (between which he sees little difference), or the Forms and Essences of other philosophic systems. At modern " Categories " and Hegelian " Notions," and all such fond things vainly invented, he would doubtless have been inexpressibly shocked, had he troubled himself to read German philosophy. He cannot understand why so much " mystery " should have been made about the process. The individuals included in a class have, in fact, nothing in common whatsoever. To say so is to use a misleading figure of speech. We do not—as the ancient philosophers tell us, and as even Hartley appears to think—leave out of view the variable accidents and surroundings attaching to different particulars, and fix our attention exclusively on the essential qualities in which these particulars agree. This is not the process at all: Abstraction is not the foundation of Classification. Even the Nominalists, who thought that so-called General Ideas were nothing but Names, saw that this was not the case, and (so far) were more in the right than the Realists, who attributed to a General Idea—though that Idea was regarded by them as entering into the composition and partaking in the nature, of the several members of the class represented by it—an independent and separate existence. Just as Class-names were invented according to Mill (though probably all schools of philosophy would now hold his view to be erroneous), solely for purposes of convenience and economy; so Classification, or the construction of a class, is merely the forming of a very complex, and therefore necessarily somewhat indistinct, idea compounded of the ideas of that large aggregate of individuals, with which, from those motives of economy, the class-name has been successively associated. Mill thus apparently believes the idea of a class to be a complex idea in every sense in which the idea of a horse, or the idea of a centaur, is ; and that whenever a class is thought of, a hazy idea of a mass of undefined individuals, to which the class-name has habitually been applied, is instantly called up. Whether this explanation of the process of Classification is more or less " mysterious " than the accounts given by Plato, Harris, Cudworth, and the other Platonists from whose works Mill quotes long extracts, we must leave the reader to judge.

The process of classification, says Mill, is only one among other modes of forming a complex idea by means of association. By association the name of an individual external object—say St. Paul's—is connected constantly with the idea of it : the name never occurs without calling up the idea, or the idea without calling up the name. This is the simplest case of all. To take a rather more complicated instance :— a child hears the word " foot " pronounced first in connexion with the sensations which he derives from one of his feet, then with those which he derives from the other : and by degrees he finds the name pronounced indifferently in connexion with either set of sensations. Consequently, the word " foot " soon begins to call up in his mind the idea of either of his feet—at one time the one, at another time the other. It has already been explained—to take another example—how the ideas of *synchronous* sensations are so welded together by frequent association as, though in fact several, to appear only one (Sensible Complex Ideas). So, too, of the ideas of several *successive* sensations, the same law holds good ; and we thus get the complex ideas of a musical tune, a hunt, a horse-race, &c. And, to proceed further, several sensible complex ideas may be combined into a yet more complex, but still sensible, idea ; as (e. g.) the ideas of several trees into the idea of a forest, or the ideas of several soldiers into the idea of an army ; and also the different complex ideas of successive sensations may be united into a still more complex idea—the ideas of several tunes into the idea of a concert, the ideas of several sentences into the idea of a discourse, or the ideas of several days into the idea of a year. And we may even obtain a very complex idea in both respects—complex, that is, both as regards the union of synchronous and the union of successive sensations. Such an idea is the idea of Humanity (in one of its senses), which comprises the present together with all successive generations of men, past and to come. It is only a step further to the process of forming a class, which is nothing more or less than the process of associating one name, say " vegetable," with one external object after another,[1] to save

[1] With this further peculiarity, that the idea of, or sensation derived

the trouble of calling the several objects by several names, and so swelling the extent of language beyond all capacity of remembering it. The name " vegetable," therefore, in this case, is not a name having a very simple idea—the idea of a quality perceived by a certain special activity of the mind to be common to a variety of objects (as the Realists thought); nor, on the other hand, is it a name having no idea at all (as the Nominalists held) ; but it is " a word calling up an indefinite number of ideas, by the irresistible laws of association, and forming them all into one very complex and indistinct but not, therefore, unintelligible idea." [*Anal.* vol. i. pp. 265, 266.]

Classification, then (so far), Mill has pronounced to be merely a device for purposes of abridgment. He even distinctly says [p. 260] that " it is obvious and certain that men were led to class solely for the purpose of economizing in the use of names. Could the processes of naming and discourse have been as conveniently managed by a name for every individual, the names of classes and the idea of classification would never have existed." But later on in the chapter he seems to become somewhat conscious that this hypothesis will not suffice to account for the facts. After all, men classify according to some *principle.* There is something that not only leads them to classify, but guides them in classifying. We have a tardy recognition of this defect in the theory at p. 268. But, in answer to the question, What is this principle of classification ? he first tells us again what the *purpose* is—naming with greater facility than would otherwise be possible. But experience teaches us what method of grouping will best advance this end. Under the guidance of that experience it is that class-names are, by a somewhat perfunctory and unreflecting

from, each such external object, is, on each successive occasion, associated back again with the name.

process—though Mill calls classification a "mighty operation of the human mind"—determined. But we are still unanswered as to the principle of classification. We have been told its object—economy; we have been told its basis—association; and we have been told that experience supplies the principle. But what, then, *is* the principle? We are finally told in the last pages of the chapter. [Pp. 270, 271.] "It is easy to see what principle it is which is mainly concerned in classification, and by which we are rendered capable of that mighty operation; on which as its basis the whole of our intellectual structure is reared. That principle is resemblance." If this is Mill's view, it is more than ever inexplicable why he should have stopped short here, and have refused to entertain the theory which is the logical and legitimate issue of that view—the theory which most philosophers up to the present time, including Hartley, and even the Nominalists,² have held—namely, that according to which abstraction is made the ground of classification. Abstraction is as necessary to classification, according to almost all philosophers, except Mill, as classification itself is—according to several, such as Mr. Herbert Spencer—to ratiocination. Mill, however, marks off classification from both the one and the other by a broad and distinct line—indeed, is compelled to do so by his peculiar view of the former as subserving solely the uses of economy in naming. However, our business is not to criticize here, and we proceed to Mill's account of Abstraction, which, if not acceptable, is at all events clear, definite, and consistent with the rest of his philosophy.

In the operation of naming—as has been pointed out above —we first assign names to clusters of sensations, or individual

---

² Mill is mistaken in supposing that the Nominalists denied any idea corresponding to a class-name, or any process corresponding to Abstraction.

objects; next, we generalize these, to represent classes of objects; lastly, finding that the class-names have served the purposes of economy at the expense of adequate representation of important varieties of feeling, we carve sub-classes out of classes, and species out of genera, by framing adjectives. But, having done this, we are led to extend the operation in another direction. Having carved out of the class "rose" the sub-class "yellow rose," we perceive that for the very same reason that we call a rose yellow, we may call a gate yellow, or a ball yellow. In the cluster of ideas represented by the name "rose" I single out one, that of colour, and colour of a particular kind, for special attention. But the sensation and the idea of yellow occurs in connexion with other clusters; consequently, by degrees the name "yellow" tends to call up not only the idea of yellow rose, but also the ideas of classes of other yellow objects; and thus the adjective applied to one class of clusters after another, in all of which the idea corresponding to that adjective is an ingredient, is associated with all those classes indifferently, just as the idea corresponding to a class-name is associated with all or any of the individuals of the class indifferently. The word "yellow" is therefore associated with numberless qualifications of the idea of yellow by other ideas which in different cases are combined with it. These different qualifying ideas, together with the idea itself of yellow, are at last commingled, or massed, into one indefinite and vague complex idea, just as the ideas of the different individuals composing a class are welded into a complex idea of a similarly indeterminate character. In the former case, we get the formation of the idea corresponding to the adjective, in the latter, of the idea corresponding to the substantive, in language. And, in both cases, the idea and the name exert a reciprocal influence on one another. As the substantive "man" calls up the ideas of a variety of indi-

vidual men, while any individual man calls up the idea of the
name "man," and it again calls up another individual man;
so the adjective "yellow" calls up a variety of classes of
clusters where yellow colour is an ingredient, any of these
clusters calls up the name "yellow," and the name again calls
up the idea of some other cluster in which the idea of yellow
is a prominent feature. The adjectival name, it will be
observed, *notes* (in James Mill's language), or especially
marks and is associated with, the constant and invariable
sensation or idea of yellow; it *connotes*, or marks along with
this principal idea, certain secondary ideas, to wit, those of the
variable clusters with which the name is indifferently associated. Drop the variable and connoted clusters, the connotation, as Mill calls it, from the adjectival names or the
concretes, "yellow," "bitter," "large," &c., and the process
of abstraction is performed; and if a suitable mark is appended
to the adjectives to indicate this elimination of the variable
clusters, such as (in English) the suffix "-ness," the abstract
names "yellowness," "bitterness," &c., are formed. Abstraction is this, according to Mill, and it is nothing more.
It is thus, though analogous to classification, a perfectly distinct process; and the latter is not necessarily related to, or
dependent upon, the former.

Hartley's numerous corollaries resemble the postscript of a
lady's letter in this, that his best guesses and suggestions
are often contained in them. Accordingly, we find in some
corollaries to Proposition lxxix. [vol. i. p. 273] some interesting
reflections on the process of abstraction. He notices, first, how
a particular element in a cluster of sensations or ideas, to
which a name is attached, may force itself on the attention
more than its other ingredients. Generally this element is a
visible idea, but sometimes it is otherwise. This prominent
idea, he further remarks, will generally be found to be a

prominent idea, not only in one, but in several kinds of clusters. Hence such ideas as " white," " whiteness," for instance, after having been associated with the different visible appearances of milk, linen, paper, &c., " get a stable power of exciting the idea *of what is common to all,* and a variable one in respect of the particularities, circumstances, and adjuncts." Thus, though Hartley does not sufficiently recognize the mind's activity in paying special attention to the common element in a variety of objects, and speaks rather of that element forcing itself upon the notice of the mind, yet he particularly asserts that it *is* this something common to all the objects of which the mind takes cognizance, when it performs the function of abstraction. He, in fact, adopts the most considerable feature in that theory which his successor pronounces to be " mysterious."

To return to Mill. Having expounded what in his view Abstraction is, and what was the purpose for which it was primarily resorted to, namely, the formation of subordinate classes, he admits that this mental operation does, in fact, serve a still more useful purpose. [*Anal.* vol. i. p. 314.] The relation or order of ideas and sensations most important to mankind is the relation of antecedent and consequent, or the order of succession. On the knowledge of this relation between the various phenomena presented in the natural and the mental world, depends nearly all that part of human science which is available for the uses of life, and, through it, the welfare or the reverse of men. If, therefore, we observe a certain sensation, or cluster of sensations, follow another cluster of sensations, it becomes of paramount importance to us to mark what particular ingredient of all those which go to form this latter cluster produces the former sensation, or cluster of sensations. Now for the purpose of experimenting on the effects of any such ingredient, we must

be able to isolate it as far as possible not only from the remaining ingredients of the particular cluster, in which we first
observe its existence, but from the remaining ingredients of
other clusters in which it is equally to be found.   It is necessary, therefore, to mark the ingredient thus found in company
with these different "variable adjuncts," as Hartley would
call them, by a special name, and separate it in our thoughts
(where we cannot separate it physically), in order to reason
out its effects (where we cannot watch them).   And this is
Abstraction; which is thus seen to be one of the necessary
preliminaries to Prediction, while Prediction is necessary to
Science, to Happiness, to the business of life—even to Life itself.

We now come to those processes of mind which, though
closely marked off from one another by most schools of philosophy, James Mill, owing to his having committed himself to
certain rigid principles relating to the formation or the having
of ideas, experienced some difficulty in satisfactorily distinguishing.   We allude to Imagination, as contrasted with
Belief on the one hand, and Memory on the other.

Imagination, in Mill's view, differs from Conception in that,
whereas the latter relates to the having of complex ideas, the
peculiarity of which generally is that their component simple
ideas are synchronous, the former represents the combining of
ideas in a less or greater number (whether simple or complex)
successively.   This is the *process* of Imagination : any *particular* imagination (the term being, like sensation, used in two
senses) is, therefore, a train of ideas, while any particular conception (here again there is a corresponding double meaning)
is a single, though a complex, idea.

Imagination, like Conception, is often loosely used in as
wide a sense as Consciousness itself.   But in strictness, of
course, both the one and the other are far less extensive in
scope than Consciousness, and are related to it only as species

to genus. Imagination is often applied in an exclusive sense
to the poet's special gift, but this is merely a popular restric-
tion which philosophy cannot notice. In the essential meaning of the term, there is no person who has not Imagination,
because there is no person who has not trains of ideas in his
mind at any given waking moment. The poet differs from
other men in his imagination, because to him trains of ideas
and the formation of such trains are ends in themselves,
whereas to the lawyer, soldier, or physician, it is ordinarily
otherwise. But this does not make the constitutive features
of imagination any the less identical in all these cases. Imagination is none the less the having or entertaining of successive ideas, whatever may be the nature, interest, or object
of these ideas. In a philosophical sense, the lawyer who considers how he will frame an opinion or conduct a case, the
general planning a campaign, the scientific man solving a
problem, the chess-player at his game, is as much exercising
his imagination as the poet, who sees before him " shapes
more real than living man, nurslings of immortality."

Another inexact use of the term Imagination is apparent,
whenever it is applied (as it was by Dugald Stewart) solely to
the putting together of ideas in new combinations—in such
combinations, that is, or successions of ideas as have not been
suggested by previous combinations and successions of sensations. Dugald Stewart further thought that such combinations should be destined and directed to some end : and this
latter element also Mill very properly repudiated.

Hartley's views on this subject differed little if at all from
those of Mill. He too was of opinion that the term Imagination simply represents a succession of ideas linked together
according to certain laws of association, often unknown or
unobserved by us. But, following his usual method, he
treats this operation of the mind more physically, perhaps,

than psychologically, and has proceeded in his investigation a very short way, when he informs us [vol. i. p. 383] that "in all the cases of imagination and reverie the thoughts depend, in part, upon the state of body or mind," and he goes on to allude to the importance of "a pleasurable or painful state of the stomach," &c.   He flies off at a tangent to those unexplored fields of physical inquiry (such as dreams, prophecies, visions, and the like), and embarks on those "strange seas of thought" which had such a fascination for him.   He does not keep to Mill's severe and philosophical view of the essence and office of Imagination.   It may suffice, therefore, just to call the reader's attention to his occasional acute observations, such as that the various scenes in a dream are linked together .by association, and, to a certain extent, according to the laws of association, but that we are not offended at the wildest sequences of images, because the counter-associations, which would under ordinary circumstances dispel them, are in abeyance during sleep;—to his explanation of the phenomenon in dreaming which has within the last few years been discussed under the name of levitation, and of somnambulism;—to his curious and intelligent remark that the wildness of dreams is necessary to the health of the intellect in one sense, because they tend to break down the accidental associative links, which otherwise might become so cemented by continuance as to be rendered indissoluble, without having, so to speak, any title to this durability, and thus induce even madness in time ; and to the characteristic physician's caution, with which he concludes the chapter, to the effect that men may test their health by the pleasantness or the unpleasantness of their dreams.   We now pass on to the two philosophers' analysis of Belief, that of James Mill being almost the turning-point of his whole system, while Hartley's is full and exhaustive, though not so clear as that of his successor.

CHAPTER V.

BELIEF, AS INTERPRETED BY THE LAWS OF ASSOCIATION.

IN Belief are included Memory and Judgment; and with Judgment are connected the steps and means by which we arrive at it, Evidence and Ratiocination. But after considering Belief, the genus, it will be necessary, before considering Memory, the first of the two species mentioned, to investigate the elements which have to be added to those comprised in the mental operation of Belief—(the differentia, that is)—in order to constitute Memory. This will involve an examination of the Ideas of Time and Personal Identity. We propose accordingly in this chapter to give Mill's and Hartley's account of the following intellectual states, and in the following order :—Belief [Time, Personal Identity] : Memory : Judgment [Evidence, Ratiocination].

Belief, we have implied, is related to Memory, on the one side, and to Judgment on the other, as genus to species. This, however, is not strictly in accordance with Mill's views, at least as regards the relation of Belief to Memory. He says, indeed, in the chapter on Belief, that "it encroaches on the provinces both of Memory and Judgment :" and even in one passage [vol. i. p. 359] admits Memory to be "a case of Belief," but in the chapter on Memory he nowhere uses such language; and he appears not to hold this view seriously, at all events to the extent to which J. S. Mill holds it, who thinks that Memory necessarily implies Belief, and cannot exist without it.[1] Moreover, while he treats Judgment under Belief, in his arrangement of intellectual processes, he treats Memory quite apart as a thing by itself: though, according to the more sound view of the editor and commentators of the *Analysis*, there was no reason why the latter should not have had the same rank and place assigned to it as the former. It will be convenient for purposes of exposition to adopt what should logically have been, rather than what was, James Mill's classification of Belief and the states connected with it. The accompanying table may serve as a clue to our succeeding observations.

Belief: I. Belief in *events, real existences.*

    1. Belief in *present* events or existences :

       (*a.*) Belief in immediate existences present to our senses.

       (*b.*) Belief in immediate existences not present to our senses, either

           (*a*) Which we have not perceived [Testimony].

           (*β*) Which we have perceived.

    2. Belief in *past* events or existences :

       (*a.*) When the event or existence has been the object of our senses at some past time. [Memory, Time, Personal Identity.]

       (*b.*) When it has not.

           (*a*) Belief of Testimony [Evidence].

           (*β*) Uniformity of Law of Nature [as in 3].

    3. Belief in *future* events or existences : [Anticipation— inseparable association of like consequents with like antecedents].

  II. Belief in *the Truth of Propositions:* Judgment. [Ratiocination and Evidence.]

Belief in events or real existences is, then, the first of

---

[1] See *Analysis*, vol. i. p. 342, note, and pp. 411—413, where Belief and Memory (as involving it) are both contrasted with Imagination.

Mill's two grand classes of Belief. And, first, as to belief in *present* events and real existences, which may either be in immediate relation to my senses at the time of belief, or not.

Of belief in the former kind of existences Mill's account is brief and perfunctory. It is based on the ever-recurring formula—" to have a sensation or idea, and to believe that I have it, is one and the same thing." The two states of consciousness are not in any way distinguishable. Consequently, belief in *the sensations derived from objects present to my senses* is neither more nor less than the experience of those sensations. If it be objected that belief in a sensation implies something added to the sensation, namely, the associated idea of the Self; and that, in this sense, sensation may be distinguished from the belief in it; Mill replies that the idea of the Self is associated with the former just as much as with the latter. It, like the ideas of Position and Unity, is as much, and as inseparably, combined with the sensations of sight, for instance, derived from an object, as with the belief in the sensation. Sensation, then, in such cases, is itself belief. The curtain here *is* the picture.

But belief in the external object from which we derive the sensation is not the same thing as, and contains more elements than, belief in the sensation. When I am said (in ordinary language) to see a rose, I actually see colour alone : but the object, rose is a combination of colour, extension, figure, &c. Therefore, though I imagine that I see extension, figure, &c., I in reality only infer them ; and that I fancy to myself that I see them, is due to association in one of its strongest forms. Rapid and continually repeated passages of thought from the sensation of colour to the ideas of extension, form, distance, position, bulk, &c., lead us to suppose that we become, in the very experience of the sensation, immediately possessed of

G

that information as to the object, which is really the result of
association of (in the first instance) visual sensations with
tactual sensations, sensations of muscular pressure and resistance, and so on. The association in this case produces
each of the well-known effects which always follow its operation, when very forcible : namely, first, the blending of the
associated feelings into a single complex feeling ; secondly,
the riveting of the associative link so fast that it cannot be
broken, and that the mental illusion is rendered permanent and
indissoluble ; just as the optical illusion of seeing a stick present a bent appearance in the water is permanent and innate,
so to speak, though the appearance is all the time known not
to answer to the fact. This mental illusion is more especially incidental to the sensations of sight, because sight is the
primary and leading element in the clusters of sensations impressed upon us by external objects ; though there are also
similar illusions of less power connected with the other senses,
as (for example) when we fancy that we hear distance, whereas
we hear only modifications of sound, and *infer* the distance of
the object. Visual sensations, however, call up the resi-
dues of the clusters with greater facility, frequency, and
certainty than any of the sensations proper to the other
physical organs.

Therefore, when I see an external object, my belief in its
existence amounts to nothing more than this : that, with the
sensation of colour impressed upon my organs of sight, I have
inseparably associated the ideas of a variety of other sensations ; and with them I further have inseparably associated
the idea of myself as having them ; that is, I believe that in
certain circumstances I should have any one of these sensations. By walking to the object, I should have the sensation
of distance ; by touching it, that of hardness or softness ; by
the putting forth of muscular energy, I should have the

sensations of resistance, solidity, or impenetrability; by touching, and the expenditure of muscular force combined, I should have that of extension and figure.

To our supposed perception, inference, or belief of the existence of an unknown cause of such a cluster of sensations as is described above, nothing *in rerum naturâ* corresponds. The Substratum, as it is called, of certain qualities in the object, which produce sensations in us, is merely a fiction of association. We are always observing sequences. The order of succession in phenomena, or rather in our sensations and ideas, is more important to us than any other order. The tendency, consequently, in our minds is to find an antecedent to every consequent, and, if we cannot find one, to invent one. We are compelled by a law of our nature "to look before and after." This is another case of inseparable association. "The perception or idea of an event instantly brings up the idea of its constant antecedent: definite and clear if the antecedent is known, and indefinite and obscure if it is unknown." [*Anal.* vol. i. p. 352]. Now constant antecedent is Cause, and Cause is nothing else. Therefore the habit of seeking for such constant Antecedents is of itself quite sufficient to account for the belief in the existence of a supposed Object, as Substance, Cause, or Substratum of its various qualities (corresponding to the various sensations in us), though that Object or Substratum, except as a convenient and comprehensive name for the clusters of sensations with which we are simultaneously affected, is non-existent.

Now as to the belief in the present existence of objects not in immediate relation to our senses. Of this there may be two cases, according as the objects have or have not been previously at any time perceived by us. The former is the only case which it is necessary to examine now; since the latter, being an instance of Belief in Events on Testimony, may conveniently be considered below in connexion with the subject of Belief in *Past* Events on Testimony.

What then is implied in my belief in the present existence of Westminster Hall, which, though not now present to my senses, I have seen at some previous time in my life? I imply (for one thing) that if I were at this moment at or near Westminster Hall, I should derive the same sensations from it as I have derived on previous occasions. Put in this form, the belief is a case of Anticipation of the future on the analogies of the past, which will be considered as the third main head of beliefs in real existences. But it may be put in another way. In the belief in the present existence of Westminster Hall is involved my belief, that if any creature endowed with organs of sense like my own is at this moment in or near Westminster Hall, he or it has sensations analogous to the sensations which I myself have experienced when so situated. The explanation of this mental condition is to be found once more in the laws of Association. There is an invincible association between the idea of an animal body and sensation. First the association is created between the idea of my own human body and the ideas of my own sensations,— then between the ideas of human bodies other than my own, and the ideas of sensations analogous to my own,—then, similarly, as to the other creatures lower and lower in the scale of the animal kingdom, till we stop short at vegetables, and there the association, to any considerable extent (except in fetichism and poetry, the lowest and the highest intellectual states), fails us. " It is apparent," Mill therefore concludes [*Anal*. vol. i. p. 358] "that the case in which I believe other creatures to be immediately percipient of objects, of which I believe that I myself should be percipient if I were so situated as they are, resolves itself ultimately into this particular case of my belief in certain conditional sensations of my own," that is, again, to the case of Anticipation, which we reserve for the present.

Our Belief in Past Existences is, in other words, our present idea of something existing, and the assignment of it to a time past. Here again we have an obvious ground of subdivision into the two cases,—first, where the object in the past existence of which we believe has, secondly, where it has not, been present to our senses. The former of these kinds of Belief is, according to Mill, neither more nor less than Memory. Just as the belief in the *present* existence of an object *now* in relation to my senses is Sensation, and nothing else, so the belief in the *past* existence of an object which was *then* present to my senses is Memory, and nothing more.[2] Remembering a past event, and believing it, are merely two different names for one and the same state of consciousness. What, then, we have to ask, is involved in the process of Memory? Hartley and Mill both give answers to this question from their respective points of view,—Hartley, as usual, looking to his favourite vibration-theory, and relying largely on physical analogies and proofs, Mill looking to the principles of Association alone, which he wisely accepts as elementary, without seeking to go behind them for a more recondite solution.

Memory, says Mill, can only take place through the medium of ideas. Every act, or (as he would prefer to call it) state of memory, involves an idea. But it also involves more than this. The state of memory cannot exist without the idea; but the idea can exist without the state of memory. A further necessary element is association—association of ideas in trains according to its ordinary laws. This is manifest on

[2] Here Mill plainly declares Memory to be a species of Belief, and though it is not treated by him in this connexion, this is clearly its proper and philosophical place.

an analysis of the process called "trying to remember" (Aristotle's "ἀνάμνησις," as opposed to passive memory or "μνήμη," the mere recurrence of associated ideas without the exercise of any volition on our part). When we try to remember a thing, we run over every idea which we think may have a chance of recalling to our minds, by means of its previously contracted associations, the idea of which we are in quest. Each idea which we have experienced has, we know, been the centre of several threads of association; we therefore try several ideas at random, in the hope of one of them eventually having a path to the idea which we require. In some cases, of course, we take the precaution to determine the associations beforehand, as in the familiar devices of underlining passages in a book, tying a knot in a handkerchief, &c. Similarly, in order to remember the sequence of words, we repeat them, because we know that repetition is one of the most effective agents in generating association. Hence it is, that if we try to remember words which we have learnt, in any other order than that in which we committed them to memory, we find it difficult, if not impossible, to do so. Mill gives an interesting example of these predetermined associations for the purpose of securing accurate remembrance, in the practice of some of the ancient orators, who used to create an artificial relation in their own minds between the different parts of a temple, or other building, in the sight of which they were about to speak, and the heads of their intended discourse. By means of occasional glances at the temple, they were thus enabled in a double sense to work up from the foundation to the coping-stone of their orations. Of course, the success of such an experiment would depend on the relation which the speaker's power of remembering pictorial simultaneous representations bears to his power of remembering audible successive sounds. Men vary very much in this respect. Some will remember a lecture better than an essay, and an acted than a written play. Even in reading a book some men, with more or less conscious effort, shape to themselves audible ideas of the sounds of the words ; illiterate persons even reproduce the audible sounds them- selves; while others read so rapidly that they are not con- scious to themselves of forming any other than a visible idea of the written symbols.[3]

Ideas and Association, then, are necessary to constitute Memory. But are these all ? Imagination involves these, as we have already seen ; and, if these were the only essen- tial ingredients, receptive or representative imagination— imagination, that is, of clusters of sensations, Aristotle's " αἰσθητικὴ φαντασία"—would involve as much as " μνήμη"; and the active or creative imagination, which frames and deals with clusters of ideas after its own fashion—Aristotle's " βουλευτικὴ φαντασία"—would, if this were the case, be tantamount to " ἀνάμνησις." What, then, must be added to ideas and their association in trains to make passive imagination equivalent to passive memory, and active or deliberative imagination equivalent to active memory or re-

---

[3] Professor Max Müller notices an ingenious attempt (by Don Sinibaldo de Mas in his *Idéographie*) to create direct associations between ideas and pictorial or visible emblems, by constructing a language consisting of 2600 figures, framed on the pattern of musical notes, and capable of innumer- able variations in meaning, corresponding to those effected by the parts of speech, according to the position of the head of the note (*Science of Language*, vol. ii. p. 48). This would have commended itself to Hartley. Mr. Shute (in his *Discourse on Truth*) is, however, afraid that, even as it is, men are more and more losing their power of associating ideas with audible emblems, and tend more and more to assimilate visible signs in preference to them. The whole subject of the differences between the pictorial or local, and the successive or eventual memory, is gone into by Mr. Francis Galton, " Mental Imagery," in *Fortn. Rev.*, September, 1880, and *Mind*, July, 1880.

collection?   The answer is: The element of recognition.
" Suppose that my present state of consciousness is the idea
of putting my finger in the flame of the candle. I recognize
the act as a former act; and this recognition is followed by
another, namely, that of the pain which I felt immediately
after. This part of my constitution, which is of so much
importance to me, I find it useful to name. And the name
I give to it is Memory." [*Analysis*, vol. i. pp. 319, 320].
But this recognition is a somewhat complex process. What
are its elements? Can it be reduced to a case of Association?

We may remember either sensations or ideas formerly experienced by us. In remembering a sensation—say, the having
seen an object at some past date—the following conditions are
implied : first, a visible idea of the object; secondly, the idea
of my having seen it.[4] And the former irresistibly calls up
the latter idea, and in this we have (so far) merely another
case of inseparable association.

But into what elements is the idea of my having seen an
object resolvable? First of all, we may break it up into :
(1) the idea of my present (the remembering) self; (2) the
idea of my past, the then sentient, and now remembered, self.
These two ideas are connected at the moment of memory.
How?   By running over the intermediate states of consciousness, and (by means of a rapid process already referred
to) uniting the two terms and the intervening links into one
very complex idea. And this, again, is association.

The remembrance of ideas admits of an exactly similar

---

[4] To these J. S. Mill would add—the *belief* (independent of the evidence
of others) of my having seen the object. And in this he would be clearly
right; but James Mill thinks that there is nothing elementary or unanalyzable in Belief itself, which he regards as in every case reducible to
Association of ideas in the last resort, as will be seen in the sequel.

explanation. I remember, for example, my idea of Charles I.'s execution. In doing so, I have,—

> (1) The ideas of the various acts and objects related and described in the account of the execution ;

and

> (2) [Inseparably associated with the above], the idea of my having had those ideas.

And (2) again includes,—

(*a*) The idea of my present self remembering : ⎫ United by asso-
(*b*) The idea of my past self conceiving : ⎬ ciation into one
(*c*) The idea of the intervening states of consciousness : ⎭ complex idea.

To put the matter comprehensively (so as to include the remembrance both of past sensations and of past ideas), the necessary elements in the memory of our past experiences, of whatever kind, would seem to be as follows :—

i. The idea of my past self
  sentient or conceiving = ⎰ The idea ⎰ of a past sensation : or,
        ⎱   ⎱ of a past idea.
        ⎱ The idea of the Self.

ii. The idea of my present
  self as remembering = ⎰ The idea of the Self
        ⎱ The idea of [Remembering =] Asso-
        ⎱ ciating.

iii. The intervening trains
  of ideas, the calling
  up of which depends
  upon   Association.

So that the memory of past experiences has now been resolved to Ideas (one of which must always be the Idea of the Self), and Association. Nothing, therefore, now needs eluci-dation, in connexion with memory, except this constant factor, the Idea of Personal Identity, after analyzing which we may (since there can be no Memory without involving it in some way) examine the idea of Time.

Neither of the two important metaphysical problems of modern times connected with the investigation of the conceptions, ideas, or forms (as they are variously called) of the Ego and of Time, attracted the attention of Hartley; consequently we must be taken as here presenting the views of James Mill alone.

Personal Identity, or the Identity of the Ego, must be explained on the same grounds and by the same method as the Identity of other human beings, and this again on the same grounds as the Identity of other animal existences; and the Identity of animal existences in general can be explained in no other way than the Identity of inanimate objects. [*Anal.* vol. ii. pp. 164—170.] It is necessary, then, to satisfy ourselves as to the essence of Identity, generically considered, before we can show the nature of that particular species of it called Personal Identity.

Now when I say, that the object which I now see is the same which I saw ten years before, or that the words which I now read were written by a certain author 2000 years ago, or that the object which was seen 2000 years ago by one man was the same which was seen 1000 years ago by another,— Belief is involved, and nothing else. The first example presents one case of Belief, the second another, and the third another; but all alike are Belief. The reader will be somewhat surprised to find here what looks very like the interpretation of a thing by itself. One of the kinds of Belief, namely, Memory, is alleged to involve, among other elements, the Idea of Personal Identity; and this idea, as being merely a case of Identity in general, is then found to be a case of Belief. The definition in a circle is rendered still more conspicuous when we find that, of the three instances of Identity given above, Mill would call the first an instance of that specific kind of Belief which is called Memory [the other two being cases of Belief in Evidence or Testimony, or of Belief in the Uniformity of Nature, or of a combination of both]. And as to Identity in general, Mill's own statement is :— " As we have already shown wherein Belief, in all its cases, consists " [it must be remembered that the chapter on Identity was written after all the cases of Belief had been examined— an arrangement from which we have seen reason to depart] " we have implicitly afforded the explanation of Identity " [*Anal.* vol. ii. p. 165] :—while, in the chapter on Memory, he says, " It is in this process that Memory consists . . . . . No obscurity rests on any part of this process, except the idea of *self*, which is reserved for future analysis. . . . . . All this will be more evident when what is included in the notion of Personal Identity is included." [*Anal.* vol. i. p. 360.] Belief and Identity cannot, on Mill's own showing, be both capable of analysis. Either Belief must involve the idea of Personal Identity as an ultimate and irreducible element, or this latter must similarly imply Belief. In the face of the contradiction in terms patent in Mill's own language, we will not attempt to guess which element he really thought the unanalyzable one.[5] Let us examine, however, his reduction of Personal Identity to a case of Identity in general.

We have already seen what is implied when we say that the inanimate external object which we now perceive, is the

---

[5] J. S. Mill, in his notes to the *Analysis*, evidently considers that the idea of the Self involves Memory, while Memory involves Belief, and that this Belief is the ultimate element. Judging from the frequency with which he insists on this view, by way of correction on numerous other occasions where James Mill leaves out of account this ultimate factor in a variety of mental processes, we may, perhaps, conclude that it was Personal Identity which the latter, if pressed, would have admitted to be irreducible.

same object as that which we have previously perceived. But what do I mean when I say that some object *having growth and life* is the same now, when present to my senses, as it was when I perceived it at some former date? Whether that object be a vegetable, an animal of the lower orders, or a human being other than myself, I mean the same thing : I express my belief that there is a certain series (known by experience) of antecedents and consequents, which is called the life of that object; that this series is capable of being marked off and distinguished from all other similar series; and that my present perception is the last link in that particular series, and no other. In all these cases the Belief involved is one thing, and the essential thing : the evidence for that Belief is another thing, and may be of various kinds. The belief in the identity of another human being is often evidenced by observation, that is, sensation and memory of sensation ; or, in other words, it is often evidenced by itself; but more often it rests on evidence and testimony of another kind as well. Now, when I use the word "same" in connexion with my own life, do I imply anything beyond this belief? Nothing whatever. The Belief is the same, and the evidence is the same. So far as my memory extends, my belief in my own identity rests on consciousness and memory, that is (as before), it rests on itself; it is its own evidence. When I get beyond reach of my memory, then my belief in my own identity is supported by exactly the same kinds of external testimony as my belief in the identity of any other person, as to whom observation has not been possible.

We have said that, within the range of memory, the evidence for my own identity is Consciousness and Memory, the evidence for the identity of other men is Observation and Memory. In the latter case we have the memory of past observed facts, in the other we have the memory of past states of consciousness, added, in each case, to a present sensation. But observation itself is nothing but a state of consciousness. Therefore the memory of a series of states of consciousness, coupled with an existing state, is the evidence in both cases.

But the states of consciousness remembered in the two cases, though they are equally evidence, become evidence in different ways. And here we come upon a real distinction between the intellectual phenomena of the two processes. In the one case, we remember past states of consciousness in ourselves as pointing to the contemporaneous or prior existence of states of consciousness in others, or as marks of those states in accordance with the laws of association which decree that certain signs, to wit, impressions of certain sensations in us, shall call up in our minds the ideas of certain sensations of others signified by them : whereas, in the other case, we remember states of consciousness in ourselves for their own sakes, and not as pointing to anything else. To use the language of the law-courts, our own states of consciousness are equally the evidence in either operation ; but in the former they are secondary evidence, in the latter they are primary. In the former, they are imperfect means of inferring the continuity and separate existence of a series of states of consciousness, constituting the thread of life of the person (other than the Ego), in whose identity we assert our belief : in the latter, they *are*, in fact, *themselves* the thread of life of the person (the Ego) in whose identity we believe. The difference then between Belief in the Identity of others, and Belief in Personal Identity, is not in the evidentiary materials, but in the *manner* in which these materials evidence the existences or events to which credence is given.

In the idea of Time, which falls to be considered in connexion with Memory, Mill sees none of the mystery

which, according to him, other philosophers have found
in it. Its supposed necessity he regards as merely another
result of inseparable and irresistible association, since the
idea of succession, or of the relation of antecedent and consequent, is inseparably associated with the idea of every
object. Any theory of Time, as one of the forms imposed by
the mind on the matter furnished by sensation, he would,
consequently, reject; though he agrees with Kant so far
as to deny with him that Time is an inherent property
or attribute of objects. Time is nothing but the abstract
name of all successive order, just as Space is of all simultaneous order, [*Anal.* vol. ii. p. 132], and it is formed no
otherwise than as other abstract names are formed. With
the idea of every present event we associate the idea of an
antecedent, with this latter idea the idea of an antecedent to
that, and so on 'ad infinitum.' The idea of the present
event, coupled with the ideas of the antecedents so associated
with it, make up our idea of the Past, which therefore implies
infinite concrete past successions of objects; it notes, that is,
in Mill's phraseology, or primarily marks, successions; it
connotes, or secondarily marks, objects. Omit the connotation, as must be done to form any abstract name, and we get
the successions, without the objects,—or Time Past in the
abstract. In the above process put consequent for antecedent,
and by similar steps we arrive at Time Future in the abstract.
Next, regard all real or possible events (or objects, in Mill's
language), whether past, present, or future, as successive,
lump them together, and we obtain the idea of *concrete* Time
in general; that is, the successions with the objects. Take
away the objects, and we have left the successions without the
objects, or the idea of *abstract* Time in general. Thus Time
is an abstract name, the corresponding concrete to which is
ultimately built upon an indissoluble association, which forces

us, in contemplating any event, to go beyond it and look on both sides of it. Whether the above process would not rather give us the abstract idea of Successiveness, and not that of Time at all, we will not here stop to inquire.

The connexion of Time with Memory in Mill's system will be best seen in his own words [*Anal.* vol. ii. p. 120];— " Pastness is included under the term Memory. . . . Memory is a connotative term ; what it notes is the antecedence and consequence of the several parts of that which forms the chain of remembrance; what it connotes are the feelings them-selves, the objects remembered. When what it connotes is left out, and what it notes is retained, we have the idea which is expressed by Pastness." Mill would presumably consider an analogous connexion to exist between Anticipation and Futureness. But Anticipation (as we shall see presently) rests on Belief in the Uniformity of Nature, and this again on Association, and the association is based on felt and re-membered cases of succession. There is nothing, therefore, as we are expressly told, in Time distinct from Memory and Sensations.

Hartley differs with Mill, and agrees with Reid and most other philosophers, in considering Memory to be a faculty, and not an idea framed in a particular way. It is "that faculty by which traces of sensations and ideas recur, or are recalled, in the same order and proportion, accurately or nearly, as they were once presented." [*Obs. on Man*, vol. i. p. 374]. After this somewhat loose and unsatisfactory definition, Hartley gives us some desultory remarks, prin-cipally of a pathological character, on the relation between the state of the faculty of memory and the state of the brain ; in the course of which he takes occasion to notice that such a connexion would tend to support the vibration theory, since vibrations in the medullary substance of the brain may be presumed to be affected by such causes as disease, concussions, liquors, poison, &c.

Hartley appears to hold with Mill, that the exercise of Memory depends almost entirely upon Association; but he does not enter into any examination of the idea of the Self in connexion with this part of his theory. He answers the inevitable query as to the nature of the difference (on this hypothesis) between Memory and Imagination in much the same way as his successor. "Let it now be asked," he says [vol. i. p. 377], "in what the recollections of a past fact, consisting of an hundred clusters" [complex ideas] "differs from the transit of the same one hundred clusters over the fancy, in the way of a reverie? I answer, partly in the vividness of the clusters, partly and principally in the readiness and strength of the associations, by which they are cemented together." The notions of Personal Identity, Belief, Time, as incidental to Memory, are here ignored; whereas Mill would say that, in every such process as is above described, the idea of the Self, then sentient, and now remembering, would be irresistibly called into being. Hartley supports his contention, by instancing the remarkable fact,— which Mill also notices, but explains more completely and philosophically,—of a man, by frequent repetition, coming at last to believe a fictitious story told by him to be true. This phenomenon, says Hartley, is attributable to the "magnifying" of the ideas and the associations by the narrator. Mill on the other hand, in accordance with his more careful exposition of the idea of the Self as one of the constituents of Memory, asserts the operation to be due to the loss of one association, and its replacement by another. The narrator used to associate the ideas of the events imagined by him with the idea of himself as imagining or inventing them: this association becomes weaker and weaker, till it finally expires altogether, and a new association, namely that between the ideas of these events and the idea of himself as *experiencing* them, takes its place. It must be admitted, however, that the cause of this latter association supplanting the former, would appear, from Mill's account, to be something very like Hartley's "magnifying" the one, and ceasing to pay attention to the other.

Hartley also refers sagaciously to the case of a man in doubt as to whether his trains of ideas are recollections or reveries. But this phenomenon too might be accounted for more satisfactorily on Mill's, than on Hartley's, hypothesis. The latter is of opinion that such a doubt, (when the ideas are in fact those of remembered events), represents a diminution of the associations *between these ideas,* and (when the ideas are in fact merely imagined) an increase of the same : but Mill would maintain that such a state of mind would in the two cases respectively indicate either a diminution or an increase of the association *between the ideas of the events and the idea of the Self as percipient of them.* In madness and in dreams, to both of which Hartley is particularly fond of referring, the vividness mentioned is often magnified to an extent which causes the mental picture or image of an action or object to appear the recollection, in some cases, and, in others, the present sensible experience, of it. Mill [*Anal.* vol. i. p. 324] explains such phenomena in delirium, madness, or dreams to be the result of a mistake of *present* ideas for present or past sensations, just as in the above-mentioned case of repeated fiction *past* ideas are mistaken for past sensations.

Hartley's account of the attempt to recollect a thing (ἀνάμνησις) proceeds on the same lines as the foregoing notices of intellectual phenomena. When a person desires to remember the name of a visible object or of a person, he

" recalls the visible idea, or some other associate, again and again, by a voluntary power, *the desire generally magnifying all the ideas and associations;* and thus bringing in the association and idea wanted at last" [vol. i. p. 381]. He points out, however, with his usual accuracy of observation, but with no attempt at explanation, that if the desire be very great, an opposite effect is produced. Mill's analysis of this operation we have already noticed. Though more precise in his language than his predecessor, he probably meant much the same thing.

The state of the memory on recovery from concussion of the brain, or as existing in aged people (where it is retentive of old, and oblivious of recent, impressions), in idiots (where, in a mechanical form, it is often very extraordinarily developed [6]), and in children, is explained by Hartley for the most part on the principles of the theory of vibrations. In this part of his subject we have the usual abundance of disconnected, but ingenious, observations, and hints, often not worked out, but always containing much suggestive matter. He remarks, for instance, in one place [vol. i. p. 376], "that the visible impressions which concur in the past fact" [remembered], " by being vivid and preserving the order of place, often contribute greatly to preserve the order of time, and to suggest the clusters which may be wanting:" [the help afforded to one another by pictorial and audible images is, as we have seen, made a subject of particular attention by Mill]. Again : " when a person relates a past fact, the ideas in some cases suggest the words, whilst in others the words suggest the

[6] Instances of this are given by Mr. Verdon in his Essay on Forgetfulness in *Mind*, vol. ii. p. 412. See also on Memory, and its different kinds, Mr. Francis Galton in his *English Men of Science.* The latest views (those of Taine, Maury, Wundt, &c.), as well as his own, on the subject of dreaming, are given by Mr. Sully in his article on " The Laws of Dream-Fancy " in the *Cornhill Magazine* (November, 1876).

ideas. Hence illiterate persons do not remember nearly so well as others, 'cæteris paribus.'" The statements that there are limits beyond which the separate powers of the memory to receive readily, and to retain ·durably, cannot coexist [vol. i. p. 381]; and that all our voluntary powers are analogous to memory, and usually decay and increase " pari passu "—whence he concludes that the whole powers of the soul may be referred to the memory in a large sense, and that, though (as explained above) a strong memory may co-exist with a weak judgment, a strong judgment cannot co-exist with a really weak memory—are also deserving of attention.

We next come to the case of Belief in those past existences or events, which have not at any previous time been present to the believer's senses. For such a form of Belief, either Testimony, or faith in the Uniformity of Natural Laws, is the foundation. First, as to Testimony or Evidence. In some cases (as has been pointed out), namely, where the event or existence is believed in from our own experience, sensation or memory is both evidence and belief. But, in the class of cases now under consideration, the Evidence is distinct from the Belief. It is none the less, however, Association which, according to Mill, constitutes the Belief,—the asso-ciation, that is, between the ideas of the evidencing facts or events and the ideas of the facts or events evidenced.[7]

The evidentiary circumstance may be in immediate relation

[7] Sir T. Browne [*Religio Medici*, p. 45, edit. supracit.] marks off the two classes of Belief here distinguished, with his usual delight in laying aside large tracts of faith in which his simple soul may spatiate : " I am confident," he says, "and fully persuaded, yet dare not take my oath of my salvation : I am as it were sure, that there is such a city as Constan-tinople, yet for me to take my oath thereon, were a kind of perjury, because I hold no infallible warrant from my own sense to confirm me in the certainty thereof."

to the thing evidenced, or it may be several removes from it, and
only connected with it by means of a long train of associated
links, uniting together (as in so many other instances) to form
a single complex idea. When a sailor sees the print of a man's
foot on the sand in a desert island, and concludes that a man
has recently been there, there is immediate association of the
evidence with the event evidenced, of the idea of the mark of
a foot as consequent with the idea of the advent of a man as
antecedent. But if the sailor tells his experience to his companions who have not yet set foot on the island, *to them* the
belief is founded on the association of the idea of their in-
formant's affirmation with the idea of the footprint, which
idea is again associated with the idea of the existence of a
man in the island. Human testimony, it is to be observed, is
quâ Testimony, the same as any other Testimony. The
Watchman calling the hour is evidence in no other sense than
the clock striking it. The links in the chain may be, and in
complicated inferences are, extended to great length; but
nothing, according to Mill, is implied in the inference constituting this mode of Belief, beyond Association, however
numerous the links may be. What then, it will be asked, is
the state of Doubt, when two conflicting hypotheses suggest
themselves to the mind? Simply a struggle between an association and a counter-association, wherein the weaker eventually goes to the wall; but, meantime, the conflicting
associations hinder each other from acquiring the fixity and
inseparability necessary to produce Belief. Thus, if our ship-
wrecked sailor should happen to see a monkey on the island,
he will begin to doubt; that is, the idea of the footprint in
the sand will now call up two ideas instead of one, the idea of
a monkey and the idea of a man; and it will call up either
indifferently, and therefore will be associated permanently
with neither, till further evidence comes in on one side or the

other, such as, for instance, the discovery of some instrument, a kettle or a knife, which could only have been constructed by human agency. There would then be two ideas to call up the idea of a man, which would therefore acquire greater fixity and permanence; since the two exciting ideas, after frequent repetition, will (as has been explained already) "run together," as Hartley says, into one complex, or rather decomplex, idea calculated to call up the idea of a man with greater vividness and force, than the single complex idea of the footprint will call up the idea of a monkey. There is nothing in any inference as to the reality of a past event or existence beyond what is involved in the above simple instance. There is, according to Mill, merely "the antecedent, consisting of all the events which are called evidence," and "the consequent, consisting of the event or events evidenced," together with "that close association of the antecedent and consequent, which we have seen already in so many instances, constitutes belief." [*Anal.* vol. i. p. 432].

We may also believe in past events of which we have had no experience, owing solely to our faith in the Uniformity of Natural Laws: and, in so doing, we rely on precisely the same grounds as those on which we rely for our belief in *all* future events. This latter is the third of Mill's forms of Belief in real existences, and to its consideration we now proceed.

In anticipation, then, is anything to be discovered beyond Ideas and Association? Mill answers once more in the negative. The basis of our Belief is, in such cases, the inseparable association of like consequents with like antecedents, and nothing beyond. In believing that an event will happen, I have an idea of that event, in the first place,— that is, the event must be such as has been suggested to me by the analogies of past experience,—and, further, inseparable association between antecedent and consequent comes into play. I cannot think of an event without the idea of its consequent on the one side being called up, as naturally and constantly as the idea of its antecedent on the other ; to do so would be, according to Mill, to have an idea and not to have it at the same time. And there are two good reasons for the inseparability of the conjunction :—the constant recurrence of successive phenomena in experience, with nothing to suggest counter-associations or counter-analogies ; and also the interesting character of such successions to us, determining, as they do, our pleasures and pains, and, through them, our happiness in life. "The union has in it all that I mark by the word necessity ; a sequence constant, immediate, and inevitable." [*Anal.* vol. i. p. 366]. I cannot, therefore, have the idea of the present, without having the idea of its consequent, the future : I cannot think of the events passing before me to-day, without thinking of those which will follow to-morrow. And, when I think of these, owing to an irresistible compulsion put upon me by Association, I am said to believe in them. Thus there is found to be nothing special in that form of Belief called Anticipation of the Future from the Past : it, like every other case of Belief in Events or Existences, rests on Indissoluble Association. When we believe that the sun will rise to-morrow, or that a stone just hurled will fall to the ground, we perform, or rather undergo (as Mill might prefer to put it), the same mental process, as when we infer the distance of objects from the manner in which the eye or ear is affected by certain modifications of light or sound, or when an association otherwise separable by sensations and will becomes for the nonce indissoluble during the absence of these sensations, and the abeyance of the will, as in dreams, or during the temporary belief in ghosts which takes possession of a child in the dark. It remains to be seen whether anything other than Ideas and Association can be found to form the basis of the second great branch of Belief, namely, that in the Truth of Propositions, or Judgment. And here we shall be able to resume company with Hartley, who devotes several pages to this head of Belief, though under it he includes a variety of matters, which Mill more philosophically treats as cases of Belief in events.

The Belief in the Truth of Propositions is, in the opinion of James Mill, Belief in *Verbal* Truths merely. " Propositions consisting of general names are all merely verbal; and the belief is nothing more than the recognition of the coincidence, entire or partial, of two general names " [*Anal.* vol. i. p. 392]. But what the recognition of a coincidence is has already been seen. Having an idea, or cluster of ideas, and then having that idea or cluster of ideas again, is itself neither more nor less than the recognition of their identity. " To have two clusters of ideas, to know that they are two, and to believe that they are two, this is nothing more than three expressions for the same thing. To know that two clusters are two clusters, and to know that they are . . . . . the same . . . . . is the same thing with having them " [vol. i. p. 433]. When we express our assent to the proposition that "an oak is a tree," or that "all oaks are trees," we recognize a partial coincidence between the two general names "oak " and "tree." When we say that we believe that "all men are rational animals," there is a recognition of entire coincidence between the general name "man " and the general name " rational animal." In the latter proposition, the first of the two names calls up the complex idea of man,—this is a case of ordinary association,—the second name calls up the complex idea of " rational animal,"—this is another case of ordinary association. The next and only remaining step in the process of Belief is that wherein the two successive ideas are recognized as identical in the mere fact of their succession to the same mind. In assenting to a proposition of the former kind, the process is a little less simple, but still generically the same. The association of the two general names with the two complex ideas is of course the same : the difference consists merely in the fact that only a part instead of the whole of the complex idea called up by the Predicate is recognized as identical with the whole of the complex idea called up by the Subject. One part of the first complex idea is recognized as being the same as, the other part as being distinct from, the whole of the second cluster, in one and the same event, namely their succession to the same mind.

After this exposition of the nature of assent to propositions, we shall not be surprised to find that Mill's account of the syllogizing process—on which his successors have expended so much pains, and evolved so elaborate and various theories—was summary in the extreme. As has already been noticed, he believes that the credit given to the conclusion of a syllogism is given in no other way, and for no other reason, than the credit given to a proposition. The association is mediate instead of direct; but it is none the less association of ideas called up by names on which the belief is grounded. To infer that, because statesmen are men, and men are mortal, therefore statesmen are mortal, is simply to recognize the identity of a part of the complex idea suggested by the name "man," a part (only a smaller part) of the complex idea suggested by the name "mortal," and the whole of the complex idea suggested by the name "statesmen;" and to recognize this identity is the same thing, under another name, as having the ideas "man," "mortal," "statesman," in succession.

Hartley's doctrine of Assent to Propositions is somewhat different from that of Mill, and even more crude. Just as words have complex ideas attached to them, so sentences,

being composed of words, have decomplex ideas attached to
them. Such a decomplex idea often, and notably in the case
of propositions, contains other elements than the complex ideas
suggested by the separate words composing the sentence : that
is, the mere combination of these complex ideas is the cause of
an additional complex idea—that, namely, of assent or dissent—
being added to them.[8] The association is analogous to chemical
composition, where two elements when mixed together produce
a substance possessing additional properties to those possessed
by either of them in their original and independent state.
"And," he adds, "it would be of the greatest use, both in the
sciences, and in common life, thoroughly to analyze this matter,
to show in what manner, and by what steps, i.e. by what impressions and associations, our assent and dissent, both in
scientific and moral subjects, is formed." [*Observ. on Man,*
vol. i. p. 79]. Later on in the work he devotes several pages
[vol. i. pp. 324—367] to the consideration of the subjects
sketched out above, and makes some attempt of a not very
systematic kind to furnish the sort of analysis indicated. The
assent which is capable of being accorded to propositions may,
in Hartley's view, be either rational or practical. It is practical, when made the basis of action. In this sense, it may be
remarked, according to some later exponents of the Association theory (such as Professor Bain) *all* belief is practical;
indeed, is only determined to be belief by the sole criterion of
its sufficiency to support and give birth to action. Hartley
says that some propositions, such as those of mathematics,
admit only of a rational assent; whereas others receive only
the practical, without the rational. It will be, perhaps,
thought more true to say that every proposition, of whatever

---

[8] In his Latin Treatise, *Conjecturæ Quædam de Sensu, Motu, et
Idearum Generatione,"* he lays down boldly that "Assent and Dissent
are nothing but decomplex ideas excited by propositions."

kind, whether scientific, religious, or moral, admits of an assent
or dissent both rational and practical; and that, where it admits of the one, it must necessarily admit of the other. The
mathematical axiom that "things which are equal to the same
thing are equal to one another," or that "two straight lines
cannot enclose a space," is quite as much practically believed,
that is, acted upon, by any one who chooses between two
diverging roads in a country walk, as the proposition that
" benevolence is lovely, and selfishness odious " is practically
believed by the philanthropist in doing an act of charity.
One element or side of the assent may be thrown into the
shade by the other, the practical by the rational, or the internal
by the external : but every practical assent must rest ultimately, however unconscious or unquestioning the believer may
be, on a foundation of rational assent; and every rational assent,
or body of beliefs, or creed, must necessarily express itself in
action, except where there are counterbalancing or restraining
influences which deflect it from the straight line of motion
which it would, of its own accord, follow. In this case the
practical assent is given none the less, but other practical
assents, resulting from other rational assents, work with it.

Hartley's formal definition of rational assent, with which
only of course we are at present concerned, is somewhat per-
plexing. " Rational assent to any proposition . . . . . . is a
readiness to affirm it to be true, proceeding from a close association of the ideas suggested by the proposition, with the
idea, or internal feeling, belonging to the word truth ; or of
the terms of the proposition with the word truth." [*Observ.
on Man,* vol. i. p. 324]. This is unsatisfactory enough : nor
are we much helped when he explains why he calls such assent
rational, and not verbal, as (like Mill) he would himself have
apparently proposed to call it. He does so because " every
person supposes himself always to have sufficient reason for

such readiness to affirm or deny." Judging from these words alone, something more than association would appear to be suggested by Hartley himself in order to constitute belief in propositions. Nobody can suppose himself to have a reason for the association of two ideas. They are, or have become, associated ;—and that is all that can be said about them.

It will be seen that Mill explains Assent to Propositions on his own theory of the equivalence of Recognition of the Identity of two ideas to the mere succession to one mind of the ideas recognized as identical. Hartley had evolved no such theory to fall back upon; and, in consequence, is reduced to the necessity of committing himself to the doctrine that the ideas conveyed by the terms of a proposition, when combined together, propagate or strike out another idea which is not in any of the former ideas taken singly. Both Mill and Hartley repudiate necessity in propositions, and consider so-called axioms and necessary truths to be, in fact, merely verbal. Here again, however, there is a difference discernible in the two views. Hartley appears, unlike Mill, to mix up with his association theory of assent to verbal propositions, such as axioms, what is known as the experiential theory of their origin. Thus though he speaks of such propositions as " $2 + 2 = 4$ " being merely verbal, he also talks of " the entire coincidence of the visible or tangible idea of twice two with that of four, as impressed upon the mind by various objects," and says :—" *we see everywhere* that twice two and four are only different names for the same impression."

There is no more difficulty in the complicated than in the simple cases of assent to mathematical propositions. The coincidence of ideas is the basis, in the latter; the coincidence of ideas and terms together, or of terms alone, in the former. But rational assent to propositions, it may be said, is often based on memory, authority, &c. Here, says Hartley with

James Mill, the working of the association-process is only thrown a step further back. The memory or authority, on which we rely itself achieved its credit on the strength of association.

Just as in analyzing rational assent, Hartley feels himself bound to discover the presence of a new factor, after the combination of the complex ideas suggested by the terms of a proposition,—namely the idea or "internal feeling" of truth; so also he resorts to an equally forced and awkward explanation of practical assent, in holding, that the decomplex idea, together with the "internal feeling" of truth called into being by it, somehow tack on to themselves another complex idea—that of utility—before practical assent (in the large majority of cases, at least) is granted. To this extent, he allows that a practical assent even to mathematical propositions is possible.

Under the heading of Assent to the Truth of Propositions, Hartley, as we have before remarked, includes Belief in the Reality of Events, apparently on the ground that every event may be expressed as a verbal proposition. It would have saved a great deal of confusion, if both Mill and Hartley (instead of devoting themselves, the one almost exclusively to the verbal side of propositions, and the other to the experience and inferences from particulars, on which these propositions are based) had recognized the double point of view from which every belief of whatever kind may be regarded, first, as a belief in an event, fact, or existence; secondly, as a belief in the identity of the terms of the proposition stating it. In the proposition, for example, "all men are animals," it is the ignoring of the fact underlying the verbal statement which makes its explanation so apparently easy. If Hartley and Mill (for, in this case, Mill shares in the peculiar error of his predecessor) had gone on to treat of the belief in the fact, they would have dived deeper into the experiential basis of knowledge (symbolized by propositions) afterwards so elaborately discussed by modern philosophers, such as J. S. Mill and Mr. Herbert Spencer, and might have discovered that the proposition is just as much the epitomized result of a previous process, and the counterpart of a belief in events or existences based on inference, as the Syllogism (which James Mill also treated as purely verbal) is the epitomized result of a series of inferences from particular phenomena. Mill would further have seen that, conversely, the forms of Belief in real existences, which he treats with such systematic and pains-taking analysis, may be expressed and summarized in verbal propositions,— indeed in the latter part of his chapter on Belief in Verbal Propositions, he seems half-conscious of this,—and that Belief may be treated from two *sides*, but cannot, philosophically, be split up into two *classes*, one of which is to be called verbal, and the other real.

Hartley shows, in a variety of ways, what importance he attaches to the particular terms in which propositions are made to represent events or facts. " Terms or words are absolutely necessary to the art of reasoning," [*Observ. on Man*, vol. i. p. 330]. A sceptic is merely a man who varies from the generality of his fellows " in the application of a certain set of words, viz. truth, certainty, assent, dissent." This last very curious expression shows the hold which the " verbal " theory had obtained over his mind;—an influence which is also reflected in the long disquisitions on Language in which he is perpetually indulging, and in the frequent claims which he puts forward (in this very connexion, amongst others) for a philosophical language, to fix the ideas to be associated with words on clear and intelligible principles. We shall see that this influence was by no means without its effect even on

James Mill, though his error was usually in the opposite direction, when we find him treating some of the most obscure and intricate intellectual processes and faculties, and metaphysical conceptions, as merely "names requiring explanation."

And not only would Hartley like to see all beliefs in events and natural laws reduced to the recognition of identity in terms, but he would go further, and have them expressed algebraically. Algebra, he says in an earlier part of his work, is only a superior kind of language, and language an inferior kind of algebra: and in accordance with this view, he here devotes a section of his work to the algebraical expression of the laws of evidence, and brings in the theories of De Moivre and others to illustrate his views.[9] He has some interesting remarks (adopted by Bentham and J. S. Mill) on the distinction between a chain of dependent, and a centre of corroborative or independent evidence, the one becoming weaker as the number of links or media are increased, the other gaining strength with the multiplication of independent sources of evidence contributing their several streams to the same destination. Valuable hints are also thrown out on Induction, Analogy, and Hypothesis, which have long since been developed into exhaustive theories in the hands of recent philosophers. These we may have to notice hereafter.

[9] "It appears not impossible," he says on p. 352 of vol. i., "that future generations should put all kinds of evidences, and inquiries, into mathematical forms, and, as it were, reduce Aristotle's 10 Categories, and Bishop Wilkins's 40 Summa Genera, to the head of quantity alone." On Bishop Wilkins, and his Philosophical Language, vid. sup.

CHAPTER VI.

LEADING METAPHYSICAL CONCEPTIONS, FORMS, AND RELATIONS, AS ACCOUNTED FOR ON THE THEORY OF ASSOCIATION. SAMENESS—SIMILARITY—SUCCESSION—CAUSALITY—EXTEN-SION — MOTION — QUANTITY—QUALITY—ANALOGY—INDUC-TION.

THIS part of his subject James Mill calls " the explaining of certain marks or names." The title is peculiar—(" it is almost," says J. S. Mill, in the *Anal.* vol. ii. p. 2, note, " as if a treatise on chemistry were described as an explanation of the names air, water, potass, sulphuric acid, &c.")—and quite in ac-cordance with the general tenor of his views. Equally characteristic is his method of treating the above-mentioned metaphysical conceptions. They are all, from his standpoint, merely abstract relative terms. Now all abstract ideas are, as we have seen, merely concretes with the connotation dropped. Mill therefore first of all sets to work to unravel the different concrete pairs of related terms, and then shows how, in this, as in other cases, the corresponding abstractions are formed from them.

In analyzing relative terms Mill (following his usual plan) begins with the most simple and ordinary instances. What, he asks, is implied in the relations, Father-Son, Husband-Wife, Light-Dark, Greater-Less, Convex-Concave, Trustee-Cestui que Trust, &c. (where the related ideas are differently named) ; or again in the relations, Equal-Equal, Like-Like,

Sister-Sister, Friend-Friend, &c. (where the related ideas bear the same name)? The peculiarity of such sets of names as the above is that they always exist in pairs. "There is no relative without its correlate, either actual or implied"— implied often in modern languages, but usually expressed in the ancient.[1] Now we give names in pairs for no other reason than because the things corresponding to the names are found in pairs. We associate in name what we frequently perceive associated in fact: and we give pairs of names to some pairs of things rather than to others on grounds of convenience: in this, as in other cases, language abbreviates where it is most useful and important to do so. Now we can only name in pairs what enters into our minds either as sensation or idea. Ideas are, as has been shown, either Simple or Complex; and Complex Ideas are either Sensible or Mental. Simple Sensations and Simple Ideas we name in pairs, "(1) when we take them into simultaneous view as such and such, (2) when we take them into simultaneous view as antecedent and consequent." [*Anal.* vol. ii. p. 8.]

In the former of these two cases, we name sensations or ideas as like or unlike one another: (for the relations Same-Same, Different-Different, are not, according to Mill, philosophically or accurately named, the former, because *no* two sensations can be the same as, but only very like, one another, the latter, because *every* two sensations are different from one another to some extent). Now—as has often been noticed before—in saying that two sensations are like or unlike, we merely imply that these sensations have occurred in succession to the same mind. To have two sensations following one another is to be conscious of a change from one to the other; and to be conscious of a change is sensation and nothing else.

---

[1] E.g. "a gift to my son," translated into Latin, would be "dono dedit pater filio," &c.

Without such consciousness, the mental life would be as non-existent as if there were no sensation at all. A sentient being is a being with sensations in a continual state of flux, as the old philosophers said: and being conscious of the flux is nothing more than being subject to it. To have the sensations, red, green, yellow, in succession, is to recognize that each of the sensations after red is a new sensation. Similarly, to have a sensation and an idea in succession is to know them severally, that is, to distinguish them. Now, if after experiencing the above sequence of colour-sensations, I have the sensation of red a second time, it immediately calls up by means of association the idea of the previous sensation of red : I therefore have the sensation of red and the idea of red in succession ; to have them in succession is to recognize their difference, whether slight or considerable. In this case the difference is recognized as slight : and slight difference is all that is meant by similarity. To have similar or different sensations is, therefore, to know them as slightly or widely different from one another. The same kind of reasoning will equally apply to consecutive ideas of sensations, or simple ideas. And in applying relative names to such sequences, (whether of two sensations, of a sensation and an idea, or of two ideas), there is nothing more involved than in the application of the absolute names, red, green, yellow, &c.— nothing, that is, beyond "having the sensations, having the ideas, and making marks for them." [*Anal.* vol. ii. p. 17.]

We are also in the habit of marking successive simple sensations and simple ideas as following one another, or standing to one another in the relation of antecedent and consequent. The following mental train takes place when a sensation A is recognized as the antecedent to a sensation B. First, sensation A, next sensation B, then, thirdly and necessarily, the

I

idea of sensation A called up by sensation B, through association in a certain manner: last comes Naming. When
three sensations A, B, C, follow one another in succession, the
process is (1) sensation A, (2) sensation B, (3) idea of sensation A called up by sensation B, (4) sensation C, (5) idea of
sensation B called up by sensation C, (6) idea of sensation A
called up by idea of sensation B. But here the idea of sensation A is not called up immediately by the sensation C.
Consequently the sensation A is not recognized as antecedent
to the sensation C. So we arrive at the following proposition
[*Anal.* vol. ii. p. 21]: " when two sensations in a train are
such that, if one exists, it has the idea of the other along with
it, *by its immediate exciting power, and not through any intermediate idea*, the sensation, the idea of which is thus excited,
is called the antecedent, the sensation which thus excites that
idea is called the consequent."

Next as to the relations of complex ideas; and first as to
Sensible Complex ideas, or the ideas of external objects.
What is implied in naming these in pairs? The modes in
which we so name them are divided by Mill into four classes,
according as we regard the members of such pairs, (1) as
having an order in space, or (2) as having an order in time,
(3) as agreeing or disagreeing in quantity, (4) as agreeing or
disagreeing in quality. Now just as by dropping the connotations of the related pairs of simple sensations and ideas,
we have arrived at the abstract relations Similarity, and Antecedence and Consequence, so by first finding the concrete related pairs proper to the above four classes, and then dropping
the connotations, we shall arrive at the abstract relatives,
[Forms or Categories they would be called in other systems],
Position [and Extension], Causality, Quantity, and Quality.

With regard to Mental Complex Ideas, we may name concrete pairs of relatives and correlates, according as we regard

the members of such pairs (1) as consisting of the same or different simple ideas (2) as standing to one another in the relation of antecedent and consequent.

Taking the three classes, therefore, of sensations and ideas above enumerated, and the Relative Terms proper to them, it will be found that we have to show how the following Abstract Relations are established,—Similarity (on which we have already said something), Causality, Extension [Position], Quantity, Quality [Homogeneity]. We propose to give Mill's account of these in the above order: with Quantity we may conveniently investigate his theory of Numbers, and Equality; while in considering Extension and Position we may also consider his conception of Space as a privative term (in contradistinction to Time, which most philosophers rank with it as analogous), as well as his views on the subject of Motion. Afterwards we may point out in their proper place some observations of Hartley on Similarity and Causality, together with their respective cognate ideas, Analogy and Induction.

The process involved in calling two sensations like one another has been explained. Now the abstract term Similarity or Likeness must, like any other abstract term, note a quality, and connote the objects possessing that quality. It is easy to see what is connoted by the abstract term in this case: it is the two sensations, or the two series of sensations,[2] compared. What is noted is that inseparable, though not indistinguishable, part of the entire process, which consists in comparing the two as like or unlike. Leave out the connoted part of the process, and retain the notative, and we get Similarity.

---

[2] Because the series " red, red," can be distinguished from the series " red, green," as much as the single sensation "red" from the single sensation "green," and in exactly the same way.

Next, as to Causality. Here too we must first discover the nature of the concrete related pairs, before we can determine that of the abstract relation. Now it is a cardinal tenet of Mill's system that, in his own words, "all our sensations are derived from objects . . . . . And, reciprocally, all our knowledge of objects is the sensations themselves . . . . . Therefore a knowledge of the successive order of objects is a knowledge of the successive order of our sensations." [*Anal.* vol. ii. p. 37]. But it has already been shown that having two sensations or ideas successively is the same thing as knowing them to be successive; or rather the latter is an inseparable and inextricable element in the whole series of sensations or ideas contemplated as successive. This element, which, though never isolated in fact, can be isolated in thought, is that which is noted by the related pair, Antecedent - Consequent: the rest of the process, that is, the having the two sensations or ideas, (so far as the having them can be distinguished from the recognition of their successiveness), together with the ideas or sensations themselves, is what is connoted. Drop the connotation, and we have Successiveness, or Priority and Posteriority (when taken together). It is to be observed that Priority or Posteriority alone will not suffice, because either has a special connotation of its own,—it connotes the other,—just as a concrete object called prior connotes an object posterior, and *vice versâ.* In the case of single-worded, as opposed to double-worded pairs of related terms, the compound names (such as Likeness-Likeness, Equality-Equality, Friendship-Friendship) would also strictly be required in order to express the corresponding abstract relations, and it is only because their use would involve a tiresome reduplication that they are dispensed with, and the single name used instead.

When we pair together two successive sensations or ideas,

and contemplate the former as immediately, as well as constantly, preceding the latter, we use the related terms Cause-Effect, and not merely Antecedent-Consequent. In expressing the latter relation, we often find it convenient to miss or slur over the intervening links, when they are not (as often happens) unknown; but in determining a causal relation, we seek to find the *immediate* antecedent, and seek so pertinaciously that (according to Mill) we often insist on inserting between the real Cause and the real Effect an imaginary Cause of our own devising, such as Power, &c., in the vain endeavour to bring ourselves, so to speak, nearer to both the one and the other of the two extremities of the chain of succession.

As instances of Antecedent and Consequent, Mill very curiously classes such pairs of related ideas as Doctor-Patient, Father-Son, &c., any of which, when taken together, he contends, makes up a complex idea consisting of a long chain of ideas of which Doctor or Father, &c., is the "*terminus a quo,*" and Patient or Son, &c., the "*terminus ad quem.*" Two brothers, or Brother-Brother, mark a still more complex idea, being equivalent to a train of ideas taken twice over, the prior extremity the Father being the same in the two cases, the latter extremity different. There are a large variety of paired names, which represent more or less long trains of ideas between, and including, the two extremities noted by them. In the relation First-Last, the extremities are as far as possible distant from one another: in Father-Son, Owner-Property, Guardian-Ward, &c., they are still very distant: in Prior-Posterior, they may be any distance from one another. But the peculiarity of Cause-Effect is that the extremities are in juxtaposition. The chain therefore consists of the extremities only, and there is either no link between them, or, if so, its existence is unknown. This pair therefore of concrete interrelated terms *notes* immediate (and constant) juxtaposition in the way of succession, of two sensations or ideas, or of a sensation and idea, and it *connotes* those sensations or ideas which are contemplated as thus immediately (and constantly) successive. Leave out the connotation, and we get that which is represented by the abstract relative compound term, Causingness (or Causativeness)-Causedness, or the corresponding single name, Causality or Causation.

As we apply the terms Antecedent-Consequent, Cause-Effect to those ideas of clusters of sensations called external objects; so also do we apply them to those clusters of ideas in the formation of which the mind takes a more active share: "thus we say that Evidence is the cause of Belief, or Villainy of Indignation." [*Anal.* vol. ii. 67]. Thoughts, as well as things, may be regarded as standing to one another in an order of succession, or in a causal relation. For in any train of ideas—and, in Mill's opinion, there cannot be more than one train present at the same time to the same individual—thoughts succeed one another;—each thought is therefore, at all events, the proximate antecedent to the rest. But can we say that it is also the constant antecedent—for constant as well as proximate antecedence is necessary to causation—in face of the fact that different minds have different series of ideas, notwithstanding that the starting-point may be the same? We can, answers Mill, for this reason. Our trains of feelings do not consist only of ideas, but of sensations also; and those sensations are impressed by surrounding objects and contemporary events, the number and different orders and relations of which are infinite, and independent of our volition in the great majority of cases. This will be sufficient to account for the variety of trains starting from the same idea in different minds. The degree of force possessed by the initial idea in suggesting its particular successor may still, for all we know, be constant; but it so happens that the results are various, because other factors and influences unite with that idea to moderate its operation. Of these factors James Mill has mentioned sensations alone, but he might just as well have added ideas, since, as J. S. Mill points out, the mind is never completely occupied by a single idea; and also the constitution, formed habits, and temporary state of the mind to which the series is present. But these qualifications, though they would have left intact the statement that one antecedent idea, *if unmodified by other circumstances*, must inevitably produce the same consequent idea in every mind—would have very much weakened, indeed utterly destroyed, the value of the proposition for purposes of psychological analysis. It is all very well to tell a marksman that, if no other laws were to act in company with the First Law of Motion, his arrow would inevitably hit the bull's-eye. The proposition is true, but trivial. So here.

Thus much, then, on the causal relation between successive thoughts. The relation called Position, and the cognate relation of Extension, next demand attention. As before, the related concrete terms must be determined before the relation. Examples of such related terms are naturally among the most familiar to us of any—High-Low, Right-Left, North-South, Behind-Before, &c. These cannot be defined except in terms involving the thing to be defined. But that which cannot be defined so as to avoid a circle may, notwithstanding, often be conveniently described in other ways, for the purpose of bringing its meaning home to us with clearness.

The Synchronous differs from the Successive Order,—Space from Time,—in one very important respect. The latter is always, as it were, in one direction; and when a series of successive events is represented figuratively in terms of space, no other symbol can be used but that of a line : whereas objects in synchronous order can stand to one another in several other relations than that of Lineness or Linth.[3]   But as being in a line with one another is the simplest of all spatial relations between objects, let us examine what this is a little more closely.   If we take a single particle of matter as centre, and attach to it another particle, we get the most elementary case of synchronous order.   Add to these successive particles along the direction of the same radius, and we still have the same relation between the various component particles of the line thus formed, which will be of greater or less length, according to the number of the particles.   Now the name of this supposed physical line notes, according to Mill, the particles of which it is composed, and *connotes* the direction.   On taking away the connotation, we get the abstract relation, for which some such name as Lineness is required.   If we then attach to the imaginary central particle other particles not only along the direction of one radius, but along those of every possible radius, an analogous account may be given of the abstract relations of Figure and Bulk.   The Position of any given particle will be its order in relation to the central and every other particle in the mass.

It remains to inquire, what are the sensations which give the cognition of synchronous order.   They are, according to Mill, tactual and muscular.   And in the very complex idea of

---

[3] These are the terms that Mill coins, to avoid, as he says, the ambiguity of the double use of the word Line, first to represent a concrete and physical, secondly, an abstract or mathematical line.   It is obvious that he is here confusing two very different things,—an abstraction and an ideal, the former representing a *quality* of which concrete objects of a class are all more or less in possession, the latter a *limit* to which they more or less nearly approach.   This confusion vitiates Mill's whole theory of spatial relations.

muscular resistance is included at least this much :—the will to move the muscles, the exertion of that will, and certain sensations in those muscles, in virtue of which we call an object hard or soft, resisting or non-resisting. These, then, are the sensations capable of being derived by a sentient being from any particle of matter. Now let us take our central particle again, and the radius of which that particle forms one extremity; and let us suppose a person endowed only with tactual and muscular sensibility (in order to exclude foreign and non-essential conditions) to be brought in contact with the aggregate of particles composing the line in question. Then such a person, just as he would have two different states of feeling according as the finger touching the line was still or in motion, or according as the motion of his finger was slow or swift, so would he have two different states of feeling, according as the finger moved along the whole line or only along half of it. And thus it is that "after certain repetitions of particular tactual sensations, and particular muscular sensations, received in a certain order, I give to the combined ideas of them this name Line. But when I have got my idea of a line, I have also got my idea of extension. For what is extension, but lines in every direction ?" [*Anal.* vol. ii. p. 34]. The explanation of Plane Surface is analogous.

It is to be remembered that we never perceive objects except in space, that is, except in the synchronous order. Position therefore becomes so inseparably associated with the idea of any object, that belief in the necessity of the relation of space has thereby, and thereby only, according to Mill, been engendered. It will be convenient now to examine the supposed necessity, and generally the nature of that which we call space.

Space is held by Mill to be not an abstract relative, but an abstract privative term. By " privative " terms Mill really means negative: (the term "privative" being properly limited to indicate the absence of some element or quality usually present in an object and necessary to its completeness as such object); and in the ensuing exposition, to avoid misunderstanding, we shall use the term "negative."

In the idea of an object, (such as Light, Sound, Knowledge) is included the idea of its existence, or the belief that a sentient organism existing at such and such a time and place would have certain sensations or ideas. In using the corresponding negative terms (Darkness, Silence, Ignorance) we couple with the idea of the object the idea that such an organism would not have those sensations or ideas at any time or place, or at all events at the time and place to which we refer the term. Now the latter idea,—its association with the former being, so to speak, strained and violent,—is forced into a prominence which overshadows it; whereas, in making use of the corresponding positive terms, we find that the idea of the object so completely absorbs the accompanying idea of its existence, that we should never, except on careful analysis, notice that the former idea co-exists with the latter at all. The comparatively small number of negative terms in a language is accounted for, in the same way as the comparative paucity of relative terms, by reference to the principles of convenience which led men to name only what was most important to name,—(though some languages, the ancient Greek for instance, are richer in negative terms than others).

From the above distinction between Presence-affirming and Absence-affirming Names, Mill devises a simple explanation of those bugbears of the ancient, to whom we may add some modern, philosophers, Being, Nothing, &c. From the notion that a name must represent some positive existence, "τὸ μηδέν" and the like, have often been elevated to the rank of Substances and Entities of much mysterious importance. It is true that even Nothing must name something; but what it names is the idea of Everything—all possible objects—coupled with the idea of their non-existence.[4]

On these principles Mill proceeds to expound the somewhat more complex negative idea of Emptiness, which is the idea of Fulness together with the idea of its absence. But the idea of the absence of Fulness Mill shows, by a curious process of reasoning, to be equivalent to the abstract name corresponding to "solid extended body" or "bulk." For the ideas of linear, superficial, and solid extension are in each case the ideas of linear, superficial, and solid surfaces or bodies, with their connotation (which in each case is Resistance) dropped. But in the last case of "bulk" or "solid extended body," we obtain a strange result;—we seem, in dropping the connotation of the idea Resistance, to drop everything that constitutes the idea. This, however, is not so: we have remaining the place for Bulk, namely Position, or Space with a limitation. If we drop the connotation of *infinitely* extended solid bodies, we get the abstract term Infinite Space.

It will be seen from the above account that, in defining such notions as Nothing, Space, &c., Mill seems to hesitate whether he shall call them abstract names derived from concretes in the ordinary way, or negative ideas, equivalent to the ideas of the corresponding positive terms coupled with the idea of their absence. It cannot clearly be gathered from his exposition, whether he regards Space as the abstract term corresponding to all concrete extended objects, or, like Emptiness,

---

[4] J. S. Mill here points out the insufficiency of this explanation, and says (what is unquestionably true) that negative terms do signify something positive: they signify a state of consciousness: Silence, for example, a state of consciousnes, when there is no sound affecting the organs of hearing, and Nothing a state of consciousness when we are not affected by sensations from any object.

to be the negative of an idea of infinitely extended bulk. To
have said, with J. S. Mill, that it is the *ideal* negative of an
ideal positive would have been the simpler and truer way out
of the difficulty : but he was precluded from taking this course
by his peculiar and rather confused views on the subject of
abstract terms.

Mill concludes his observations on Space by a neat summary
of the various indissoluble associations which combine to engender and form our ideas of that abstraction. " First of all
with the idea of every object, the idea of position or place is
indissolubly united. Secondly, with the idea of position or
place, the idea of extension is indissolubly united. Thirdly,
with the idea of extension the idea of infinity is indissolubly
united.[5] Fourthly, by the unfortunate ambiguity of the
Copula " [see above, ch. iii.] " the idea of existence is indissolubly united with Space, as with other abstract terms." And
all these elements, the ideas of Position, Extension, Infinity,
and Existence, " forced into combination, by irresistible
association, constitute the idea of Space." [*Anal.* vol. ii.
pp. 114, 115].

Intimately connected with Space is Motion. It is also, as
appears on analysis, closely related to Time. It is the abstract
name corresponding to the concrete " moving body," the idea
of the body being dropped, and the idea of that which constitutes it a moving body being retained. Now the idea of a
moving body comprises the following ideas (1) the idea of a
line, whether straight or otherwise ; since every moving body

---

[5] In this way : we can never think of a finite line, surface, &c., without
thinking of something beyond it, just as we can never think of an event
without the idea of its antecedent or consequent being brought up, or of a
number without thinking of one more beyond it. Infinity is, therefore,
that state of consciousness in which the idea of something beyond is associated with the idea of any given finite line, surface, or bulk, &c.

must move in a line of some sort,—(2) the idea of a body,—
(3) the idea of position (or extension in every direction, which
taken abstractly, is Space), since the particles composing the
line have each of them position,—and (4), since the body must
move successively from one position in the line to another, the
idea of Succession, which in the abstract, coupled with the
idea of infinity, is Time.

Now how do we acquire our knowledge of moving bodies?
Not by the sense of sight, any more than we see figure or
distance: that we imagine sight to be the source of our perception of moving bodies is due, as in the other cases, solely
to association. We in fact derive the idea of moving bodies
from the same kinds of sensation as those from which we
derive our idea of extended objects, that is, from tactual and
muscular sensations. If we touch a (physical) line at any one
point we experience the sensations in virtue of which we call
it tangible. If we move our finger along the line we have the
sensations (tactual and muscular) and the ideas—(for in all
cases of succession, the ideas of past sensations must co-exist
with or rather follow immediately upon present sensations)—
in virtue of which we call it extended. But these are the
very sensations and ideas in virtue of which we call our finger
a moving body. So that according as we regard the object
or the finger principally, we have the idea Object Extended,
or the idea Finger Moving. Drop the connotation, and
the result is the abstract name Extension, on the one hand,
and the abstract name Motion on the other, [that is the four
elements mentioned above, excluding the second].

The term Quantity is, like the others, an abstract relative
term. The concrete related terms corresponding to it are As-
Great, So-Great, Quantus, Tantus. These are equivalent to
Equal-Equal. Then what use have the former terms? If
they had no use, says Mill, somewhat gloomily, it would not

be surprising, "considering by whom languages have been made." But in the present case there is a use. In the pair of related terms Equal-Equal, either may be taken as the standard of the other. But of the other pair, Quantus must always stand for the measure of Tantus. Quantitas then, if it had kept its original meaning, would (dropping the conno-tation of Quantus, which has reference to some specific body taken as a standard) involve the idea of some amount of body being taken as the standard of some other body; and it would thus connote Tantitas, just as Priority connotes Posteriority. But the idea so implied has been dropped, and there has been substituted for it the idea of some amount of body being taken as the standard of all other bodies; or rather, not even this has been permanently substituted, but Quantity has at length become an absolute, instead of a relative, abstract term; and is used to represent any portion of extension, weight, number, heat, or anything, in fact, which can be measured by a part of itself.

What do we mean when we use the terms More-Less, Longer-Shorter, &c.? Such names may be applied to a variety of things, the simplest of which to take, for purposes of ex-planation, is Extension. Tactual and muscular sensations give us the line. We have certain sensations of this kind in ex-tending the arm a certain distance, and certain other sensations of this kind in extending it further. To have these different sensations in succession is to recognize their difference. Having recognized the difference, we find it important to name it. The pair of sensations are accordingly named in relation to one another Shorter-Longer. So of superficies, and bulk. When we apply the terms Part-Whole to objects, the idea of division is involved. The term Division when applied to a physical line comprises the ideas of the feelings of contraction of the muscles, and resistance after the contraction (the act of dividing), the idea of the sight of the line before division (the antecedent of the act), and the idea of the sight of the line after division (the consequent of the act). It is found convenient to assign a pair of related terms to the antecedent and consequent above indicated; the former we call the whole line, the latter the part of it. Whole and Part, of course, connote each other. Taken together they make a complex idea involving the three stages or elements of the above process. The same remarks hold good (*mutatis mutandis*) in the cases of Surface and Bulk. The division, of course, need not be physical in all cases : it may be imagined.

Similar reasoning applies also to Weight, Heat, &c. "More heavy," "Less heavy," are names given to objects from which we have derived separate and successive sensations differing from one another by the more or less muscular resistance, in a particular direction, which they involve. "More or less muscular resistance" must, it would thus appear, be accepted as ultimate and unanalyzable. Whether any very important object is gained by stating the expression "more or less heavy" in other terms—for that is what the alleged analysis comes to—may very well be doubted. It is true, as J. S. Mill says, that this, like all other relations of quantity, exists only as it is felt,—and to this extent James Mill's description, rather than explanation, is important—but it must be understood that differences of quantity are really irreducible, however much we may choose to translate them into different language.

Mill's conception of Numbers proceeds faithfully upon the foregoing lines. He does not regard them as the names of objects, but as expressing and naming a process,—the process of addition, of putting one object to another. "One" is merely the name of this operation once performed; "two," of the operation once more performed; "three," of the operation once more performed, and so on. Mill seems to have been quite unconscious that, in this account, he was interpreting the thing by itself. It may be, however, that he meant the above as a description, not as an analysis. But, if so, he ought to have recognized, more emphatically than he has, the ultimate character of numbers; and not have left his statement, that there is nothing mysterious about numbers, open to the construction—"there is nothing unanalyzable about numbers." Of course, in one sense, there is nothing mysterious about them, any more than there is about Time, Space, an Idea, or a Sensation; that is, we all know when we experience a sensation, or have an idea, and what is the difference between walking one mile and ten, and what is the distinction between missing a train and catching it. But in the only other sense which the word "mysterious" can bear in this connexion, namely, that of ultimateness, Numbers—judging from the fact that Mill himself is driven to define them in a circle—are "mysterious."

Numbers (Two, Three, Four, &c.) connote, says Mill, the objects to which these numerals are applied. When we drop the connotation we get the corresponding abstract names; but, unfortunately, there is only one name for both the concretes and the abstracts. When we say, "two roses and three roses are five roses," we use the concrete names; when we say, "two and three are five," we drop the connotation, and retain only the idea of the process; and it would be more correct to say, "twoness and threeness are fiveness." It will strike the reader that in this, as in other instances, Mill has formed a wrong conception of abstract names. Numerals are always concrete names.

The ordinal numbers (First, Second, Third, &c.) note a certain position, (if the objects, one of which is described in relation to the others, are in synchronous order), a certain link (if they are in the successive order): they connote the object which has the position, or forms the link. The abstract term is derived in the ordinary way from the concrete.

Quality is the last metaphysical category, or (to keep to Mill's own phraseology) abstract relative term, which has to be discussed. Qualities of objects are the names of the sensations which we derive from them—(the name "quality" *notes* this much)—and also of the unknown causes of these sensations—(and this is the connotation). We *know* about objects only the sensations, the effects, but we suppose a cause to produce these effects, owing to what some would call a mental instinct, others a "category," or law of thought, others, the actual independent existence of the Cause, but what Mill would ascribe to the working of association, and association only.

There are, it is to be observed, two kinds of qualities, strictly speaking: there is that kind, in virtue of which we say that an object has a certain colour, form, consistency, &c. —the "sensible" quality: and there is also that kind, in respect of which we are not properly said to derive our sensations from the objects themselves, which possess them, but from certain powers or properties in the objects. Thus, when we say that aqua regia dissolves gold, or has a gold-dissolving quality, the aqua regia is not itself the immediate antecedent of my sensation, but is one remove from it. The order is: Antecedent, aqua regia; Consequent, gold dissolved by aqua regia; Second Consequent, myself perceiving the gold so dissolved. But, in the other sense of the word "quality," the object is not distinct from its qualities: beyond the qualities, it is nothing.

Qualities, in this latter sense, are, as we have seen, the sensations which we derive from the objects, together with the association of their ideas with the idea of something as tho cause. This something turns out, on analysis, to be nothing but sensations regarded as antecedent to those experienced by us at any moment from an object. When I am affected by any object, say, through the sense of smell, I associate with the idea of such sensation the ideas of the sensations of colour, figure, size, weight, position, &c., which I imagine myself capable of deriving from the object, and presuppose their indissoluble union. And this is all that really takes place in the mind, according to Mill, during a supposed reference of sensations to an unknown cause, or to the object as their cause, however much we may be led by the permanent illusions of association to fancy otherwise.

When we affirm that one object is Talis-Qualis another— of like nature with another—we mean that we derive from the two objects like sensations,—whether of one kind only (that is, in respect of one quality), or of several (that is, in respect of several qualities), or of all those kinds which we are capable of deriving from the objects compared (that is, entirely, or in respect of all the qualities which constitute the object, excepting only the relation of dimension).⁶ And what having like sensations is, has already been shown.

Talis-Qualis, then, are names applied to objects in respect of every kind of sensation derivable from them, except that of dimension. And they differ from Like-Like in the one peculiarity, in which Tantus-Quantus differ from Equal-Equal,—that is, the objects denoted by Qualis and Quantus are always taken as standards, whereas in the case of the other two pairs either member is the measure of the other. The abstract name Quality is formed in exactly the same way as the abstract name Quantity. Qualitas, moreover, (like Quantitas, and all relative, as distinguished from

---

⁶ For which a special pair of related terms, viz., Tantus, Quantus, has been invented.

ordinary, abstract terms) did originally connote something, namely Talitas, its abstract correlate: but from its having been from the beginning employed to express first one feature in an object which required to be specially marked, and then another, the term acquired in its rapid locomotion a migratory tendency, so to speak, which eventually enabled it to slip the bonds imposed by its original connexion with its correlate, and it thus became "the generical name of everything in objects, for which a separate notation is required." [*Anal.* vol. ii. p. 60.]

Mental, as well as sensible, complex ideas can, when put together in pairs, be contrasted as same or different, like or unlike, &c. We call them by these names, when the members of any such pair are composed of like or unlike simple ideas.[7] And what it is to call two simple ideas like or unlike, has been seen already.

We may even style one complex idea greater than another, as when we say that the delicacy of Portia is greater than that of Antigone, or the statesmanship of Julius Cæsar than that of Charlemagne. We make such quantitative comparisons on analogous grounds to those, on which we call three yards greater than two. Just as in using the latter expression, we mean that one yard would have to be put to two, in

---

[7] Or because there would have to be added to, or subtracted from, the idea of one member of the pair, some generically different idea or ideas, in order to make it like the other of the two complex ideas compared: e.g. to the idea of a horse has to be added the idea of wings in order to constitute that of a Pegasus: from the idea of a man has to be subtracted the idea of an eye, and other ideas substituted, in order to frame the idea of a Cyclops: from the idea of Firmness the idea of sound judgment has to be subtracted, in order to establish the idea of Obstinacy. It is for this reason only that we call the sensible complex ideas Horse, Man, and the mental complex idea, Firmness, different from the mental complex ideas, Pegasus, Cyclops, Obstinacy, respectively.

order to produce in us the same muscular and tactual sensations which we experience in moving our finger along a physical line of three yards in length : so, in the former mode of speech, we mean that further ideas of statesmanlike qualities would require to be added to, or associated with, those suggested by the name of Charlemagne, in order to realize or come up to the combination of qualities, which we connect with the idea of the character of Julius Cæsar.

Hartley does not formally discuss Qualities, and the cognate relative terms so elaborately handled by his successor. His incidental remarks, indeed, on this head show him to have been (as far as he went) substantially at one with Mill. His analysis, however, was not very penetrating or detailed. The general conception of Quality was common to the two philosophers, though Hartley puts his case in a somewhat different form from that of Mill. He lays down that the explanation of the assent to the proposition, "Gold is soluble in aqua regia," is that the idea of gold has come to suggest the idea of solution in aqua regia, and vice versâ. (*Observ. on Man*, vol. i. p. 329). This is tantamount to saying, with Mill, that the name "solubility in aqua regia" notes the specific quality, and connotes the other properties of gold, from which we derive sensations, regarded as the antecedent or cause of that specific quality. Hartley, however, makes no distinction between such propositions as the above, and such as "milk is white," &c., which Mill carefully marks off from one another; and therefore presumably would not discriminate between the kind of quality called whiteness in milk, and the kind of quality, or power, called gold-dissolving in aqua regia, or solubility by aqua regia in gold.

In connexion with the subject of Quality, we ought not to omit to mention Hartley's observations on a relation which is intimately bound up with that of Similarity in Qualities, namely Analogy.

Hartley uses the term Induction as equivalent to a higher type of analogical reasoning. When we see a piece of coal before us, and observe that the sensations in us (and, therefore, qualities in the object) of Form, Colour, Consistency, &c., are mostly similar to those derived from, or noticeable in, other pieces of coal, we immediately infer that, if fire be applied to it, it will burn and be reduced to ashes. Such an inference is grounded on what Hartley calls "the highest probability, which may be termed induction, in the strict sense of the word." But when the qualities, in respect of which the similarity between the objects is observed, are comparatively few, we call the process analogy and not induction. In science Analogy can only be admitted provisionally, and where induction is impossible. "Coincidence in mathematical matters, and induction in others, wherever they can be had, must be sought for as the only certain tests of truth" [vol. i. p. 313]. Hartley's view of analogical inference as that mode of reasoning, whereby we argue that, where A has one or more of its properties or qualities similar to one or more of the properties or qualities of B, therefore A will resemble B in some or all of their remaining qualities, coincides very nearly with J. S. Mill's account of *one* of his modes of the argument from analogy.

On Hypothesis (which does not come within Mill's scheme, and would probably have been relegated by him to the "Book of Logic," which he mentions in the last page of his "Analysis," as distinct from analytical psychology), Hartley, who in this, as in so many other matters, follows Newton, makes a number of sound observations. He notices its different kinds; the provisional hypothesis, awaiting tests and "experimenta crucis," before its validity can be established, and the hypo-

thesis sanctioned by analogies, but not yet elevated to the
rank of an ascertained law : he distinguishes also between
that form of hypothesis, in which the supposed cause is a real
one, or is known to operate in the natural world, while its
causal connexion with the phenomenon to be explained is
assumed, and that other form, wherein the effect is known,
and the law governing it, but the cause (e.g. an impon-
derable æther in astronomy) is assumed, though not met with
among physical phenomena. In connexion with this branch
of his subject he shrewdly remarks—(what has since been
observed by Faraday, and other scientific men most competent to judge from their own experience)—the dangerous
fascination of a hypothesis which has once been allowed to
dwell in the mind, and explains it on principles of association.
"The ideas, words, and reasonings belonging to the favourite
hypothesis by recurring and being much agitated in the
brain, heat it, unite with each other, and so coalesce in the
same manner, as genuine truths do from induction and
analogy" [vol. i. p. 346]. In this statement is wrapped up
a warning especially useful in these days of hypothesis run
mad. On much the same principle Mill, as we shall see
below, explains the operation of the Will, and of a desired
End in connexion therewith, as giving rise to action.

In Hartley's interesting, but somewhat ill-arranged "farrago
libelli," we are constantly coming across matters and hints
which take us by surprise. Here, for instance, at the end of
the section on "Propositions and the Nature of Assent," we
somewhat unexpectedly meet with a topic, which has had an
important place in the systems of various philosophers from
Plato to Mr. Herbert Spencer and Comte, namely, the Classification of the Sciences. Hartley's division is rudimentary,
of course, but not without interest, as reflecting his general
views. He distributes knowledge in general into seven
leading branches. The first of these is significant as an illus-

tration of the belief, common to him with Mill, in the importance of names. Under Philology, or the knowledge of words
and their significations, he places together, oddly enough,
Grammar, Criticism, Rhetoric, and Poetry. In ancient
treatises on Poetry (as in Aristotle's *Poetica*), there is certainly a good deal of grammatical disquisition; but we should
scarcely have expected from Hartley an arrangement so un-
scientific, as to include in one class of science both Grammar
and Poetry. The second branch is Mathematics or the doctrine of Quantity; the third Logic, which he defines, quite in
the Baconian manner, as the art of using words as symbols,
("as counters, not as coin," Hobbes would say), for the
purpose of discovery in all departments of knowledge. Logic
presupposes the two foregoing classes to some extent. The
fourth branch is Natural History, which he terms, as Bacon
again termed it, "regular and well-digested accounts of the
phenomena of the natural world." Civil History is the next,
(in which are comprised histories proper of every kind), followed
by Natural Philosophy, which depends upon the application
of Mathematics and Logic to Civil and Natural History, with
a view to the determination of the laws on which the external
and physical world is governed, and thereby the acquisition of
Foreknowledge and Power, or the means of predicting and
producing phenomena. The seventh and last sphere of knowledge is Divine Philosophy, or Religion, which treats of,
amongst other things, the Summum Bonum, the highest end
of life, and, as such, includes Ethics and Politics, and even
(Hartley appears to hint) may, through the conception of
Final Cause, be applied with advantage even to the analysis
and interpretation of natural phenomena. The insertion of
this last branch of science serves to show us how widely different Hartley's standpoint was from that of Mill, in relation
to ethical, political, and generally to practical speculations.

CHAPTER VII.

THE "ACTIVE POWERS" OF THE HUMAN MIND.

WE now come to an entirely new section of the Association Theory, that, namely wherein are discussed our sensations and ideas, not merely as existing in our minds, but in their effect upon action. We have done with the intellectual faculties and phenomena, and now come to the moral energies or active phenomena, of human nature.[1] And in the Association system of philosophy, as in all others, we shall see that the practical doctrines follow closely the lines of the theoretical.

Sensations may be either pleasurable, painful, or indifferent. They are known to be such only as they are felt: they are distinguished from one another in the feeling them, and by no other process. We do not, however, attach so much importance to our ideas of the pleasurable and painful sensations as we do to the causes of them, because, as Mill says, the sensations, so to speak, "provide for themselves," whereas it is of the greatest interest to us to discover their causes or constant antecedents in order that we may learn how to produce or remove them, according as the sensations consequent upon them are pleasurable or painful. Moreover, the conse-

---

[1] "Active phenomena of Thought" is a very loose expression: but it is obvious what Mill means by it. Instead of intellectual and active phenomena, Hobbes expressed the distinction by the terms, Cognitive and Motive Powers.

quent sensations are not nearly so numerous or various as their actual and possible antecedents. These considerations are sufficient to account for the absorbing attention paid by us to the antecedents of sensations, whether proximate or remote, and for the fact of the association between the sensations and the causes throwing the interest so heavily on to the side of the latter, as even to lessen or completely obliterate the interest originally attached exclusively to the former,—a phenomenon instanced by the familiar case of the miser.

Ideas of pleasurable or of painful sensations are, like the sensations themselves, known only by being experienced. They are respectively identical with those states to which we give the names of Desire and Aversion. To have the idea of a pleasurable sensation is, according to Mill, one and the same thing as to have a desire for it : to have the idea of a painful sensation one and the same thing as to have an aversion to it. But these two expressions are also, by an ambiguity of language, applied to our ideas of the causes of the sensations, as well as those of the sensations themselves. We are said to have a desire for water, when in reality, the object is indifferent except in producing relief from thirst, the pleasure of which relief is what we in fact desire. From the fact that the names which, in strictness, belong only to the ideas of the sensations are (through association) transferred to the ideas of their antecedent, Hartley explains the derivative character of *all* intellectual pleasures and pains, which, in his scheme, are those of ambition, self-interest, sympathy, theopathy, and the moral sense. The "originals" which we really or primarily desire are sensible pleasures, but out of our secondary interest in the associated causes of these pleasures, are gradually generated independent desires for the "intellectual" pleasures. [*Observ. on Man*, vol. i. pp. 416, 417.]

The idea, then, of a pleasurable or painful sensation is the same thing as the desire for, or aversion to it, together with a connotative reference to the absence of the sensation, the idea of which is in our minds. The absence may be either because the sensation is past, or because it is to come,—generally the latter; Desire and Aversion however are the only terms in use to express both the one and the other of these two possible cases. It follows that the number of our desires and aversions is equal to the number of our pleasurable and painful sensations.

When a pleasurable or painful sensation is contemplated as future, but not as certainly about to be experienced, the state of consciousness with which it is regarded is called Hope or Fear. When such sensations are contemplated as certainly about to be felt, the states of consciousness, with which they are respectively regarded, may be described (though unsatisfactorily) by the terms Joy and Sorrow. When such sensations are contemplated as past, the attitude of the mind is almost neutral. But besides the sensations, the causes of those sensations, may be regarded either as past or future. If as past, the idea or thought of them, unlike that of the sensations in an analogous case, is called Antipathy or (less conveniently) Hatred, in the case of past causes of painful, and Sympathy or Love (both most inexact terms) in the case of past causes of pleasurable, sensations. If as future and certain, the state of consciousness is termed Hatred, Horror, or Aversion in the one case, and Joy in the other: if as future and uncertain, the state of consciousness is called Dread in the one case, and Hope in the other. The reason of our regarding with such interest the past causes of past sensations, while we look back with comparatively tranquil feelings on the past sensations themselves, is to be found partly in those associations to which allusion has already been made, but principally in that particular form of it, whereby the thought of a past antecedent and consequent is no sooner raised in us, than the mind becomes, so to speak, possessed with the idea of the relation of antecedent and consequent in its generic character, and divested of any limitation as to time, and so passes naturally, and even irresistibly, to the idea of future antecedents and consequents. Then from the idea of a future antecedent of a painful sensation, it arrives finally at the idea of a future painful sensation : "and thus the feeling partakes of the nature of the anticipation of a future painful sensation." [*Anal.*, vol. ii. p. 202]. The cause of a past pleasurable sensation is, it is to be observed, not so attractive an object of contemplation and reminiscence, as the cause of a past painful sensation is a revolting and disagreeable one ; and that because the sensation itself in the former case is not so pungent as in the latter. But of course the cause of the extinction of a past pain is often a subject of the most lively and absorbing interest.

Just as the causes of pleasures and pains are more interesting, for the reasons already given, than the pleasures and pains themselves; so the remote causes of them are often more interesting than the proximate,—both for the same reasons, and owing to this further fact, that the more remote causes, such as Money, necessarily carry with them a larger number of associated ideas of pleasures and pains; since they are associated primarily with all the proximate causes of them (Money, for instance, with Food, Health, Comfort, Power, Art, &c.), and through each of these mediately with several sets and combinations of sensations. After these preliminary remarks, Mill discusses the different causes of our own pleasures and pains in separate classes. Wealth, Power, and Dignity have this feature in common, that they all advance our happiness as instruments in securing for us the good offices of our fellow-men, and hardly at all in any other way.

In the achievement of these results, Wealth operates mainly through the opportunities which it affords of rewarding others; Power (according to Mill) through the opportunities which it affords of inflicting evils and imposing burdens on others; while Dignity expresses "all that in and about a man which is calculated to procure him the services of others, without the immediate application of reward or of fear," together with (though in a less marked degree) a disposition to make a good use of Wealth and Power (which is Virtue), and Knowledge and Wisdom, which enable him to direct the disposition into proper channels.   All the three conditions above enumerated procure for their possessor respect and admiration even beyond the sphere of their operation, or of the possibility of their operation.   This noticeable fact—which other schools of philosophy would explain on other grounds, and instance as justifying a deduction of the phenomena in question from anti-selfish principles—Mill, of course, regards as only another example and effect of association.   We associate the idea of the power of doing good and harm enjoyed by other persons, with the idea of pleasurable and painful sensations inflicted in the exercise of that power; and with this latter idea is associated the thought of such sensations inflicted on ourselves : and, though this association may be only momentary, yet even a momentary association—one no sooner formed than forgotten—may be such as to give "its whole character to a phenomenon of the human mind;" since, according to the theory which Mill emphatically endorses and repeats in this connexion, there can be no idea present to the mind without at least a momentary belief in its existence.

The opposites of the above causes of pleasures, namely, Poverty, Weakness, and Contemptibility, admit of the same analysis.

The Affections, or the feelings, with which we regard the

above causes of pleasures and pains, whether as past or as future—unfortunately we have no names to distinguish affections according as they refer to the one or the other—are named Love of Wealth, Power, Dignity, and Hatred of Poverty, Weakness, Contemptibility. It is only in this roundabout manner that we can express them.

When the element of comparison enters into our state of consciousness while contemplating the above causes of pleasures and pains (that is, when we compare the degree in which they are enjoyed or endured by ourselves with the extent to which they are enjoyed or endured by others), the affections called Pride, where the comparison is favourable to ourselves, and Humility, where it is unfavourable, are engendered. This is where the reference is primarily to such causes as possessed by ourselves—when the Self is the standard of comparison : when another individual is the standard by which we measure ourselves, the respective affections are those of Contempt and Admiration.

On the pleasures and pains connected with the sentiments of Power, Dignity, &c., Hartley has something to say, though, as usual, of a descriptive, rather than a deeply analytical, character. He does not formulate distinctions so nicely, or dissect with so keen a scalpel, as the later philosopher. But, under the head of the Pains and Pleasures of Ambition, he makes some penetrating observations covering much the same ground as Mill's treatment of Wealth, Power, and Dignity. Of these pleasures and pains of ambition he recognizes several varieties, according as they are referred to, and connected with, External Advantages or Disadvantages, Bodily Perfections and Imperfections, Intellectual Qualities (accomplishments or defects), or Moral Qualities (virtue and vice). Under the first of these he includes riches, titles, &c., and their opposites, most of which Mill would consider as incidental to Wealth and Dignity; under the second, Beauty, Health, and Strength, which Mill would probably refer to Power and Dignity. The last two classes speak for themselves; and without the one to supply the right means, and the other the right end, Mill (as we have seen) would hardly admit that Dignity could properly be said to exist.

In common with Mill, Hartley is of opinion that, in seeking the good offices and opinions of others, the primary object in the first instance is the acquisition of the pleasures, and avoidance of the pains, likely to result to us from their attitude towards us;[2] but that, by association, we accustom ourselves to seek those good offices and opinions independently of immediate results, and even when results of any kind are almost or entirely beyond the range of probability or even possibility. He takes account, accordingly, of the fact that counter-associations may equally well be generated, whereby poverty, instead of riches, low instead of high birth, may be identified in thought with the pleasures and aims of ambition (as, for instance, in the history of monastic orders); and notes that the common element in all the pleasures of ambition, of whatever kind, is the prominence in their constitution of the " videri," as compared with the " esse," and the greater richness of the former in the interesting associations and ideas which it is able to bring before the mind. [*Observ. on Man*, vol. i. p. 446, sqq.] It is to *be thought*, not to be, rich, of high birth, strong, beautiful, intellectual, virtuous, &c., that men rise so early, and so late take rest—in so far at least as they are actuated by ambition, which is all that we are at present considering.

To *be thought* intellectual is considered desirable by most

---

[2] " All the things," he writes [vol. i. p. 455], " in which men pride themselves, and for which they desire to be taken notice of by others, are either means of happiness, or have some near relation to it."

men, chiefly (says Hartley) owing to the association in their minds of the eagerly pronounced opinions of learned men in their books to that effect, apart from a consideration of the more obvious and external advantages accruing from such a reputation. Hartley seems to insinuate that the world is in a gigantic conspiracy to suppress and degrade the dullard; and that, in discussing the comparative merits of ignorance and learning, the controversy has always been entirely on one side. While Learning has always a series of recorded opinions with which to support its case, and so a link of association in its favour is formed—a link which becomes stronger every day from repetition—the dullard, on the other hand, "ex vi termini" cannot write books himself, or plead his own cause. Many a learned man could write a "*Ship of Fools,*" but no dunce can write an "*Encomium Moriæ.*" The scholar does it for him occasionally, but, unfortunately, only in such a way as to show that his real object is to attack other learned men, and not at all to elevate the fool. In his serio-comical way— we often cannot be quite sure whether he is amusing himself or in earnest—Hartley alludes, in this connexion, to "the high-strained encomiums, applauses, and flatteries, paid to parts and learning, and the outrageous contempt and ridicule thrown upon folly and ignorance, in all the discourses and writings of men of genius and learning" [perhaps Hartley had been reading the *Dunciad* of his friend Pope]; "these persons being extremely partial to their own excellences, and carrying the world with them by the force of their parts and eloquence" [vol. i. p. 449]. In considering those kinds of the pleasures and pains of ambition which relate to the reputation of virtue or vice, it is to be noticed that Hartley, like most of his successors in the Associationist School, universally adopts the Sensational or Selfish theory of morals, that is to say, the theory which derives in the last resort the love of virtue and repugnance to vice from the desire of the real and supposed pleasures associated with the idea of the practice of the one, and the aversion to the real and supposed pains associated with the idea of the practice of the other. He maintains the reward-and-punishment doctrine of ethical action. Thus it is the "many advantages resulting from the reputation of being benevolent," which causes most people to desire that reputation : and the honour in which the virtue of Benevolence, as contrasted with that in which Piety, for instance, is held, is explained on egoistic and utilitarian principles combined (since it does not very clearly appear whether the advantages spoken of are advantages to the individual agent, or to others). Military glory he deduces from a more exclusively utilitarian starting-point, coupled of course, with association. Humility he divides into negative and positive, the former being "the not thinking better, or more highly, of ourselves than we ought," and the latter "a deep sense of our own misery and imperfections of all kinds " [vol. i. p. 455], and here sagaciously observes that men are often impelled by the grossest motives of vanity and ambition to seek the reputation of that which contradicts it, namely, humility.[3] In this he finds an instance of the tendency of vice to destroy itself.

Not only are the prospects of praise or blame incentives to or deterrents from a particular course of action or a particular habit, but (as is acutely remarked by Hartley) it is considered praiseworthy to be influenced by praise and blame, and censurable to be unsusceptible to those influences. And thus " praise and shame have a strong reflected influence upon

---

[3] One is reminded of the story of Diogenes theatrically stamping on Plato's rich carpets, with the words, "thus do I trample on the pride of Plato ; " to which Plato retorted, "with yet greater pride yourself, Diogenes."

themselves," and " praise begets the love of praise, and shame increases the fear of shame." The latter part, however, of this proposition may be considered doubtful. It is rather to be gathered from experience, and would certainly be supposed *à priori,* that it ought to stand as the converse to the other part, and that a succession of ignominies heaped upon a man produces as shameless a callosity and indifference as a succession of encomiums and rewards fosters, if it does not engender, a refined and delicate sense of honour.

Self-Interest Hartley divides (not very philosophically) into three kinds, Gross, Refined, and Rational. The exposition of Gross Self-Interest covers the same ground as those observations of Mill on the Love of Wealth, on which we have already commented. It is defined as " the cool pursuit of the means whereby the pleasures of sensation, imagination, and ambition, are to be obtained, and their pains avoided," and he refers to the love of money as a crucial and interesting example, both of the pursuit of Gross Self-Interest, and of the general principles of association. In this latter reference, his language is almost identical with that of both the Mills, the younger of whom relies largely on the phenomena of avarice to support his utilitarian theory. There can be no original desire for money in itself. But from being regarded as the measure, standard, and exponent of a large variety of the pleasures of common life, it comes, by association, to signify, and stand for, " the thing itself, the sum total of all that is desirable in life." And so completely and rapidly is this mental process accomplished, that even a child will prefer a piece of money, as the symbol of a choice of pleasures deferred, to the immediate fruition of any specific pleasure.

Wealth, Power, and Dignity, are only mediately the causes of our pleasures and pains—through the intervention, that is, of the actions and attitude towards us of our fellow-men. Having

L

examined the ultimate causes, Mill proceeds to treat of the
(relatively to them) proximate causes, of our pleasures and
pains—in a word, our Fellow-men. And with this view, he
discusses successively Friendship, Kindness, Love of Family,
of Party, of Country, of Mankind, according to the extent of
the various circles and sections of humanity whose actions may
be supposed to affect our happiness. These sentiments are
expounded on principles, with which the reader by this time
will be sufficiently familiar ; and we need not stop to examine
his account in detail. Suffice it to say that in each case,
according to Mill, the ideas of services rendered and to be
rendered, benefits derived and to be derived, pleasures enjoyed
and to be enjoyed, are associated, directly or circuitously, consciously or unconsciously, but always strongly, with the ideas
of the individuals or portions of mankind who are the objects
of the sentiments in question. And the sentiments are the
outcome of, and depend for their force and durability, upon
that association.

One or two views, however, colouring all the different parts
of Mill's exposition of our Fellow-men regarded as the causes
of our pleasures and pains, should be noticed. To begin with,
Mill has a somewhat peculiar notion as to the manner in which
a person prompted to do a kind action regards a fellow-creature
in pain, or in which a Father or Husband regards his Son or
Wife, as the cause of his own pain or pleasure. His theory is
that we cannot see a man in pain, without associating with
the idea of his pain the idea of ourselves as suffering it ; that,
this latter idea being painful to us, we hasten to remove it by
removing the man's sufferings ; and that it is thus only that
he can be said to be the cause of our pain, or we to be prompted
to do a kind action. This, however, can hardly be said to
answer to the experience of most men ; and J. S. Mill, in cor-
recting the error (which, however, he is inclined to regard as

lying rather in expression than in meaning), carefully points out that there is probably no conscious association of the kind described, but that the idea of another person in pain is to most people *in itself* a painful idea. Benevolent and compassionate impulses may be in the last resort reducible to such an association; but this is a different thing from saying that it is actually experienced on each occasion of performing kind actions. "An association does not necessarily act in all cases, because it exists in all cases" [*Anal.* vol. i. p. 218. Editor's note].

The Parental and Marital Affections are very minutely analyzed: and it is shown how, apart from the parental and sexual instincts involved in them, association contributes a large share to their formation and development, as appears in the case of a man rearing orphan children, and in similar instances, where such instincts cannot exist.

In connexion with the discussion of these affections, some shrewd observations are to be found: as, for instance, that a man is prone to love the person on whom he has frequently conferred benefits—(which is the converse of Aristotle's observation that there is something in human nature which impels a man to hate one from whom he has *received* frequent and great benefits, and to whom he is under lasting obligations);—also the remark that one among other strong incentives to a mother to love her child is the recollection of the pains and hopes and fears connected with parturition, (which again corresponds to another quaint Aristotelian dictum to the effect that maternal affection, like the artistic pride of the poet and sculptor in his own works, is a case of the law, according to which that is most loved, which has been produced with the greatest pain and anxiety). In the case of the Family Affections, as in that of the Love of Wealth, and the Desire for Posthumous Fame (noticed later in the Analysis), which seem to be the most typical illustrations, Mill draws attention to the tendency of association to render the means more acceptable than the end, and the disposition, by exercising which we achieve pleasures, more desirable than those pleasures themselves.

The associations connected with the ideas of Party, Country, or Mankind in general are merely enlargements of those connected with the ideas of Family, Friends, persons in distress, &c. Any one of the various affections dependent upon these associations may of course militate against one or more of the others. To subordinate them to one another properly, giving each its just weight and proportion of influence, is to order life well. A man may "give up to party what is meant" for country, and to country "what is meant for mankind,"—or conversely he may give up to mankind what is meant for country, party, friends, family, or those whose calls on his assistance are the most immediate and urgent; and (like the elder Mirabeau) call himself the Friend of Man, in order to dispense with being the friend of wife and family: in such cases, life is ordered badly. Class-feeling, Esprit de Corps, Party-Spirit, Codes of Honour, "honour among thieves," &c., all these are so many recognitions of our dependence upon some circle of our fellow-men, some portion of humanity, wider than the limits of the domestic hearth, not only for our pleasures and comfort, but for social, that is human, existence itself. It is only when not corrected by the higher and broader associations that the Spirit of Caste, devotion to Church or Order, becomes reprehensible and, in extreme cases, even wicked and hateful.

We have seen that Hartley divides Pleasures and Pains into—apart from those of Imagination, which will be treated separately in a later chapter—those of Sensation, Ambition, Self-Interest, Sympathy, Theopathy, and the Moral Sense.

This is not a very philosophical division : for, on examination, the pleasures of Self-Interest seem to be not properly included in the list, but rather to stand outside it, because they are nothing more or less than (to use Hartley's own words) the pleasures " generated by attention to and frequent reflection upon, the things which promise us " the pleasures of Sensation, Imagination, Ambition (in which cases the Self-Interest is gross), Sympathy, Theopathy, and the Moral Sense (in which cases the Self-Interest is refined). In fact they are only the pleasures of the other six classes with a special reference to the Self. The motive would thus appear to constitute the distinction. In the one case the pleasures are contemplated merely as attendant and consequent, as a matter of fact, upon certain sensations and acts ; in the other, as consciously pursued by the agent, in the doing of certain acts, or the putting one's self in the way of receiving certain sensations. So that we may pass over Hartley's Refined Self-Interest for the present,[4] and proceed to his account of the Pleasures and Pains of Sympathy, which covers the same ground as Mill's theory of our Fellow-creatures regarded as the causes of our pleasures and pains.

Hartley distributes the sympathetic affections into (1) those by which we rejoice at the happiness of others, (2) those by which we grieve for their misery, (3) those by which we rejoice at their misery, (4) those by which we grieve for their happiness. It is a somewhat over-subtle refinement which separates the first of these classes from the second, and the third from the fourth. Two classes are quite sufficient.

---

[4] Rational Self-Interest (as distinct from Gross and Refined) appears to be tantamount to the judicious ordering of life as a whole, as contrasted with the acquisition of particular pleasures,—the pursuit of happiness instead of momentary gratifications of sense,—eudæmonism as opposed to hedonism.

Sociality, Benevolence, Generosity, Gratitude (of which "a lively sense of favours to come" is recognized as one constituent element, though not the absolute equivalent, as in the proverb), Compassion, and Mercy are treated under the former of these two heads much in the same way, though not so minutely or accurately, as they are analyzed by Mill. The force of association in producing " pure disinterested benevolence" (a slightly contradictory expression in the mouth of an Associationist) is insisted on by him, as by the later philosopher.[5] In his remarks on Compassion and Mercy, Hartley speaks of the sight of another's pain directly exciting disagreeable sensations in the percipient, which act on his nervous system,[6] giving rise to "painful internal feelings," and calling up, immediately or by association, unpleasant ideas. He nowhere resorts to the needless and artificial desire of inferring an association between the idea of the pain of another, and the idea of the self as suffering that pain, which is Mill's explanation of the phenomena; and, to this extent, he is the more satisfactory of the two. Mercy, he observes, is a higher quality than Compassion, because it has to overcome a repugnance founded on retributive justice or a legitimate vindictiveness.

In the second of the two classes (amalgamated as above) are comprised Moroseness, Anger, Revenge, Jealousy, Cruelty, Malice, Emulation, and Envy. Into the ideas productive of these tempers of mind, those (already considered) attendant upon the Love of Power and Dignity and Wealth largely enter. The idea of another's happiness or power, when combined with acquiescence in it, constitutes (in relation to our-

---

[5] It is a recognition of this process which induces even Epicurus to say of his ideal wise man, that " he will sometimes die for his friend."

[6] " Persons whose nerves are easily irritable . . . . are, in general, more disposed to compassion than others." [*Observ. on Man*, vol. i. p. 475.]

selves) the affection of Humility, and (in relation to the other person, as we have seen) Respect and Admiration. But, when not so combined, and when the Love of Power and of Dignity is strongly developed, Envy and Jealousy are the Affections which result. It is this Love of Power, and the ideas associated with it, which often lead us (involuntarily, and against our better natures) to feel that degree of complacency in contemplating the fortunes of our friends, which the proverbial moralizers tell us that even the best of men are apt to feel at times.

Having discussed these varieties of the sympathetic temper, and the share which association has in producing them, Hartley first notices the different materials on which such tempers may be exercised ; and in his arrangement he is at one with Mill. His analysis of the marital and parental affections [vol. i. pp. 483—485] is followed closely, almost word for word, by Mill, as also his account of Friendship, Devotion to Country, Mankind, &c. Nothing need be added here to what has already been said.

We have now considered (1) the proximate causes of our pleasures and pains, namely sensations (2) the remote causes, namely (*a*) Wealth, Power, and Dignity, (*b*) the dispositions of our Fellow-Creatures, to which Mill here adds, (*c*) the acts, as distinguished from the dispositions, of our Fellow-creatures.[7] It remains now to examine in order these several causes (whether proximate or remote), considered *as consequents of our own acts*, in connexion with which the corresponding Motives will come under consideration.

[7] The remaining class of Remote Causes, namely "the objects called Sublime and Beautiful and their Contraries," we reserve for separate consideration in the chapter devoted to the æsthetic, as distinguished from the intellectual and ethical, sides of the association theory represented by Hartley and James Mill.

Mill defines Motive in the following terms: "when the idea of a pleasure is associated with an action of our own as its cause; that is, contemplated as the consequent of a certain action of ours, and incapable of otherwise existing, ... a peculiar state of mind is generated, which, as it is a tendency to action, is properly denominated Motive." [*Anal.* vol. ii. p. 258.] More strictly, the association above mentioned as leading to action is the association of the idea of an action of our own as cause, with the idea of a cause of our pleasure (whether proximate or remote) as effect; while, as has been already shown, the mere contemplation of the cause of our pleasure or pain, whether past or future, when regarded as independent of our own actions, is called Affection. A readiness to obey the Motive—a facility of being acted upon by it—is the corresponding Disposition.

A motive must necessarily produce action, where there are no counteracting motives; and, in all cases, must *tend* to produce action, even when eventually overcome by other moral forces. Every pleasure being desirable, for otherwise it would not be a pleasure, the idea of any pleasure associated with the idea of action on our part producing it, must necessarily lead to that action, and so possess motivity, (though the term Motive is often loosely and incorrectly used to denominate the pleasure, without the accompanying idea of our own agency). The comparative strength of different motives in the case of any one individual depends upon the comparative strength of the associations, engendered by habit and education, (Aristotle's ἔθος and διδαχή), between different pleasures and different actions or courses of action. The right thing to learn is how to make the abstractedly desirable equivalent to the actually desired, how to make the values and the associations correspond.

In this part of his exposition, Mill carefully points out the distinction between the Motives, the Affections, and the Dispositions in each of the classes of causes of pleasures already mentioned, notwithstanding the almost invariable identity of name to denote all three states of mind, or at least two of them, the Motive and the Disposition,—an identity extremely embarrassing in any attempt at analysis. The following tables will show the Motives, &c., in each of the four classes alluded to, and exhibit the results of Mill's careful analysis :—

I. SENSATIONS, THE PROXIMATE CAUSES OF OUR PLEASURES AND PAINS.

Affection = Motive.	Disposition.	Object.
a. Love of Eating (Gluttony when in excess). β. Love of Sex (Lust, when in excess). γ. Love of Drinking (Drunkenness when in excess).	The same names.	Palate. Sex. Drink.

It will be noticed that in the above class the Affection *is* the Motive in fact as well as in name, because our own acts are here the *direct* antecedents of our pleasures (regarding the pleasurable sensations as equivalent to the pleasures, as, following general usage, we may do), and not (except for purposes of strict analysis) the causes of the causes of our pleasures. A generic name for all the cases of excess above noted is Sensuality, which, like the names of its various species, stands both for Disposition, Motive, and Affection. Each of the senses, of course, has its separate motive, but only the above have names in common use. Temperance and Intemperance are names of Dispositions only, and have reference to Pleasures and Pains generally. The former Mill defines as " an equal facility of associating with any act both its pleasures and its pains.' [*Anal.* vol. ii. p. 262]. In the case of the latter Disposition, the pleasurable associations overbalance the painful. We now come to the remote causes of our pleasures and pains, and first as to—

II. WEALTH, POWER, AND DIGNITY.

Affection.	Motive.	Disposition.	Object.
a. Love of Wealth—Avarice, Rapacity, (when in excess). β. Love of Power (Ambition). γ. Love of Dignity. δ. Pride. ε. Humility (Envy).	The same names. Emulation. Envy.	The same names. { Emulation. { Ambition. Envy.	Wealth. Power. Dignity. All the above as compared with the Wealth, &c. of others, to our own advantage, or to our own disadvantage.

The last two of the above affections (with their corresponding motives and dispositions) require some explanation. When we contemplate our own wealth, power, and dignity as small, and slightly productive of pleasure, in comparison with those of other men, the Affection is Humility; when we contemplate them as large, the Affection is Pride. But when we associate the idea of an increase to our wealth, &c., as compared with those of others, with an act of our own as causing that increase, the Motive is Emulation; when we associate the idea of our own poverty, &c., as compared with the riches &c., of others, with the idea of some act of our own detracting from the superior influence of others, the Motive is Envy.

III. The States or Attitudes towards us of our Fellow-men, and alterations in those States or Attitudes.

	Affection.	Motive.	Disposition.	Object.
a.	Friendship.			Friends.
β.	Kindness (or Compassion when the immediate object is removal of pain).			No class.
γ.	{ Love of Family. Parental Affection.	The same names.	The same names.	} Family.
δ.	Patriotism.			Country.
ε.	{ Esprit de Corps. Love of one's Order, Church, &c. Party-spirit.			Class.
ζ.	Love of Mankind.			Mankind.

Here too the distinction between the Affections, Motives, and Dispositions is manifest, though the names are again, unfortunately, the same. In speaking of the last of the above motives, Love of Mankind, Mill takes occasion to observe that large conceptions, such as those of Country, Mankind, and the like, not being directly objects of sense, can only be brought home to men's minds through the medium of General Terms. For this purpose, as "an aid to the senses," in Baconian language, Philosophical Education is necessary.

IV. The Acts (as distinguished from the States) both of ourselves, and of our Fellow-creatures, which cause us
pleasure or pain.

Object.	Affection.	Motive.	Disposition.
a. Acts primarily useful to the agent, secondarily to others :—			
(*a*) when the acts are our own,	{ Courage. { Prudence.		
(*b*) when the acts are those of others.	Moral Approbation.		
β. Acts primarily useful to others, secondarily to the agent:—			The
(*a*) when the acts are our own,	{ Justice. { Beneficence.		same
(*b*) when the acts are those of others.	Moral Approbation.		names.
γ. Acts comprehending all the above :—			
(*a*) when the acts are our own,	Virtue.		
(*b*) when the acts are those of others.	Moral Approbation, Moral Sense, Moral Intention, Moral Faculty, Sense of Right and Wrong, &c.	Love of Approbation, &c.	

The fourth and last table demands a somewhat detailed
explanation. It is to be noticed in the first place that Mill,
conformably to his ethical theory as developed in the *Fragment on Mackintosh* and *Miscellaneous Essays,* holds the
generic element in the four cardinal virtues to be the conferring
of benefits on men, whether ourselves or our fellow-creatures,
primarily on ourselves in the case of Fortitude and Prudence,

primarily on others in the case of Justice and Beneficence. But—and here he seems to be following Gay very closely—since Prudent and Courageous acts best enable us to perform acts of Justice and Benevolence to others, and since, further, our own acts of Justice and Benevolence best dispose others to perform similar acts towards ourselves, it follows that each of these two main classes of acts, the primarily self-regarding, and the primarily altruistic, may be said to have a double aspect.

And not only this,—but there is another difference to be observed, according as the acts which cause us pleasure or pain are our own, or those of other men.

First let us consider the case where the acts in question are our own. We associate with any of our own acts of Prudence and Courage, as its immediate consequence, some advantage to ourselves, either Pleasure, that is, or the cause of Pleasure: and, moreover, we associate with the ideas of our own acts of Justice and Beneficence the ideas of the pleasurable feelings of a fellow-creature (ideas which are pleasurable in themselves), and also the ideas of the benefits which we secondarily derive from our fellow-creatures by the performance of such acts, (the ideas, that is, of causes of pleasure to ourselves). Now to contemplate a Pleasure, together with its cause (however remote), is to have a complex idea, which, after repetition, ceases to be an indifferent, and becomes a pleasurable, idea, that is, an Affection. And to contemplate, in addition, an act of ours as causing that cause, is to have the corresponding Motive. But in this case there is no act of ours to be associated as cause of that cause, because our own act is the cause. Therefore, in this case as in that Class (I), the Motive is the Affection, and the Affection is the Motive. The Disposition in this, as in all instances, is the ready capability, induced by habitual exercise and education (the ἕξις induced

by ἔθος and διδαχή in Aristotelian language) of being influenced by the Motive, or, to use Mill's curious phraseology,
of " performing the associations."

Now as to another man's acts of Prudence, Courage, Justice,
and Beneficence. These, though (as we have seen) primarily
useful to the agent himself, are also secondarily useful to
others, as being the causes or conditions of the performance
by him of acts to their advantage, if not (as often in the
case of Fortitude) acts directly useful in themselves to others.
As such, they are attended by agreeable associations. Our
ideas of such prudent or brave acts of another,—of acts, that
is, related to our pleasures as causes (however remote) to
effects,—become in this way complex pleasurable ideas, or
Affections. It is of course still more obvious how Affections
are generated, where the ideas of Just and Beneficent acts on
the part of others is associated directly with pleasurable ideas
of the advantages to be derived therefrom primarily by
persons other than the agent himself, and how strong such
Affections will become. The generic name for them is Moral
Approbation or Disapprobation, Moral Sense, and the like;
and this is also the name of the corresponding Motive, or of
the association not only of the Prudent, Brave, Just, and
Beneficent actions of others as causes with our pleasures as
effects, but also of our own acts with, and as causing, these
causes. For by what means can we, through our own acts,
cause those causes? Firstly, by performing similar acts ourselves; but, secondly, by conferring praise on those acts of
others of the nature specified, and affixing the stigma of
Blame or Dispraise on the reverse. When we associate acts
of praise or condemnation on our part as causes with the acts
of our fellow-creatures as effects, and these latter acts as
causes with our pleasures as effects, such an association will
lead to action, and is therefore a Motive, which has received

some such name as that designated above. The same term, or perhaps better Love of Approbation, (it must be admitted that, in all this part of his work, Mill's terminology is terribly confused), serves also for the corresponding Disposition.

Some further remarks of Mill on the subject of the special motives and virtues fall to be noticed here.

Since Prudence expresses, according to Mill, " the choice made, among all the innumerable acts within our power, of those, the consequences of which, when the pleasurable and painful are balanced against one another, constitute the greatest amount of good " [vol. ii. p. 282], it follows that to be prudent, a man must have knowledge and experience of all or most of the possible consequences, or successions of consequences, which any given act has produced or may produce. Judgment is therefore requisite, as well as a certain disposition, and state of the will : and hence the semi-intellectual character of Prudence. So far most persons would agree : but when Mill goes on to say that knowledge is a condition of Courage as well as of Prudence (in this following Plato), and that Courage is but incurring the danger or possibility of evil for the certainty of ultimate good,—is, in fact, (for Mill, like Plato,[8] goes this length) only a species of Prudence, the analysis will probably be thought faulty. Courage is all the more courage when there is most to be lost, and most chance of its being lost. On any other explanation Mill would be obliged to call the death of the Spartans at Thermopylæ an act not of courage but of fatuity, an " immoral act " (as he himself says, when speaking of cases in which no ultimate good to the agent is probable) ; and the courage of a beast (as having less to lose) would be superior to the courage of an Athenian of the age of Pericles. The very fact that we often

[8] Plato defines Courage as " a right judgment concerning things to be feared and not to be feared."

call an action brave, but rash, shows the vital distinction
between Courage and Prudence.   It is when a highly civilized
being possesses the greatest appreciation of life, and is bound
to it by the strongest and most various ties, that his courage
is most peculiarly and markedly courage.   As Professor Bain
observes in his note [vol. ii. p. 284 of the *Analysis*], " the
courageous soldier is not he who maintains a post of *apparent*
danger unmoved, knowing that there is no real danger. . . .
Something very different is exacted in return for the epithet
of a brave man."

Justice is similarly considered by Mill to be a section of
Beneficence, and just acts to be carved out of the class of
beneficent acts merely by reference to the particular legal
system in use in a particular country at a particular time.
In point of fact, the conventional theory of Justice is adopted.
Out of all the various acts of individuals which are productive
of good to others, some are so in virtue of their conforma-
bility to the laws of the state in which they are performed.
There is no place in Mill's system for any theory of mental
construction in the matter, of any constitution by the individual of an equity within himself, or even of adaptation of
mathematical processes and proportions to the facts of the
moral world.   Mill is a philosopher in this respect resembling Plato's litigant, and is obliged to go to the law
courts for justice, because he has none of his own making.

In connexion with the subject of the influence of Praise
and Blame on moral action, Mill notices that the very names
of the cardinal virtues and of Virtue itself, signify not only
the qualities characteristic of virtuous acts, but also the pleasurable ideas of the benefits resulting from the exercise of
those qualities, and the performance of those acts.   They are,
in Bentham's phraseology, eulogistic terms, while their opposites are dyslogistic.   This alone is of immense power in

attracting men to Virtue; and every one knows the kind of homage which Vice is forced to pay to it, in assuming the properties and titles of its opponent, in order to secure a tolerable status. The importance of such names is not to be overlooked. History teaches us how much depends on whether the name of assassination or that of national deliverance is assigned to a deed immediately after its committal; and that this often has its appreciable share in determining whether a human being is to be execrated as a Guy Fawkes, or exalted as a Harmodius, a Jael, or a Charlotte Corday. Many important effects may be traced to the designation of a disturbance of constitutional relations in a country as a revolution, or as a rebellion; and much depends on whether a body of reformers succeed in getting themselves called a Constitution or a Convention, a Party or a Faction. Eulogistic terms then, having by themselves alone so much significance and influence, it may be imagined what a degree of controlling power is exerted on the deeds of our fellow-creatures by the systematic diffusion of applause and condemnation. Praise, as Mill says, extends to all men : whereas our own acts (the alternative means of securing the performance of virtuous acts by others) extend only to a few. In the former case we not only express our own favourable disposition towards the person who is its object, but we at the same time point him out to others as a fit object of a similar affection on their parts towards him. From the pleasurable ideas connected with the being praised by others, springs not only that extraordinary case of association, which has already been noticed, the desire of posthumous fame, (when the idea of advantageous consequences to ourselves is so firmly associated with the idea of the performance of virtuous actions, that we cannot dissociate the two *ideas*, notwithstanding that a very little reflection tell us that the two *things* cannot coexist after death), but also the desire of being deserving of praise, and the dread of being deserving of blame,—the Love of Praiseworthiness, and the Fear of Blameworthiness; as also the state of misery attendant on the consciousness of being blameworthy in reference to past actions, which is called Remorse.

Hartley makes the pleasures and pains of the Moral Sense a special class of the various pleasures and pains of which human beings are susceptible. He places them at the end of his list, after those of Sensation, Imagination, Ambition, Self-interest, Sympathy, and Theopathy; and all these latter must, in his view, have been experienced before those of the Moral Sense can be properly appreciated. In his account of this Moral Sense, he differs slightly from Mill, in so far as he bases it less on a conscious regard to the utility of actions. He speaks of "a pleasing consciousness and self-approbation" rising up in the mind of a person who believes himself to be possessed of virtuous qualities, "exclusively of any direct explicit consideration of advantage likely to accrue to himself" [*Observ. on Man,* vol. i. p. 493]. Like Mill, he remarks on the eulogistic character of the names of virtue and the different virtuous qualities; and also how the pleasurable ideas incidental to the frequent use and application of these names are gradually impressed by education on the minds of children. Like his master in this department of his subject, Gay, he notices the rival theories of Hutcheson, as to the instinctive character of the moral sense, and of the mathematical Platonists, Clarke and Cudworth, as to its alleged foundation in the eternal relations of things; and he contends that if it be meant that the supposed instinct, or the supposed relations, exist or operate independently of association, then no indubitable instances or proofs of such existence or operation have been produced. All moral judgments, approbations, and disapprobations are, in his opinion, deduced from association alone; though it is admitted (as we have implied above), that these associations may be "formed so early, repeated so often, riveted so strong," as, in a popular way, to deserve the name of "original and natural dispositions or instincts," or even of "axioms and intuitive propositions."

CHAPTER VIII

It is characteristic of the Association Theory of Hartley and James Mill, that the Will occupies a very late place—in Mill's analysis, the very last—in their examination of moral phenomena. In the systems opposed to the derivative theories of ethics, it comes into prominence at the very outset of the inquiry. Kant, for instance, begins at once with its definition, from which, as a starting-point, he evolves his entire speculations on morals. Schopenhauer, again, a philosopher of a very different type, although he professes to be following out Kant's doctrines to their legitimate issue, considers that this all-powerful Will, the centre of Personality, should be suppressed in favour of the impersonal Intellect, if happiness is ever to be achieved for men. But whether as the mainstay and foundation of morals, or as the incessant obstacle in the path of tranquillity, all philosophers, except Associationists, have concurred in placing the Will in the forefront of their ethical systems. With Hartley and Mill, on the other hand, after everything else is determined, and not till then, the Will follows as the necessary result. Given Association, Affection, Motive, Disposition, to find the Will is, according to this school, not very difficult. The Will, it is to be observed, is, in their view, not a faculty but "a peculiar state of mind or consciousness" [Mill, *Analysis*, vol. ii. p. 328], that, namely, which precedes an action. It is the cause of the action, in the proper sense of the word, that is, its immediate antecedent. The notion that it is a faculty has arisen from the common mental illusion in subjection to which, not content with having found the cause of a phenomena, we proceed to invest it with a certain imaginary Power, in virtue of which alone it is said to produce its effect. This emanation from, or property of, the cause Mill pronounces to be a fiction. To determine the nature of the Will, we have merely to "discover which is the real state of mind which immediately precedes an action."

Now actions, says Mill, may be either those of the Body, or those of the Mind.[1] The former are muscular contractions, and may be preceded either by Sensations—as in the familiar cases of sneezing, vomiting, coughing, and other involuntary or instinctive movements—or by Ideas, as in yawning, laughter, convulsive fits, on seeing another person yawn, laugh, or fall into convulsions; or again in the case where a person rapidly shuts his eyelids on seeing an object approach them, which action is consequent on the idea of pain called up by the sight of the object. This last is a good example of association, because an infant will not wink if anything is passed rapidly before its eyes, while an adult will.[2]

When these contractions of the muscles are preceded by Sensations, the steps are (1) sensation originating in the extremities of the nerves, (2) "something, we know not what conveyed by the nerves to the brain," (3) a consequent state of the brain, (4) something (also unknown) conveyed by the brain through another set of nerves to the contracting muscles,

[1] " A vile phrase " this—" actions of the mind." It is curious how, in this instance, Mill shows himself under the bondage of that habit of constructing metaphor, which he elsewhere (using, too, this very example) so severely reprobates in others.

[2] The experiment was performed by Mr. Darwin on his own child, with this result. See his interesting account of these psychological observations in *Mind*, No. 7, (*a Biographical Sketch of an Infant*).

followed by (5) muscular contraction. When they are preceded by Ideas, the first two steps are not present, and the
process begins with the third, or with a certain state of the
brain. It will be seen, therefore, that in both cases the state
of the brain is, strictly speaking, the immediate *mental* antecedent of the contraction : but, for purposes of the present
investigation, that state may be distinguished as Sensation or
as Ideation, according as it is, or is not, produced by external
causes operating directly upon the nerves. The principle of
those mental phenomena of the latter class which result from
the tendency to imitate the actions, and experience in our
own persons the sensations of another,—a species of phenomena familiar to physicians, under the name of imaginative
diseases,—is that the action, motion, or bodily state, the idea
of which is conveyed to us by what we thus perceive in others,
"calls up by association the idea of the feelings which precede" that action, motion, or bodily state. "The idea of the
feelings exists, and the action follows." [*Analysis*, vol. ii.
p. 343.]

Sensations and Ideas, then, are to be considered as the
immediate mental antecedents of muscular contraction. Now
over sensations we confessedly have no control : they may
therefore be dismissed from consideration : and the kind of
ideation, hitherto discussed as antecedent to action, clearly
does not answer to what we mean by an exercise of the Will.
So much only has been established up to the present point :
that muscular contractions follow ideas, that to obtain a command over the former we must obtain a command over the
latter, and that to produce certain sequences of associated
motions, we must have acquired the power, through repetition,
or otherwise, of readily calling up the correspondingly associated ideas. The power of the Will is not, therefore, exerted
over the motions, but over the ideas, or trains of ideas which

precede those motions. The motions or actions which we will must of course be our own, and therefore one at least of the ideas constituting the state of volition must be the idea of such an action as our own.

Is there anything more involved in Volition than the above elements? Now in the cases already noticed of the ideas of our actions preceding these actions, whether in the way of automatic imitation or of repetition, we cannot be said to will them. They are as involuntary (at all events in the adult mind) as those motions which are excited by our own sensations in the manner already indicated. But it is ideas alone in any case which give birth to action : there must therefore · be something in the process by which these ideas are generated, when we are said to exercise volition, different from the process whereby these ideas are generated when the acts which follow them are, as in the above instances, styled involuntary. In the latter case they are produced in the way of ordinary association whether by sensations of our own, or by the ideas of the sensations of others (as when we yawn or laugh on seeing another person do so), or by our own ideas, as when we weep on reading a tragedy. But in none of these instances, can we be said to will the performance of the acts. But where strictly voluntary actions are concerned, the ideas of them,— the ideas which precede them,—are accompanied with Desire, which is their distinguishing feature. Now Desire is the idea of a future pleasurable sensation, or exemption from pain. Therefore in the state of mind which precedes what are called voluntary actions, there must coexist, (1) the idea of the action, and the idea of it, of course, as our own, (2) the idea of the pleasurable condition to be enjoyed by us consequent on the performance of the action. In other words, we must have the idea of a future pleasurable state coupled with the idea of an act of ours as causing it. But this is exactly what

Motive was defined as being. Is then Motive the same as
Will? No. The difference is the following.

In the train of thoughts constituting the Motive, (as Mill,
in a careful elaboration of a well-known Aristotelian principle,[3]
points out), we start with the idea of the pleasurable sensation to be obtained, proceed from it to the idea of the action
of which it is contemplated as being the immediate result,
then to the idea of the step next preceding it, and so on
through the ideas of a series of means, till we come to the last
link in the chain which ends with ourselves, that is, to the
idea of some muscular contraction on our part. Now when
mere Motive, unaccompanied by Volition, is present, the process of association stops at this point; whereas when the
Motive is sufficiently powerful to generate volition, it does
not cease, but the mind passes from the idea of some muscular
contraction on our part, to the idea of the internal sensations
preceding the muscular contraction, which sensations originally produced similar muscular contractions. On this the
action follows. It may seem somewhat over-subtle to draw
such a fine line of distinction between the idea of the outward
appearance of our own action and the idea of the internal sensations which precede that action. But Mill explains that
these sensations, and their ideas,—though scarcely ever noticed
or even thought to exist, owing to their inevitable absorption
in immediately subsequent sensations and ideas, of far greater
interest to us,—are yet real. Why the visible idea of an
action should at one time call up the idea of the internal
sensations preceding it, and at another time not, can only be

---

[3] "ὃ πρῶτον ἐν ἀναλύσει ἐσχατὸν ἐν εὑρέσει." The order of execution is
the reverse of the order of thoughts in volition. In the former case, we
begin with a muscular contraction on our part, and end with the pleasurable
condition. In the latter, our first idea is that of the pleasurable condition,
from which we work backwards.

explained on principles of association. A strong connexion between the two ideas is formed in some cases, so that the one cannot come into existence without exciting the other, whereas, in others, no such indissoluble, or nearly indissoluble, association has been generated. This analysis of the Will regarded as a state of mind preceding muscular contraction is partly an amplification, and partly a condensation, of Hartley's theory of the association of motions,[4] and of the growth of voluntary out of automatic motions, (such as are produced by internal sensations), and again of "secondarily automatic" motions out of voluntary.[5] [*Anal.* vol. ii. pp. 355, 356. J. S. Mill's note.]

But we have yet to consider the Will as a state of consciousness antecedent to what Mill calls "the actions of *the mind.*" We seem to ourselves to have the power of calling up an idea at will, or of forcing one train of thought into existence to the exclusion of others. Is this power over our mental associations real or imaginary? Are the processes of Recollection, as distinguished from Memory, and of Attention, as distinguished from mere passive thought or reverie, cases of Volition or not? If they are, then can the Will in these, as in the other cases already examined, be reduced to association, or is it something which controls association itself?

If the Will controls association, it must do so in one of two ways,—either in virtue of some power which it possesses of calling up an idea "ex nihilo," so to speak, or in virtue of a power of making one idea present to the mind at any time

---

[4] These Hartley considers *pari passu* (in the earlier part of his work) with the association of sensations and ideas. The title of his short Latin tractate, *De Sensu, Motu, et Idearum Generatione,* shows the triple application which he designed for his system.

[5] E.g. a child moves, first of all, spasmodically and under the stimulus of sensation; then it learns to *regulate* its movements, lastly to employ them without conscious volition, as in walking.

call up another, not then present to the mind, to succeed it, and of simultaneously excluding all ideas which would interfere with the sequence of ideas desired. But we have already explained that we cannot will to evoke any particular idea, without already having that idea in our minds. And to will a particular sequence of ideas equally, of course, presupposes the presence of that sequence to our minds. We can no more will the introduction of an idea into a train at a particular point, than we can will its presence at all, indeed, much less. In either case we may be said to desire, but never to will. We desire, for instance, to recollect a thing; we are not properly said to will to recollect it. The discovery of the lost idea is contemplated by us as the cause of future pleasure, or is associated with the idea of that future pleasure, and, as such, becomes interesting to us. Now interesting, as contrasted with indifferent, ideas have this peculiar property, that they call up trains of great length, rapidity, and complexity, and are themselves suggested by most of the ideas which may enter the mind from whatever quarter. In the attempt to recollect, accordingly, the idea of the alleviation of an existing unsatisfied state of mind obtrudes itself into every train of ideas which would otherwise run its usual course, and itself excites a large variety of trains of all kinds, until that alleviation is obtained, and, with it, the wished-for pleasurable sensations. This phenomenon, a familiar enough one, has already occupied our attention.

In regard to the process of Attention, there certainly seems at first sight to be more plausibility in the view of those who hold that we can will to attend, or not to attend, to a thing. But here too, according to Mill, the so-called act of Will except as a case of association, is found not to exist.

We may attend either to Sensations or to Ideas. Sensations are either in themselves indifferent, that is, apart from any ideas associated with them, or interesting (whether as pleasurable or painful).

Now to attend to sensations interesting in themselves is, as has often been remarked before, the same thing as having the sensations. "To attend to sensations indifferent in themselves" is on the other hand as palpably contradictory an expression, as "to attend to sensations interesting in themselves," is redundant and tautological. If sensations are attended to, they are not indifferent in themselves : if they are interesting in themselves, they must necessarily be attended to in the fact of experiencing them. But we may attend to sensations indifferent in themselves, but rendered interesting by the ideas associated with them; just as, conversely, we may feel, without attending to, sensations which, though interesting under ordinary circumstances and in themselves, are on the particular occasion absorbed in stronger sensations or more vivid ideas (as in the well-known example of men in battle fighting while quite unconscious of their wounds). The attention to a sensation rendered interesting by association no more differs from the having the *association*, than the attention to a sensation interesting in itself differs from the having the *sensation*, or, again, than the non-attention to a sensation interesting in itself differs from the having that sensation accompanied by, and swallowed up in, stronger simultaneous sensations or ideas.

Exactly the same reasoning applies "*mutatis mutandis*" to the phenomenon of attention to Ideas. Attention to an interesting idea is merely the having it;—to an indifferent idea, merely the associating it with some idea which is not indifferent. By way of illustrating his theory of attention as applied to ideas, Mill takes the case of a man composing a treatise or discourse with a given object, where the discovery of a single idea (as in the attempt to recollect) will not suffice

to accomplish the desired end, but where the discovery and
selection of a variety of trains of ideas is necessary.   Here the
interesting idea of the pleasure consequent upon the attainment of the end is continually being suggested by, and
suggesting, large varieties of ideas and sequences of ideas, in
precisely the same way as, but to a greater extent than, the
idea of such a pleasurable state calls up a single idea in successful, and tends to call it up in unsuccessful, efforts of recollection.   Of the same kind as this is the still more complicated example of an aim of life ruling a man's actions from
day to day, where the Idea of the End to be obtained associates itself in his mind with all the ideas and trains of ideas
of all those actions of his which may contribute to the realiza-
tion of that end.   The conclusion is that, when we attend to
Ideas, just as when we attend to Sensations, the attention is
due to the occurrence or recurrence of interesting sensations
or ideas, whether interesting *per se*, or as forming part of
an associated cluster, some of the other ingredients of which
are interesting *per se*, and, as such, have given a reflected
interest to the entire cluster.

We cannot better sum up the results of this analysis of
Volition than in James Mill's own words [*Anal.* vol. ii.
pp. 378, 379] :—" In regard, then, to that state of mind
which precedes action, we seem to have ascertained the
following indisputable facts : That actions are in some
instances preceded by sensations; that, in other instances,
they are preceded by ideas ; that in all cases in which the
action is said to be willed, it is desired as a means to an end ;
or, in more accurate language, is associated, as cause, with
pleasure as effect : that the idea of the outward appearance of
the action, thus excited by association, excites in the same
way, the idea of the internal feelings which are the immediate
antecedent of the action, and then the action takes place ;

that whatever power we may possess over the actions of our muscles, must be derived from our power over our associations ; and that this power over our associations, when fully analyzed, means nothing more than the power of certain interesting ideas, originating in interesting sensations, and formed into strength by association."

Mill disposes of Intention in the same way as Bentham. It differs from Will, in that an action willed is some action of ours contemplated as immediately about to take place ; whereas the action intended, though still some action of our own, is contemplated as about to take place after the inter- vention of a certain train or series of events. To look forward to or anticipate a certain chain of antecedents and conse- quents, the last consequent of which is an action to be first willed by us, and then performed, is all that is meant by Intention. We believe that at some future time we shall will to perform, and shall eventually perform, the intended action. We cannot, of course, properly be said to will such an action, or even to will to will at some future time to perform the action. Such a fancy arises from the illusory character of the term, which, being active in form, appears to imply some activity in fact ; whereas, in reality, intention is merely a case of belief : it is "the strong anticipation of a future will" [*Anal.* vol. ii. p. 399]. A promise, consequently, is merely a declaration of this belief,—a declaration of such a character that it derives from customary, legal, and moral sanctions, and carries with it, a strong guarantee that the declared anticipation will be realized. But, besides intending an action, we are frequently said, in the language both of law and of morals, to intend the consequences of an act. By this is meant the foreseeing or anticipation of the consequences, at the moment of willing or intending the act. By this latter, again, as we have seen in discussing that form of Belief which is called Anticipation, is meant that the idea of the action calls up the idea of its consequences. Though Mill does not specifically refer to the questions of Free Will and Necessity, which have so vexed the minds of moralists at different times, there can be little doubt—judging from his analysis of Volition—that he would have adopted what Hartley calls the theory of the Mechanism of the Human Mind, as opposed to that of Free Will, in any but the popular use of the word. For Hartley carefully distinguishes the philosophical doctrine of Free Will, according to which it is held possible for a man to will either of two actions while the circumstances attendant upon, and previous to, the exercise of his will, remain the same, from the popular doctrine, which amounts merely to the tautological proposition that a man has the power of doing that which he wills or desires, or has the power of "deliberating, suspending, choosing, &c.," between various courses of action. The latter Hartley does not dispute, but maintains in opposition to the former, what on examination appears to be equally tautological, that a man is infallibly determined by the strongest motive to action, and that when the motives are the same the action consequent upon them must be the same in the same man. This appears to be nothing more than the statement that a man wills what he does will, desires what he does desire. The further question as to who or what determines the motive, granting that the motive determines the action, is not satisfactorily answered by Hartley, because (in common with most associationists) he is inoculated with the misconception of a motive as a force operating upon the individual "ab extra," and not as an object in itself indifferent taken up into, and made part of, the Self; and so endowed by the Self, and the Self alone, with motive power. "By the mechanism of human actions, I mean," says Hartley, "that each action results from the previous circumstances of body and mind, in the same manner and with the same certainty, as other effects do from their mechanical causes." [*Observ. on Man*, vol. i. p. 500]. This proposition he supports by an appeal to each man's introspection of his own acts and states of consciousness [6] and observation of the acts of others. Neither method, he says, will discover any act to be unmotived, nor in the event of conflict will the weaker motive ever be seen to override the stronger.[7] Apart from this appeal to experience and self-scrutiny, Hartley relies once more on his vibration theory. Actions result from vibrations " in the nerves of the muscles;" and these vibrations result from others which are either completely mechanical, or which, though now voluntary, have become so, from being originally mechanical, by means of association.

The sum of the objections raised against the mechanical theory was, in Hartley's time, not so much metaphysical or psychological as practical. This theory, it was said, gets rid of the notion of personal responsibility. We shall never refer actions to an Ego, if we are taught to believe that the state of the Ego which determines the action is itself determined by a series of prior circumstances. Such objections are of course quite unphilosophical, and are calculated to divert the attention from the real issue. Hartley would have done well

[6] Such an introspection has been made, and the results given in an essay called "An Introspective Investigation," *Mind*, No. 5, p. 22, seq., by Mr, Travis. He does not come to the same conclusion as Hartley.

[7] This latter statement is again tautological or circular. For how can we tell the strength of one motive as compared with that of another, except from its effect upon action? As to unmotived acts, they are recognized by no school of philosophy, no school of art even. Even in Iago we find the "motive-hunting of a motiveless malignity" (as Coleridge calls it) which testifies to this law of nature, while seeming to violate it.

not to notice them. The practical outcome of a theory has nothing to do with its truth. But it was characteristic of the times in which he lived both to advocate and to combat systems with a reference to results : and just as every new metaphysics (such as that of Berkeley, for instance) was at this period generally prefaced with some anti-atheistic flourish to gain it admittance among the ingenuous respectabilities of "thinking gentlemen," so Hartley, like the rest, was at great pains to show, first of all, that the ordinary sentiments of gratitude and resentment towards our fellow-creatures as responsible agents do in fact remain in force, notwithstanding all theories and analyses : but he added secondly, that so far as this is not the case, it is right and proper, even in a practical reference, that it should not be, and operates for the advantage, and not the detriment, of morality. For just as an infant, or a savage tribe, begins by exhibiting gratitude or resentment towards inanimate objects regarded as causes of his pleasures and pains, but gradually learns, the one on reaching maturity, the other on attaining some degree of civilization, to transfer such affections to the human beings who produce or use those objects ; so man in general will, on learning to regard his fellow-men as links in a chain,—in the light of consequents as well as in that of antecedents,— reach a still higher order of intelligence and morality. We laugh at Xerxes for lashing the Hellespont, and are amused at a child for kicking and abusing the chair over which he has just stumbled : but we have yet to learn to treat human beings with the like equanimity to that which we think Xerxes should have displayed towards the storm on the Hellespont, as the product of natural forces, or the child towards the chair, as matter misplaced.[8] Such a mental attitude

---

[8] Hartley in fact thought that there could be an exaggerated Animism (as it is now called) in relation to human beings, as well as to inanimate objects.

stimulates attention to the high interests of Education, and leads our thoughts away from resentment against individuals, to the reform of the circumstances, and mitigation of the influences, which have made them what they are.[9] It thus begets humility in ourselves, and further "tends to remove the great difficulty of reconciling the prescience of God with the freewill of man. For it takes away 'philosophical free-will,'" [as Hartley calls the imaginary rival doctrine of un-motived willing], "and the practical" [or popular] "is consistent with God's prescience." [*Observ. on Man*, vol. i. p. 510.][1]

[9] This is a more familiar idea now than it was in Hartley's time. Not philosophy only, but art and fiction (cp. Victor Hugo's *Jean Valjean*) have inculcated it strenuously. It finds its "reductio ad absurdum" in Mr. Butler's *Erewhon.*

[1] On this mechanical theory of Hartley's, see Mr. Leslie Stephen's remarks (*History of English Thought in the Eighteenth Century*, vol. ii. sect. 67).

CHAPTER IX.

THE PRACTICAL LAWS OF ETHICS AS RESULTING FROM THE PRINCIPLES OF ASSOCIATION AND UTILITY.

HAVING considered the answers of Hartley and Mill to the question—"how do we act?" it remains to collect from scattered hints their probable answer to the question, which only the former has dealt with specifically—indeed it was no part of Mill's proposed object to do so—namely, "how ought we to act?" What should be the rule or guiding principle of life?

At the end of his *Analysis* Mill suggests that, since all valid practical rules are founded on true theory, the works which ought to follow on an exposition or true theory of the operations of the human mind both in its intellectual and moral aspects, are works containing (1) rules for guiding the mind in its search after truth, (2 rules for training the individual to the greatest excellence of his nature, and (3) " rules for regulating the actions of human being." These would be respectively the Book of Logic, the Book of Education, and the Book of Ethics, to which might be added (if not included under Ethics) the Book of Politics. These would furnish the entire fabric capable of being reared on the basis of a sound theory of the human mind. On Education and Politics, Mill has a good deal of matter, elsewhere than in the *Analysis*, to which we shall have occasion to refer presently. On Logic he has nothing; and as regards Ethical rules we have to gather his views from his criticisms of his opponents contained in the *Fragment on Mackintosh;* while those of Hartley on the same topic are to be found, mixed up with a large mass of theological and other speculations, in the second volume of his work *On Man.*

Mill's conception of morality is evident from his description of ethics, as "rules for regulating the actions of human beings, so as to deduce from them the greatest amount of good, both to the actor himself, and to his fellow-creatures at large" [*Anal.* vol. ii. p. 403]. He holds not only that men do act for their own interests, but that they ought to do so ; but then Education, to which he attaches very great importance, steps in, and shows what their highest interests are. It shows that man best secures his own ultimate advantage by not directly and consciously seeking it, but by working for the good of his fellow-men. Thus though moral action is in the last resort referable to self-interest, its primary and immediate aim in practice should be utilitarian, in the modern sense of the word, or conducive to the good of the largest possible number. To adopt Hartley's phraseology, our actions at first, and during infancy, for the attainment of self-gratification are primarily automatic ; then by practice, and owing to the influence of education, we learn to associate ideas of self-interest of the higher kinds with the ideas of actions productive of good to others, and so accustom ourselves gradually to the voluntary, and at first troublesome, actions dictated by considerations of general utility ; which latter again, after frequent repetition, became automatic in the sense that we no more think of self-interest at the time of performing them, than the miser, when making an addition to his hoard, thinks of realizing the possibilities of pleasure which that hoard symbolizes. To analyze any of the complex faculties and tendencies of human nature, is not to deny their existence or effectuality, but merely to point out their ultimate justification. "Gratitude remains gratitude," says Mill, [*Frag. on Mackintosh*, p. 51], like his predecessor, "resentment remains resentment, generosity, generosity, in the mind of him who feels them, after analysis, the same as before."

For the perception of the useful results likely to flow from certain classes of actions, the ordinary feelings and understanding of men suffice. No special sense, such as the hypothetical Moral Sense, is required. [*Fr. on Mack.*, p. 11]. If and whenever a man has not contemplated the consequences of his act as likely or calculated to produce good to others or to himself, "the man's act may be a grateful act, or an affectionate act, but certainly not a moral act." [*Fr. on Mack.*, pp. 55, 236, 237]. An act has no ethical value, apart from its intended consequences; and it lies on the opponents of utilitarianism to show what morality is apart from utility.

It is no objection to the practical rules founded upon utilitarian doctrines that, according to them, calculation must precede action; but that this balancing of consequences, to be just, must be infinite, since the consequences are infinite both in extent and in time, as well as infinitely complicated; and that, therefore, action will never take place at all. It is true that every act reaches out into an indefinite future with innumerable ramifications of consequences; just as the disturbance of air by the motion of a man's hand may conceivably produce some effect on the remotest planet: but no man is expected to attempt to calculate these, though on the other hand, if he looks carelessly to the probable immediate consequences of his acts, he is justly responsible for all those which he might have foreseen by the exercise of reasonable care, and did not. In all cases where the more lengthy calculations would be impossible or inconvenient, it will be found that they have been done for us beforehand with sufficient correctness for practical purposes by the collective experience of humanity extending through past ages.? A man may act either upon certain general rules, such for instance as those of the cardinal virtues, and in accordance with certain formed habits, [*Fr. on Mack.*, p. 258], and be (so far) absolved from the necessity of reflection or computation of consequences. [p. 163]. Where however circumstances arise which do not come within the ordinary classes of moral rules, there he must balance probabilities and effects for himself: habit will not suffice. [p. 257]. The nature and complexity of the calculation must, of course, be limited by the urgency of the case. But moral sentiments, intuitions, &c., Mill utterly discards.[1] The moral agent must in all cases either calculate for himself, or accept the previously formed and recognized calculations of others or (as in habitual acts) of himself. He must proceed, like a natural philosopher, who bases his laws on proper inductions, inferences, and analogies, though no one blames him for adopting from others (without proving again) the results of mathematical processes, where it is necessary or convenient to do so. Mill follows Bentham in thinking that the morality of an act in no way depends upon the motive, which in itself is colourless, and only derives its complexion from the consequences

---

[1] Cp. *Fr. on Mack.*, 267, 268. Mill ridicules the sentiment of Andrew Fletcher (approved by Sir James Mackintosh) to the effect that "he would lose his life to serve his country, but would not do a base thing to save it." A refusal of the latter kind Mill would presumably consider immoral. So also, we imagine, would he repudiate Kant's well-known assertion of the duty of telling the truth to a murderer about the hiding-place of his intended victim.

contemplated by the agent, or neglected to be contemplated by him. [*Fr. on Mack.*, pp. 161, 315, 316].

Granting then that the proper aim of man is to contemplate, intend, calculate the good of his fellow-creatures,—the object of Education, Government, and Legislation should be to lead men to take into view wider and wider circles, in considering the benefits to be thus conferred, and their recipients. Man must be taught to put philanthropy above patriotism, patriotism above party-spirit, party-spirit above individual gratification. Imitation and Custom tend to restrict men's benevolence to the limits within which their lives and habits have grown up. The incentives to keep within these bounds are strong: it should be the function and aim of Education to supply yet stronger incentives to transcend them. [*Fr. on Mack.*, 64, 65]. "The man whom his education or other fortunate circumstances have habituated to the ideas of the good of one of the larger communities of men, a nation; and to consider the interests of small societies, and of individuals as subordinate to the interests in which each and all of the other individuals and societies composing the great communities participate; the man who has learnt to fix his esteem upon the actions which promote these great interests, and in whom the motives to the performance of such actions overpower all other motives, is the only man who has reached the elevation of true morality."

Regarding then utility as the test of morality, and not morality of utility, as Sir James Mackintosh says is possible "in another way," Mill cannot sufficiently express his contempt for the theory which ascribes aims to appetites, over which conscience has a controlling and legislative authority.[2]

---

[2] Butler's theory, approved by Mackintosh. Cp. Hooker's similar opinion about the Will:—"Appetite is the Will's solicitor, and Will is the Appetite's controller."

All this he thinks merely so much metaphor, of a very misleading character. When it is said that the appetites aim, all that is meant is that a man has a certain appetite, and aims at its gratification. When it is said that conscience possesses a controlling power over appetite, all that is meant is that the man who has the appetites has also the right to control them, which nobody denies. The question of ethics, however, is,—"in what way ought we to control them?" And to this of course Mill's answer is clear : we must control them in a manner calculated to confer benefit on others or on the agent himself. [*Fr. on Mack.*, 72, 73]. Still less will Mill allow actions to be properly called beautiful or ugly, unless their beauty or ugliness be regarded as consisting simply and solely in the character of their consequences. [p. 263]. The artistic aspect of ethics, if it exists at all, should be kept in the background, as illusionary and tending to emasculate moral energy. Similarly "Fitness," which some ascribe as their distinguishing feature to moral actions, is either the utility of their effects, or it is an unmeaning phrase. So too of Right Reason, and the like. [p. 265].

The same considerations which dictate action, also dictate and justify moral approbation. The *conscious employment* of moral approbation is grounded on utilitarian motives. Men have agreed, thinks Mill, to affix marks of praise or blame to certain classes of actions, which they have perceived to be advantageous or the reverse in their effects, in order that with them may be associated such pleasurable or painful ideas, respectively, as may induce to, or deter from, the performance of them. On the building up of such associative links depends the value of Education; since children must necessarily act largely on such associations, and not so much with a view to computed consequences. But, further, the *sentiment* of moral approbation is justified ultimately, if not immediately, by this same reference to utility,—to the consequences, that is, observed as likely to flow from the act approved of, or observed as having flown in other instances from the class of acts to which the act approved of belongs. Approbation is thus both justifiable as a sentiment, and obligatory as an action. We in *fact* extol certain acts, because of their beneficial issues: we *ought* to extol them, in order to induce others to perform acts like them. [*Fr. on Mack.*, pp. 249—254, 259—261].

Mill is careful to disavow the limitation of the words "interest," "pleasure," and the like, which the opponents of Utilitarianism seek to father on the system. When it is said that men ought to seek the benefit of others, and equally when it is said that, in the last resort, they aim in every action to secure their own interests, it is to be understood that "the principle of utility takes in every ingredient wherein human happiness consists" [*Fr. on Mack.*, pp. 271, 272], and that its advocates do not (formally at least) pretend to disregard the pleasures of taste, and the arts dependent upon imagination. In Hartley's system however even this formal disavowal, as regards art, is very qualified, if not withheld. (See *Observ. on Man,* vol. ii. ch. 3, sec. 3, On the Pleasures of Imagination).

To sum up then: every person before action, if he is to act morally, should either contemplate himself its consequences, or adopt those fixed opinions which interpret the experience of mankind in reference to the particular case: if these consequences are found to be likely to bring advantage to others, or to himself, unbalanced by evil, the action should be performed, if not, not. And under Utility, Advantage, Good, Interest is included everything from which men derive satisfaction. The object of the act is not to form good Dispositions,[3] nor is it to realize so-called moral beauty, fitness, &c., nor to produce a certain state of will; but it is simply and solely to procure good for others, or for the agent himself. There is nothing, for instance, in the disposition, habit, sentiment, or state of will, involved in the term Courage, in itself good or bad, apart from the consequences of the courageous acts which result from it. If it be asked why we do not ascribe morality to all actions which produce good to the agent (such as eating or drinking) or to others (such as the ordinary courtesies of civilized life), the answer is that Moral Approbation is bestowed "only where it is needed; not on acts the performance of which is provided for by the constitution of the individual, but on acts, the performance of which society needs, by the use of means, to secure; of which means its approbation is one of the most powerful." [*Fr. on Mack.*, p. 368]. In all actions there is nothing in itself moral or immoral in either the motive, the volition, or the external act (physically regarded). That which is moral is the expectation in the mind of the agent of consequences, beneficial or otherwise. [*Fr. on Mack.*, p. 321].

Hartley deals with the practical rules of morality in a more diffusive and gossiping manner, and with greater particularity of detail and variety of illustration, than Mill. It will not be at all necessary to follow him closely through his somewhat rambling amplification of what the later philosopher states in general and concise terms. Hartley's remarks here would equally well fit almost any moral system that could be named.

---

[3] It may be urged that one social affection strengthens another, and that therefore there is an object in cultivating affections and dispositions. But this argument too is grounded on utility in the last resort; besides which, it is not true that a man quiet and humble in private life, for instance, is necessarily so in public. Tyranny in political life may be accompanied by strongly developed family feeling.

In his case, in fact, as in that of so many other Utilitarians, the old objection at this point strikes us with peculiar force, that what is new in his opinions is not true, and what is true in them is not new. Men should pursue their own interests. What is meant by interests? Everything that for any reason or with any object in view they have at any time a desire to do. After such a comprehensive definition, the most adverse schools of philosophy must perforce agree. Then comes the further question, over which the battle is really to be fought, namely, what *ought* their interests to be? What ought a person to like or desire? The answer of Utilitarianism, both as represented by Hartley one of its earliest, and by J. S. Mill one of its latest, exponents, is the same: he should like what other people like, and do what other people do. Humanity has found out what is best for itself. Follow its experience.

Hartley expressly says that the rule of life must be extracted, firstly, from the opinions held, and secondly, though in a less degree, from the practice obtaining among mankind in general. He would add to these the testimony of religion, natural and revealed, were it not that he is anxious to lay down a basis which may equally suit all classes of thinkers. " Even atheistical and sceptical persons " can, he thinks, have no objection to his first principle, that, from the infancy of their race, men have sought happiness; that, allowing for a fluctuating margin, their methods of attaining to it in practice have been constant and discoverable; and that, where men's practice conflicts with their deliberate opinions, we have in the latter, as being unwarped by passion, even more certain guides on moral questions. [*Observ. on Man*, vol. ii. pp. 207—210].

The verdict of mankind's experience and opinions is that the right method of seeking our own advantage consists in attempts to secure the happiness of our neighbour. All mere and gross self-interest may, says Hartley, be roughly put down as vice, all advancement of the interests of our neighbour as virtue. He does not (with Mandeville) consider private vices to be public good, but public misfortune. And as to how both private and public virtues should best be practised, the common sense and judgment of mankind has determined for us already.

It will thus be seen that Hartley leaves considerably less to the calculative element in morality than Mill, and follows much more unquestioningly the common verdict of men of all ways of thinking in different countries at different times. He is not so much at variance with the ethics of the past. He, like Mill, thought the times "out of joint," and foresaw a general upheaval of society drawing near [vol. ii. pp. 440, 441], but his recipe for "setting right" the times was to revert to the old morality which, though accepting in theory, men were neglecting in fact; while Mill, on the other hand, considered the ethical principles existing in his time to be radically wrong in theory, and therefore also in practice, and for that purpose wished, as Plato wished before him, to revolutionize Politics, Legislation, and Education.

Hartley conceives the graduation of the various interests of man in point of moral dignity to be exactly in inverse order to their arrangement in point of physical and historical development. The latter order is (as has already been pointed out), (1) those of sensation, (2) those of imagination, (3) those of ambition, (4) those of self-interest, gross, refined, and rational, (5) those of sympathy, (6) those of theopathy, (7) those of the moral sense, the last-named being not so much something apart from the rest as the consummation of them all. All these classes are to be successively referred for their justification on association principles to the class immediately preceding; so that the fountain-head, so to speak, the ultimate and irreducible fact is sensation, and the interest attaching to it. We seek the pleasures to be derived from works of art, because the ideas suggested by them are intimately associated with the ideas of sensation; we pursue the pleasures of ambition because the ideas suggested by these are intimately allied with those of sensation and imagination both, and are generated by combinations of them; and so on for the rest.[4] Conversely, in point of moral worth, the pleasures of sensation are of little importance, unless informed by those of imagination, those of imagination unless informed by those of ambition, and so on, till we arrive at the pleasures of theopathy, and finally to those of the moral sense, which include, regulate, and react upon all the rest. Hartley thus works out in the department of morals the Aristotelian contrast between what is first in the order of growth, and what is first in the order of reality and dignity.[5] We begin by desiring the gratification of our most primitive instincts, and we end by the renunciation of the self in one sense in order to realize it in another. Throughout our lives we are continually rising "on stepping-stones Of our dead selves to higher things." Our own interest is always our proper and legitimate object; but the content and conception of that

---

[4] Mr. Leslie Stephen [*Hist. of Eng. Thought in the Eighteenth Century*, ii. 67] neatly expresses Hartley's meaning : " in mathematical language it may be said that six equations arise from stating each of the latter six classes in terms of all the others; and thus it is possible to determine every one of the other classes as functions of the primitive sensations."

[5] " Now which way soever we turn our view, that which is prior in the order of nature is always less perfect and principal, than that which is posterior, the last of two contiguous states being the end, the first the means subservient to that end, though itself be an end in respect to some foregoing state " [vol. ii. p. 213]. This is the Platonic and Aristotelian doctrine of τέλη or final causes.

interest widens for us with each successive advance from the merest animal passion to the "apprehension of a god."

With considerable elaboration Hartley goes through the various duties of man in connexion with the various species of pleasure, and shows that there is no one of these latter, which ought to be made a primary pursuit, at least till we come to the class of sympathetic pleasures, which may be primarily pursued, though even they should, in order to attain to perfection, be coloured and vivified by the sentiments of theopathy. The special rules laid down need not be detailed, as they are generally in close conformity with the dictates of ordinary morality. One or two peculiarities however,—of the man more than of the system—may be noticed.

Hartley has an altogether Platonic distrust of any indulgence of the imagination. He wishes it, and its works, to be curbed and suppressed to an extent which strikes one as puritanical, almost brutal. Like Plato, he will tolerate "simplicity, neatness, regularity, and justness of proportion" [vol. ii. p. 249]; but any efforts of the artistic impulse beyond this he appears to think not only unnecessary, but evil, as diverting the mind from the far more urgent interests of benevolence and the other sympathetic affections ; though he allows that, in default of any higher emotions, those excited by art draw off the mind from the grosser sensual pleasures, and fill up what would otherwise be moments of absolute idleness. Moreover, he will permit them, when brought into the service of religion.[6] But on the whole, " it is evident," he thinks [vol. ii. p. 253], " that most kinds of music, painting, and poetry have close connexions with vice, particularly with the vices of intemperance and lewdness; that they re-

---

[6] He plainly says that "the polite arts are scarce to be allowed, except when consecrated to religious purposes " [vol. ii. p. 251]. Here again we are reminded of Plato's state-mythology, and state-poetry.

present them in gay, pleasing colours, or at least take off from the abhorrence due to them. . . . . This is evident of public diversions, collections of pictures, academies for painting, statuary, &c., ancient heathen poetry, modern poetry of most kinds, plays, romances, &c.," and, further on, he adds somewhat shrewdly, that " the arts are apt to excite vanity, self-conceit, and mutual flatteries, in their votaries." Nor is he any tenderer to scientific pursuits;[7] and he enjoins temperance in these studies also. It is evident that " high priests of science," and mutual admiration cliques in art, were no more unfamiliar in his day than in ours. His whole scheme of duties inclines to severity. In connexion with the pleasures of sensation, he recommends occasional fasting. In considering the pleasures of ambition, and the desirability of humility, he counsels, in the spirit of the great satirist of the present day, the imposition on one's self of voluntary silence, and thinks it well " not to attempt to speak, unless a plain reason requires it." Another remarkable feature of his moral admonitions is the constant reference to Education as the necessary—means of developing the right associations.

[7] "Nothing," he roundly asserts, "can easily exceed the vain-glory, self-conceit, arrogance, emulation, and envy, that are found in the eminent professors of the sciences, mathematics, philosophy, and even divinity itself."

CHAPTER X.

THE ÆSTHETIC DOCTRINES OF HARTLEY AND MILL.

WE have now found the answers of Hartley and James Mill to the questions, (1) how do we come to think? (2) how do we come to act? (3) how ought we to act? Having done with Thought and Moral Action, it remains to see what our philosophers have to say,—it is not much—on the subject of Æsthetic Emotion. In this last department, as in the others, Association is brought in as the prime solvent; but no one can fail to notice with how little success, compared with that attending its application to the practical fields of human energy, and, in a less degree, to intellectual phenomena. There is something in art, and the feelings generated by the contemplation of its works, which eludes the Associationist's dissecting knife; and it is remarkable how meagre, vague, and unsatisfactory all the attempts to interpret them by the light of such principles have been.

In his remarks on the "Objects called Sublime and Beautiful and their Contraries, contemplated as Causes of our Pleasures and Pains," [*Anal.* vol. ii. pp. 230—252], Mill follows closely Hartley's section on the genesis of the Pleasures and Pain of Imagination [*Obs. on Man,* vol. i. pp. 418—442], and also Alison's "Essays on Taste," quotations from whose work he liberally introduces. These three philosophers, it is needless to say, account for the state of the human mind in the presence of the Beautiful and the Sublime, by the hypothesis that pleasurable ideas are associated with certain forms, curves, colours, or sounds in the mind of the person subject to the emotion : and that this association is due to the fact that on previous occasions, pleasurable sensations have been imparted to him by external objects possessing or emitting such forms, curves, colours, or sounds. Where such a hypothesis cannot be shown to apply directly, we must argue from the known to the unknown, and presume that patient analysis will in time prove it to hold good in these cases also.

Hartley proposes to consider under this head the pleasures arising, (1) from the beauty of the natural world, (2) from works of art, (3) from the liberal arts of music, painting, and poetry, (4) from the sciences, (5) from the beauty of the person, (6) from wit and humour, and also (7) the pains arising from gross absurdity, inconsistency, or deformity. This division is an example of Hartley's hopelessly clumsy and empirical way of treating a subject of this kind. (7) is obviously the converse of all the other classes; (5) should be included under (1), and (3) under (2), while (4) and (6) seem to be scarcely assignable at all to the pleasures of the imagination as a distinctive species. This leaves us the pleasures derived first, from the beauty of the natural world, secondly, from works of art. It is characteristic of Associationists to regard an explanation of the first of these, in which department their methods are applied with some success, as doing duty for an interpretation of the latter also, where, however, the difficulties really begin. This arises from their seeing in Art nothing but imitation of Nature, without paying any heed to the creative element. [Hartley, vol. i. p. 426]. Mill indeed scarcely seems to conceive the Beautiful and Sublime as existing outside Nature at all, and almost entirely omits Art from his examination of them as causes of pleasure.

The pleasures derived from beautiful objects of Nature arise, in Hartley's view, from the association of sensible pictures of rural scenes with mental pictures of the different comforts and advantages (such as pleasant tastes, sounds, temperature, sports, &c.), originally and repeatedly experienced in connexion with them. Novelty too excites surprise and thus produces a state of mind which is highly pleasurable, though sometimes bordering upon the limits of pain. The ideas of uniformity and variety in combination—differences in details combined with unity of law or plan—which are called up by such scenes, also produce pleasure, inasmuch as they are intimately connected with the idea of Adaptation to Ends, excited by similar properties in mechanical works and contrivances. [Hartley, vol. i. p. 419]. Other ideas associated with the contemplation of natural beauty are those of health, innocence, and the amorous pleasures, and those " which the encomiums of others beget in us . . . . . by means of the contagiousness observable in mental dispositions" [Hartley, i. 420], also those suggested by the theopathetic affections, where these are strongly developed, as well as those which scientific pursuits and investigations abundantly call forth. In support of this analysis Hartley appeals to each man's individual consciousness. "An attentive person," he says [*Observ. on Man*, vol. i. p. 421], " may, in viewing or contemplating the beauties of Nature, lay hold as it were, of the remainders or miniatures of many of the particular pleasures here enumerated, while they recur in a separate state, and before they coalesce with the general indeterminate aggregate, and thus verify the history now proposed." It is an argument moreover in favour of this " history " of the growth of the æsthetical emotions, that the kind and degree of feeling with which a person contemplates natural scenes varies with the different stages in his life, and as the stock of associated ideas gradually accumulates and becomes more firmly welded together. It is notorious that old people, as a rule, take greater delight in the contemplation of nature than young. Granting these associations to be an adequate explanation and basis of the feelings with which we behold the Beautiful in nature — a concession which, we imagine, few people who have seriously reviewed their own state of mind in such circumstances, will be disposed to accord — let us see if the emotions consequent upon the contemplation of the Sublime can be analyzed by any analogous process. The ideas which rugged mountainous scenery, for instance, excites in us must necessarily be in the first place, at any rate, as Hartley says, associated with ideas of fear and horror; so much so that certain philosophers, such as Buckle, have even founded on them important national characteristics, (such as torpor, abjectness, want of mental inquisitiveness, superstition, cruel religious rites, &c.).

Whence then the pleasure with which we contemplate the grand and awful in Nature? It is explained (rather unsatisfactorily) on the Lucretian "suave mari magno" principle. There is a pleasure, as the dramatist says, in hearing with drowsy content the winds roaring and rain beating against the roof of the comfortable room in which we are ensconced.[1] But this is a very different feeling from that consequent on the view of mountain scenery. Still Hartley and Mill consider the latter ultimately analyzable into the same primitive elements as the former. "The nascent ideas of fear and horror magnify and enliven all the other ideas, and by degrees pass into pleasures by suggesting the security from pain." (Hartley, i. 419). One might ask how it is that, if originally painful spectacles suggest by contrast the pleasurable ideas of our own immunity from pain, pleasurable ideas, such as are called up in the first instance by beautiful scenes, do not

---

[1]   ὑπὸ στέγῃ
πυκνῆς ἀκοῦσαι ψεκάδος εὐδούσῃ φρενί. *Soph. Fr.*

equally suggest the ideas of dissatisfaction at our own condition as contrasted with their tranquillity and perfection.

Mill even more emphatically than Hartley, says that the sensations which we immediately derive from Colours, Forms, and Sounds are in themselves absolutely indifferent, and only become interesting by association with ideas. In the case of Colours, for instance, the associations are either those which arise from the interesting nature of objects or phenomena permanently coloured in certain ways, such as Day, Night, &c., or those which arise from some supposed analogy between certain colours and certain dispositions of mind, or lastly, those which arise from accidental connexions, whether national or individual, e.g. the connexion of the colour of purple with ideas of dignity and majesty, or the connexion of black in some countries, of white in others (as China), with funerals and mourning. The Association in every case, and the Association alone, is the cause of the Beauty [Mill, ii. 244].[2] Underived beauty of colours is denied. No new colour introduced by fashion is (says Alison, as quoted by Mill) pleasing at first. This proposition, we think, most persons will dispute with J. S. Mill (ii. 247 n.). And still more will they dispute the statement that there are no direct physical sensations of pleasure to be derived from music at any rate, if not from the sounds of animals. Granting that the scream of the eagle or the roar of the lion is only interesting as suggestive of the ideas of lonely majesty and independence, who can ascribe the pleasure derived from a sonata of Beethoven to its association with pleasurable ideas, once connected with similar sounds emitted by animals or inanimate objects in nature? Similarly, it may very well be doubted whether there is not an original pleasure in the contemplation of beautiful Forms; and whether Alison's and Mill's derivation of the emotions with which we regard grace-

[2] Cp. ii. 250.

ful curves from the fact that, since most of our bodily motions are in curves, and most soft surfaces are round, therefore curves are suggestive of ease and comfort, and Hartley's explanation of the delight taken in beautiful architectural proportions as depending upon their association with the ideas of utility and adaptation to ends, are at all adequate. Mill as we have said, does not treat distinctively of the pleasures derived from works of art, but that he would treat these on the same principles as those on which he bases the pleasures already noticed, is evident from his somewhat astounding statement [ii. 251] that the train of ideas associated with the form of the Venus de Medicis, and this alone, induces us to call it beautiful and justifies us in so calling it. Hartley's exposition of the feelings consequent upon the contemplation of works of art consists mainly in a reference (1) to the associated ideas of fitness and utility (as in architectural and mechanical works), (2) to the pleasurable ideas, which are derived from the detection of a successful imitation, in Painting, for instance, and Poetry [*Observ. on Man,* vol. i. pp. 427, 431]. In the case of Music, however, Hartley allows that certain concords excite an original, and not a derived, pleasure : but that original pleasure is enormously enhanced by those derived from the associations of certain sounds with the ideas of "amorous pleasures, public rejoicings, riches, high rank "—we may imagine the feelings of a musician on reading this—or with " battles, sorrows, death, and religious contemplation." In reference to this latter set of associated ideas, as in the attempted analysis of the Sublime in nature, there is a failure to explain satisfactorily the great crux of the Associationists' theory of æsthetic emotion, namely, how it is that we experience a pleasure in the teeth of our pain or sadness. A cognate question would be raised by the consideration of the feelings attendant on tragic representations, where the paradox, that our pleasure consists in our pain, is still more apparent: but Hartley omits the Drama from his theory altogether. Discords, he says, are necessary and proper in music to prevent us being cloyed with the delights of "concords of sweet sounds," just as, for purposes of contrast, a certain degree of obscurity may be both justifiable and delightful in poetry. We need not notice further the views of Hartley on these subjects, as they are not of much real value, and are only of interest as one of the earliest attempts to explain æsthetic emotion on strictly associationist principles: though ingenious, they are strained in the extreme, in order to bring every phenomenon under his favourite law, as, for example, where he speaks of the pleasure arising from pictures being derived from, amongst other things, "ambition, fashion, the extravagant prices of the works of certain masters, from associations of the villas and cabinets of the noble, the rich, and the curious, &c.,"—a statement which, we imagine, would not find more favour with the painter, than would the passage quoted above with the musician.

CHAPTER XI.

As in Ethics, so in Politics Mill considers the proper end of
human effort to be Utility, and further that where really useful
objects do not appear to be so to minds warped by passion, or
overclouded by ignorance, such minds should be enticed to
the performance of the actions calculated to achieve those
objects by the instrumentality of association, and by connect-
ing with the actions desirable from such a point of view either
pleasurable sensations or pleasurable ideas. The same process
by which we explain how men act as they do should be used
and manipulated in a manner calculated to induce them to
act as they ought. The end of *any* action is always *supposed*
Utility; of right action, considered and reasoned Utility.
The object of Government, Legislation, and Education is to
make the imagined interests more and more nearly coincide
with the real interests,—"to make the values and the associations correspond" [*Anal.*, vol. ii. p. 259.]

Most philosophers agree, says Mill, in his *Miscellaneous
Essays*,[1] that the end of government is "public good," to use
Locke's expression, or, in Bentham's well-known phrase,

Reprinted from the *Encyclopædia Britannica*, 1828.

" the greatest happiness of the greatest number." These propositions, however, though true, tell us little. They are tautological, until what is meant by the "public good" is explained. To convert them from analytical to ampliative propositions, it is necessary to survey the whole field of human nature in its various individual manifestations. Politics must be based on psychology. History, and the comparison of social phenomena as existing in different ages and countries, are scouted; and Mill nowhere appears to recognize the necessity of taking them into account in determining the principles of politics or legislation. He reverses the method of Plato, who thought that when the happiness of a whole state is discovered, that of the individuals composing it is necessarily found too; and that in constructing an ideal of happiness, philosophy should begin with seeking the conditions of the former. Mill, on the contrary, distinctly says that "to understand what is included in the happiness of the greatest number, we must understand what is included in the happiness of the individuals of whom it is composed " [*Essay on Government,* p. 3]. His theory of government is, therefore, a direct application to masses of men of his theory of moral phenomena as applied in the *Analysis* to individuals.

Mill considers that in political inquiries we are bound to treat men as ruled by one motive, namely self-interest, just as in the narrower sphere of political economy we are forced to treat them as ruled by the one motive of love of wealth. We isolate the wealth-desiring and wealth-acquiring phenomena of human nature in the latter case, though we know that in practice they are intermingled with other phenomena, and that wealth is not the only thing which men desire, or the love of it which moves them to action. But after the results of this isolation are obtained, due allowances can be made, and the equation can have the proper values of its terms assigned to it. So in Politics and Legislation we must suppose, with Bentham, that every man is a knave, and will take everything he can from others by deceitful means, to obtain his own ends; or again, with Hobbes, that every man is a being of unlimited rapacity—("homo homini lupus")—and that he will take from his fellow-citizens, to secure the same ends, everything he can by force. The *value* of the method,—there is no question of its legitimacy,—depends of course on the degree of facility with which the phenomenon to be exclusively examined can be separated from those usually existing in company with it. It may reasonably be doubted whether this facility exists in the case of the study of Politics or Legislation to anything like the same extent as in that of Political Economy or the physical sciences.

Mill places the greatest happiness of society in the insuring to every man of the greatest possible quantity of the produce of his labour. [*Essay on Government*, p. 5.] The means of attaining this end is the union of a number of men to protect one another from the else unrestrained rapacity of individuals.[2] But large bodies can only effectively combine for these purposes by delegating to representatives the power necessary for protecting all. The means therefore may be more particularly described as (1) Power, to restrain instinctive rapacity and knavery, (2) checks to prevent that Power *itself* developing into rapacity and knavery,—or guards against the guardians. Developing with the utmost rigour the principle that men in power are wolves or knaves or both, Mill attempts to show, that where power is placed in the hands of either a Monarch or an Aristocracy, the One or the Few thus constituted ruler or rulers will prey upon the rest,

---

[2] "Government is founded upon this, as a law of human nature, that a man, if able, will take from others anything which they have and he desires." [*Essay on Government*, p. 8, cp. p. 9.]

and defeat the objects for which government is instituted, apart from the fact that hereditary governments, whether residing in one man or in several, are the worst possible security for the ruler or rulers possessing the requisite intellectual qualities for their office. The monarch or aristocracy will desire the acquisition of pleasure at the expense of the persons and properties of others. Desiring this as an end, they will desire to have the means of attaining it. This means is power—the ability, namely, to enforce actions on the part of others in conformity with their own will. This again is obtained by the two instruments of terrorism and favouritism. The former operates upon men's fears, and produces that dumb hopeless and nerveless kind of obedience, which existed, for instance, in France for the three or four reigns preceding the Revolution. The latter produces its effect by awarding pleasures to pliancy and obsequiousness. Thus the monarch or aristocracy is irresistibly led on, and the more irresistibly the longer he or it governs, (till, at last, as Plato says of the tyrant, it becomes with them a self-preservative instinct), " not only to indulge in that degree of plunder which leaves the members (excepting always the recipients and instruments of the plunder) the bare means of subsistence, but also to exercise that degree of cruelty which is necessary to keep in existence the most intense terror." [*Essay on Government*, p. 12.] They are impelled to seek the means of obtaining an unlimited degree of power over an unlimited number of persons. So that the common objection that the citizens of a state will be less plundered by One in a Monarchy, than by the Few in an Aristocracy, and by the Few in an Aristocracy, than by the Many in a Democracy, falls to the ground. The notion, accepted by some modern philosophers such as Guizot, of a Monarch as a Mediator between the conflicting forces of the state, removed by his exalted position from the possibility of interest or prejudice in any one direction, evidently did not find favour with Mill. With him the Monarch must necessarily be the Tyrant, according to the principles of human nature, though he admits that some historical facts (such as the Monarchy of Denmark) are against him. [*Essay on Government*, p. 9.] The conclusion is then, that " whenever the powers of Government are placed in any hands other than those of the community, whether those of one man, of a few, or of several, those principles of human nature which imply that government is at all necessary, imply that these persons will make use of them to defeat the very end for which Government exists." [*Essay on Government*, p. 8.] And the difficulty is not got over, in Mill's opinion, by a constitutional system of Government by different Orders. [*Essay on Government*, pp. 14, 15.] The Community must desire its own interest. And this can only be secured by its acting as one body, not by its having two peoples, the rich and the poor, as Plato says, encamped over against one another in one city, or within the limits of one territory. But all public business would be out of the question, if the community attempted to transact it *en masse*. A Democracy, pure and simple, is the most desirable form of government, where feasible, as in the old Greek cities; but according to the modern territorial conception of a state, it must be dismissed as outside the range of practical politics. Nothing, therefore, remains which is at once, just, proper, and feasible, but the Representative system. [*Essay on Government*, p. 16.] The power here resides in certain individuals appointed by the Representatives, and the checking power resides in the Representatives themselves, whose interest is identical with that of the Community. We have therefore the two requisites of good government. [*Essay on Government*, pp. 17—27.]

It may be objected however that the people are incapable of estimating their true interests; that though they cannot be mistaken as to what they desire, they may be, and often are, mistaken as to the real value of what they desire.[3] But the question is, Mill urges, not whether the will of the community is an ideal or perfect will, but whether it is better that the will of the community, or the will of an individual, party, or class in it, should direct and control the affairs of all the citizens. For such mistakes, in any case, there is an unfailing remedy, knowledge; and knowledge is happily capable of being increased by Education, an instrument which we now proceed to consider.[4]

It is natural that two such believers in the almost unlimited potency of Association in forming pleasures, pains, duties, motives, and affections, as were Hartley and James Mill, should occupy themselves considerably with the most obvious means of establishing and riveting associative bonds. Accordingly, even in the exposition of their general theory of the human mind, we are continually coming across references to the influence and importance of Education, accompanied (especially in Mill's case) with strong expressions of discontent at the modes of instruction prevailing in their respective times, and hints for the establishment of a better system.

" It is of the utmost consequence to morality and religion,"

---

[3] This objection besides being handled on pp. 28—32 of the *Essay on Government* is made the subject of copious extracts and remarks, under the title " People Unfit," and among the " Idola Politica " enumerated in Mill's MS. commonplace books (in four volumes) which were presented to the London Library by J. S. Mill, and are now in its possession. Objections to Aristocratical and Monarchical Government are treated of in these same books under the titles Nobility, Liberty, Innovation, Patronage, Protests of Despotism, Reform, Character of a Perfect Reformer, People's Power, Aristocracy, &c., &c. The quotations exhibit a prolonged and methodical study.

[4] In Legislation and Jurisprudence [*Essay No. II.*] Mill merely follows Bentham.

says Hartley [vol. i. p. 81], "that the affections and passions should be analyzed into their simple compounding parts, by reversing the steps of the associations which concur to form them. For thus we may learn how to cherish and improve good ones, check and root out such as are mischievous and immoral, and how to suit our manner of life in some tolerable measure, to our intellectual and religious wants. And as this holds, in respect of persons of all ages, so it is particularly true, and worthy of consideration, in respect of children and youth. . . . . The world is indeed sufficiently stocked with general precepts for this purpose, grounded on experience; and whosoever will follow these faithfully, may expect good general success. However, the doctrine of association, when traced up to the first rudiments of understanding and affection, unfolds such a scene as cannot fail both to instruct and alarm all such as have any degree of interested concern for themselves, or of a benevolent one for others." Education, then, in Hartley's opinion should be the putting together again of the pieces severed by the theory of association. The reconstructive process should be the exact reversal of the analytical. Mill follows Hartley in this view, though by no means in his sanguine estimation of the value of the ordinary precepts of the times, grounded on experience.[5] He thought the current systems wholly and radically wrong, and for

---

[5] In another passage, however, Hartley speaks of the " carelessness and infatuation of parents and magistrates with respect to the education of youth," as one of the causes which seemed to him to " threaten ruin and dissolution to the present states of christendom " [ii. 441]. And again, in speaking of the duties of parents, he " cannot but conclude the general education of youth to be grossly erroneous and perverted " [ii. 237]. He supposes [ii. 254] the proper education of a prince to be entirely out of the question, and expresses a longing for, rather than an expectation of, the appearance of some philosopher-king, after Plato's heart.

> All saws of books, all forms, all pressures past
> That youth and observation copied

in the human mind in his day, he had but little respect. We have seen how Hartley regards the influence and value of Art almost entirely in its moral and educational aspects, and what didactic significance he attaches to allegories, myths, and analogies generally. He, like Mill after him, notices more than once the educational importance of language in creating associations, and more especially the use to which such words as Bentham would call eulogistic and dyslogistic, may be put; and proposes, as we have seen, with a view to the suggestion of the proper trains of thought, philosophical languages and dictionaries. [Vol. i. pp. 319, 320]. The mechanical view of human nature, upheld by him, as the outcome of associationism, he thinks particularly calculated to abolish the notion of capricious volition, and to inculcate that of law and method in morality, and so to give better guarantees for the success of educational labours [vol. i. p. 510]. In the *Analysis* Mill deplores again and again the imperfect systems of education in vogue, and hints at what he considers the right means of disposing men to work for the good of their fellow-creatures, and allow the larger associations to guide and control the narrower.[6] But his more elaborate adumbration of the essential features of proper and philosophical education is contained in the seventh of the Essays.

In Education, as in Politics, Mill considered man from one side only, and that the side brought most prominently forward in his psychological inquiries. "In psychology," wrote

---

[6] *Analysis*, vol. ii. pp. 215, 221, 225, 227, 259, 270, 272, 276, 278, 279, 289, 293, 300, 378, 403. See his essays in the *Edinburgh Review* and the *Philanthropist* on the rival schemes for the education of the poor propounded by Bell and Lancaster.

J. S. Mill, "his" (James Mill's) "fundamental doctrine was the formation of all human character by circumstances, through the universal principle of Association, and the consequent unlimited possibility of improving the moral and intellectual condition of mankind by education." On such subjects Mill was an enthusiast. He believed that there was no limit to the number and variety of individuals which it could reach, to the age at which it was possible to begin, (in this following Rousseau,) to the things which it could teach, or to the qualities which it could inspire. All men were in his view as in that of Helvetius and Sir W. Jones, born with much the same capacity of improvement. There were no differences in the energy and ability brought to bear by various individuals on the affairs of life, which could not be accounted for by differences in education. In describing its possibilities [*Essays*, No. VII. pp. 18—29] Mill almost reaches the sublime.

The object of education is to render first the human mind, and next the human body, productive of the highest degree of happiness to their possessor and to the rest of mankind. To the body Mill did not pay very much attention.[7] In regard to the mind, everything which affects in any way whatsoever those of its qualities and conditions, on which happiness depends, must be contemplated as a possible means of its education. The reason why the theory of education is generally so imperfect is that this first principle is neglected, and certain classes of things affecting the mind are arbitrarily singled out from the rest, for the purpose of building on them an educational system.

As prerequisites, therefore, to any theory of education, it is necessary (1) to consider how things and circumstances operate

---

[7] Either as part of his theory, or part of his practice,—(witness the education of his son, so lamentably deficient in physical training, vid. *Autobiography*, p. 36).

upon minds, (2) the nature of the things and circumstances so operating on the mind as to render it productive of happiness, (3) the nature of the mental qualities productive of happiness. The first problem is answered by the Association psychology, the third by the analysis of the active phenomena of the mind. It remains to consider the circumstances and methods operating upon the mind so as to form the necessary qualities. Now the function of the mind being the having or experiencing certain sequences or trains of ideas, the object of education is to ensure the constant presence of some trains in preference to others. The means which most effectually secure this end are Custom, and the Ideas of Pleasure and Pain. The right sequences of ideas must be rendered as indissoluble as possible by the former, and as desirable, or as repulsive as possible, by their association with the latter. We have " first to ascertain what are the ends, the really ultimate objects of human desire ; next what are the most beneficent means of attaining these objects ; and lastly to accustom the mind to fill up the intermediate space between" [any] " present sensation" [taken as a starting-point] "and the ultimate object with nothing but ideas of the beneficent means." [*Essays*, No. VII. p. 147].

The qualities of the mind calculated to produce happiness are partly intellectual, partly moral. It was characteristic of Mill's philosophy, indeed of the Utilitarian system generally, to look to actions and results, rather than to sentiments motives and dispositions, in estimating moral worth : and we are not surprised, therefore, to find Mill paying considerable attention to the intellectual qualities (knowledge to supply the material, and sagacity or the power to use that material,—copiousness and energy,—fullness with readiness). Blind fanaticism working infinite evil with the best intentions was as repulsive and abominable to Mill as " the lie in the soul" was to Plato. The ethical qualities are chiefly, as we have seen above, Temperance, Fortitude (primarily self-regarding) and Justice and Benevolence, (primarily altruistic). The circumstances operating on the mind to produce and stimulate these qualities, moral and intellectual, are both of the physical, and of the moral and mental kind. A consideration of the former gives us a view of Physical Education, of the latter a view of Domestic, Technical, Social, and Political Education. In the matter of Physical Education, Mill follows Cabanis, the French physician and *philosophe*, whose name is chiefly known to Englishmen as associated in a sarcasm of Carlyle with the doctrines of "the secretion of thought," and "the production of poetry from the smaller intestines," the elder Darwin's *Zoonomia*, and Dr. Crichton's researches, besides hints thrown out by Hartley in his semi-medical capacity. [*Essays*, No. VII. pp. 22—30.]

Domestic Education in Mill's view cannot be commenced too soon. It should be contemporaneous with sensation itself. The mistake of most people is, to begin education too late. What Mill derived from the theory of Rousseau, he carried into practice in the training of his own son, whether with altogether satisfactory results any one who reads the latter's *Autobiography* may be allowed to doubt.[8]

In order that the qualities of intelligence may be early developed in children, the sequences of their ideas should be made as far as possible to correspond to the sequences of phenomena in nature. Pain and pleasure again should be made to follow on conduct with the precision of a natural law. Children should not be led to regard their parents as acting capriciously, or as propitiated by entreaties and flatteries. They should be taught to recognize, that each act of theirs

[8] On the want of physical education in J. S. Mill's case, see *Autob.* p. 36 (quoted above); on the deadening of the imaginative element and the emotions, see the *Autob.* passim.

carries its consequences with it, and thus the appropriate associations would be generated, and a foundation laid for Temperance as well as Intelligence. [*Essay,* No. VII. p. 33.]

In inculcating Benevolence, the task of the parent or educator is (at first at any rate), somewhat easier. The child will of his own accord notice that when those around him are cheerful and pleased, they will be more disposed to let their feelings overflow in little acts of kindness to himself, and that when they are plunged in gloom and sorrow, he will be forgotten or made much less of than usually. An association will consequently be formed between the pleasures and pains of those about him and his own pleasures and neglect (if not pains) respectively. He will thus have an interest in seeing other persons happy, and will on occasions be prompted to endeavour himself to secure their happiness. Next he will perceive (of himself, again, in most cases, quite as much as under the guidance of others) a new fact, namely, that when he is the cause of pleasure to other people, not only do they often in their gratified condition, exert themselves to perform kindly offices to those round about them (himself among the number), but they are peculiarly well disposed to him in particular. He is, therefore, now doubly stimulated to benevolence from the two sets of pleasurable ideas associated, first, with the happiness of others from whatever source derived; next, and specifically, with that happiness as caused or promoted by himself.

Meanwhile the child is every day absorbing by imitation the basis of future character. And here it is that the office of education is brought into play, in regard to the quality of benevolence. If by the observation and interpretation of the words and other signs, spoken or made use of by those about him, the child perceives that the trains of ideas in *their* minds connected with the ideas of the pleasures and pains of persons other than themselves, and especially when caused by themselves, appear to be

P

pleasurable and painful respectively; then the associations formed in that child's mind in the first instance will be riveted still closer by repetition and imitation. Immediately therefore on the occurrence to a child of the pleasurable ideas of power over other men, dignity, &c., it is the duty of the parent, by his words and actions, to suggest to him the ideas of the proper means to that end, that is, of acts of benevolence ; and, again, whenever the idea of performing an act of benevolence enters the mind of the child, whatever may in fact be the antecedent of that idea, to couple with it at once and as often as possible pleasurable and encouraging ideas of the command over other men's wills, as the necessary effect and reward of those acts. But this is only half the work. Another great object should be to eliminate, suppress, and discourage the formation and repetition of those sequences of associated ideas which tend to impress on the child the belief that he can obtain the good offices of others as much by threatening them with pain as by doing acts which will procure them pleasure, ideas which thus lay the foundation for tyranny. Mill takes a rather good example of this, and one which shows how early he would have the educational processes inaugurated :—he says that nearly every child is taught to associate the idea of obtaining its desires with the ideas of crying and shrieking ; and in this way, says Mill, pathetically, the cries and wailings of a child are very often an instrument of absolute tyranny. This and similar concessions on the part of parents (often from a selfish desire to remove their own unpleasant sensations by the speediest measures) begin what is known as the process of spoiling a child. In the case of Pain, as in that of Pleasure, Imitation is a potent factor in producing habitual dispositions. When children see pain inflicted everywhere about them, on themselves among others, as the means of securing power, they gradually associate the ideas of dignity with those of the infliction of pain on others; hence the frequently observed fact that the slavery of childhood becomes the tyranny of mature age, and conversely that only those who have served law well can administer it well: and that the ideal of a citizen, and we may say of a man, is ὁ κατὰ μέρος ἄρχων καὶ ἀρχόμενος [*Essays*, No. VII. pp. 31—37].

Technical Education (to which, much to Mill's disgust, the term Education is often exclusively confined), has to do mainly with the intelligence, or (as above stated) the knowledge of the order of those natural events and phenomena on which happiness depends, together with that sagacity which finds the best means to the accomplishment of desired ends. Mill's observations are here restricted to the inculcation of the necessity and duty of educating the labouring classes, the poor as well as the rich. To deny them technical education—education in the liberal arts—is to deny them intelligence (or at all events its proper development): to deny them intelligence is to deny them happiness.[9] He is vehemently opposed to the idea that happiness is disproportionate to knowledge: it may be so in individuals, where external circumstances operate as well as cultivation of the mind; it cannot be so in the case of nations. When knowledge is diffused, it will never happen that the nation will miss the best objects of knowledge, though an individual may. He strongly recommends some such discipline as Bentham's Chrestomathia, or instruction in useful objects of knowledge; of the proposed Chrestomathic Day-school, and other institutions connected with it, he rather sanguinely affirms that "of the practicability of the scheme no competent judge ever doubted," though he adds that "the difficulty of collecting funds" prevented its demonstration. For the current modes of instruction in Universities he had

---

[9] Cp. his essay in the *Edinburgh Review* on the moral systems of Bell and Lancaster for the education of the Poor.

the greatest contempt,[1] as he had for all forms and institutions which he conceived to be hostile to the distinctive feature of all true education, progression, and to be allied to clericalism and routine. He does not, however, go into details on this, or on the other two branches of Education, social and political. His sentiments, moreover, on the two last-named, may be collected from his *Analysis* and the *Essay on Government*.

The great object of Domestic Education is to enable a man to defy the evil effects of social education, as society is now constituted.[2] We may not be able at once to alter the influences of society from bad to good, but we can equip our children against them by reforming our households. [*Essays*, No. VII. pp. 43—46]. The danger of a riotous reaction in some cases, and of utter gloom and despondency in others (such as affected J. S. Mill at one period of his life), on the child's attaining mature years, and finding that the vast world outside his hearth and home has not been instructed as he himself has, and that the mode and temper of thought prevalent in society is totally strange and unfamiliar to him,—these were problems which never occurred to Mill. Not only did Mill believe in the unlimited teachability of individuals to procure and secure their common interests, but he also believed in the possibility of a similar education for nations. The scheme of an international tribunal for the arrangement of differences between communities, and the gradual elimination of war from off the face of the earth, which has given food alike for the aspirations of

---

[1] In one of his commonplace books he has several pages of very bitter declamations of his own, and extracts from the works of others (Bacon, Gibbon, &c) against university training.

[2] We are reminded of Plato's philosophical education, which however was to begin much later in life, with a view to equip the citizen-philosophers against the seductions and sophistry of the greatest of all sophists —society.

poets, and the investigations of philosophers,[3] was made by Mill the subject of elaborate practical suggestions, contained in his Essay on the Law of Nations. The tribunal was to work in conformity with the provisions of an international Code, and Mill (with all the confidence of a theorist) expresses his belief that the application of the principle which he suggests implies no peculiar difficulty, if the proper moral sentiments be implanted in nations by means of a study of the Code. Each nation will be as anxious to avoid the ill-will and contempt of other nations, as every individual is to avoid similar dispositions towards himself on the part of his fellow-men. [*Essays*, No. VI. pp. 27—73.] It is curious, however, that whereas, in treating of Politics, Mill conceives of a man or body of men as desirous only of securing as much pleasure as they can at the expense of others, in dealing with international relations, he apparently ignores the exclusive operation of such a desire, though the restraints on its accomplishment are obviously much less strong in the case of nations than in that of individuals, and the hypothesis, therefore, which should isolate such a phenomenon would be much nearer the facts, and therefore more valuable, in the former than in the latter. If a man is a wolf to other men in a community, unless effectual restraints,—restraints far stronger than moral,—are placed upon his actions, will not a community itself become a pack of wolves in reference to other communities, where no such restraints can possibly be imposed? Association can do much in the way of educating; but Mill vastly underrates the difficulty of educating a nation out of its warlike propensities by the use of such an instrument.

---

[3] Kant sketched out a plan of such a tribunal in an essay translated by De Quincey. The Abbé St. Pierre was another speculator in this direction. See Woolsey's *International Law*, for an account of some of these schemes. Shelley of the poets is the most anti-warlike. See the beautiful chorus closing the *Hellas*.

Part III.

THE VALUE AND INFLUENCE OF THEIR OPINIONS.

We have hitherto abstained from detailed criticism, in accordance with the aim of this Series, and have only offered comments here and there, where the tenets of either of our two philosophers appeared manifestly insufficient to explain what they proposed to explain, or where they were inconsistent with themselves, or where, on any other ground, brief criticism seemed not only not at variance with, but even necessary to, the interests of exposition. We are now at liberty (1) to attempt to show (very briefly) to what extent James Mill by superior lucidity of arrangement, accuracy of reasoning, or analytical penetration, made advances on Hartley, and how far on the other hand he was indebted for his impulse and starting-point to his predecessor's copious, but often ill-digested, materials; (2) to estimate the general character of the writings of the two philosophers, the distinctive mark which they left on their successors in various branches of philosophy, and their place in the history of Associationism and Utilitarianism.

I. Hartley and Mill were alike ardent and single-minded lovers of truth. And they agreed in the main on the meaning of the truth which they wished to convey. But the speculative and literary methods employed by them in the exposition of their (on the whole) common views differed considerably; as also did the matter itself in some minor details.

The styles of the two philosophers were as dissimilar as possible. Hartley was gifted with the " copia fandi," [1] while Mill's style and mode of reasoning were severely simple. The two, indeed, were alike in their formal and scholastic methods, and in their love of packing their doctrines into a syllogism or pocket formula. But Hartley was not prevented by these precise and orderly habits from giving free vent to those sentiments, which Mill and his school would have scorned as sentimentalities, nor from many a gay excursus into a variety of intellectual domains, from which the austerer bent of the latter restrained him. Hartley's rambling and gossiping style, his queer mathematical mysticism (which Mr. Leslie Stephen notices [2]), his medical fancies and digressions, his theories of biblical interpretation, his minute observations of the customs of young children, and the inferior animals, his interest in philosophical languages and dictionaries, his liking for theology and discussion of the theopathetic faculties,—all these were foreign to the mental habits and constitution of James Mill. The preciseness of method apparently reflected in Hartley's Propositions, Corollaries, and Scholia did not extend beneath the surface, whereas that observable in Mill's works was radical, and answered to a certain analytical twist in his mind. Indeed the mathematical forms of the former, when applied

---

[1] Hartley's philosophical garrulity is not so striking as that of Tucker, whom he resembles in some respects; but his book is not unlike a less well-stocked *Religio Medici* than that of Sir Thomas Browne : indeed *Philosophia Medici* would have been an admirable title for the *Observations on Man*.

[2] *Hist. of Eng. Thought in the Eighteenth Century,* vol. ii. p. 68.

to the abstrusest and most ethereal subjects, serve rather, by
quaintness of contrast, to intensify our recognition of his love
of mysticism than to suggest his predilection for formalism.
The form was conventional, and derived from without,—from
Newton's *Principia* and other mathematical and scientific
works : whereas the *matter* to which he applied the form was
really congenial to his own tastes. This curious compression
of elastic material within rigid formulæ is continually to be
met with throughout his work. His algebraical symbols and
equations are endless. He goes out of his way [*Observ. on
Man*, vol. ii. p. 282] to compare the gradual substitution of a
less and purer self-interest, in moral growth, for a larger and
grosser, to "some mathematical methods of obtaining quantities
to any required degree of exactness." The degree of happiness
which may be derived by one man from his benevolent actions
towards another is explained like a problem in Euclid [ii. 286].
All the propositions relating to vibrations and vibratiuncules are
expressed algebraically ; and even, in enouncing the proposition that in all men the love of God should be greater than
the fear of him, and the fear of him greater than the love of
the world, he is not content until he has evolved an equation

$W : F : : F : L$, therefore $W = \dfrac{F^2}{L}$, where L, F, and W re-

present the three above sentiments respectively. Language,
he often says, is merely a less perfect algebra, and perhaps
this is why he flies to algebra so often where language fails
him. The wealth of his illustrative matter is very great.
Allusions to Newton, whose *Principia* first set him on to the
Vibration Theory, and introductions of physical theories and
analogies are numerous. He never forgets that he is a physician, nor allows his readers to forget it. He culls several
examples from the field of medicine,—comparing, for instance,
a complex idea irresoluble into the separate elements of which

it is composed to Venice treacle [vol. i. p. 322], while the phenomena of disease and morbid affections are carefully considered by him in relation to his philosophical principles, whenever an opportunity offers, and he devotes a special section [vol. i. pp. 390—403] to the imperfections of reason resulting from derangements or decline of bodily powers, such as madness, idiocy, dotage, drunkenness, delirium. To the phenomena of sleep and dreaming, and also to the condition of the deaf and dumb, he pays great attention [vol. i. p. 287] ; and in the practical part of his work devotes some pages to an elaboration of the rules of good diætetics [ii. 218—228]. His medical instincts similarly led him to couple muscular motion with sensation and ideation, and to give an account of association which should embrace each branch of its triple influence on the three main elements of human nature. Nothing is too apparently small to escape his attention. " De minimis curat philosophia" is his motto: and he is quite guiltless of that misconception of the function of philosophy which the late Mr. Bagehot imputed to most of its professors, preventing them from condescending to small things, or seeing that speculation should, like some Nasmyth's hammer, be able to put the head on to a pin as easily as beat out a ton of weight. He devotes a special section to the intellectual faculties of brutes [i. 404—415, cp. ii. 226 sqq.]. By his observations of the reciprocal influence of language and thought upon one another, he is (as we have already seen) led to suggest hints for the construction of a philosophical language for all nations, founded on combinations of a certain number of primitive words, carefully selected with a view to their facility of calling up the appropriate ideas [i. 315—318],—a scheme which was first worked out in some kind of outline by one George Dalgarno (1627—1687) in his *Ars Signorum,—Vulgo Character Universalis et Lingua Philosophica,* and elaborated by Bishop

Wilkins,[3] with his six genera and 3000 radicals, on a principle noticed with much approval by Professor Max Müller.   Such a philosophical language, says Hartley, " would as much exceed any of the present languages as a paradisiacal state does the mixture of happiness and misery which has been our portion ever since the fall."   In connexion with this part of his subject, he speaks with approval of Byrom's system of shorthand, then first coming into use, as being a method of marking ideas by the most practicable, economical, and at the same time philosophical symbols as yet discovered.   In another part of his work, his busy brain is occupied with the idea of a philosophical dictionary, which should be, as he says, "a real as well as a nominal one," that is, should combine the merits of an encyclopædia and a lexicon [vol. i. p. 285].

From music Hartley derives several of his illustrations and analogies [i. 289, 321, &c.] ; and for Pope and some other of the English poets of a practical and moralizing turn (as was stated in his Life) he had a sincere admiration : but, somewhat to our surprise, we find his attitude towards the imaginative arts in their moral and educational aspects to have been decidedly hostile.   The poets in general he rarely speaks of in his philosophical writings except as " lewd," and unfit to be taught to, or read by, the young.   In his classification of the sciences, he contemptuously relegates poetry, together with Grammar and the cognate sciences, to the sphere of Philology, and he agrees (to the best of our recollection) with Mill in not having a single quotation from any poet in his philosophical " magnum opus."   But of all his pursuits theological seem to have been the favourite ; such questions as the possible

---

[3] In his *Essay towards a Real Character and Philosophical Language* (1668).   The second part of the work was strictly philosophical, the remaining three were on the artificial language proposed.   Leibnitz speculated in the same direction.

restitution of the Jews to Palestine he discussed with the greatest avidity; and did not shrink from such unortho-dox conclusions on the expectations of man as that all indi-viduals will ultimately enjoy the same degree of happiness in the future state [i. 486—492, and vol. ii. passim], and the like expressions of what Mr. Leslie Stephen[4] calls his "optimism run mad," which remind us of similar speculations on the part of Abraham Tucker.

From the above instances the varied nature of Hartley's in-vestigations will be apparent. His personal character and posi-tion shine through his writings. In them we see the patient physician professionally accustomed to "read each wound and weakness clear, And say, 'thou ailest here and here,'" but having leisure for other studies in his moments of repose, and willingly seeking relief therein;—a man of enthusiasm, but of a measured enthusiasm;—loving to speculate on the un-known future, but sober and restrained in his speculations, which generally rested on some solid basis of fact;—not eager to publish his ideas when red-hot, but preferring to accumulate, to wait, to prove and improve. His position as oscillating between two poles,[5]—between the firm ground of earth and Ariosto's moon-region of abortive fancies,—between the career of the theologian for which he was destined in the first instance and the career of the experimental physician to which he even-tually devoted himself,—is curiously reflected in the form of the first sketch of his system, the Latin treatise above referred to in the Life, which commences modestly in the character of an appendix to a medical tract *de Lithontriptico,* or on reme-dies and solvents for the disease of the stone, and ends with a

---

[4] *Hist of Eng. Thought, &c.,* vol. ii. pp. 65, 66, 120.

[5] The curious contrasts in Hartley's work are pointed out by Mr. Leslie Stephen (*English Thought, &c.* ii. 64) with his accustomed clearness and vivacity.

rhapsodical eulogium of the Christian religion,[6] reminding
us strongly of Bishop Berkeley's *Siris*, which, as Coleridge
tells us,[7] was " announced as an Essay on Tar-water, and began
with Tar and ended with the Trinity, the ' omne scibile ' forming the interspace." In the closing sentences of this little
pamphlet he augurs well for logical, ethical, and religious
studies from the combined efforts of medicine and philosophy,
based on physical science [" sociatâ operâ Medicorum et Philo-
sophorum, Lockii et Newtoni vestigiis insistentium "] : while,
in his preface to the *Observations*, he speaks of the double interest
attaching to Association,—first that of tracing it to its physical
cause, next that of following out its consequences in morality
or religion. He apologizes too for the " many disquisitions
foreign to the doctrine of association, which intermixed themselves " in the course of his work ; disclaims the office of a
system-maker ; and says that he did not look for facts to suit his
system, but adapted his system to suit the new facts which
were every day unfolding themselves to his view, as his labours
proceeded. In consequence of this, he fears that the book may
seem sketchy and incoherent, some of his doctrines (that of
necessity or mental mechanism, in particular) having forced
themselves upon him in the course of his undertaking in spite
of vehement opposition on the part of his own inclinations and
prejudices, and having been dragged, so to speak, with violence
into the main body and drift of the treatise. The fact that the
different parts of the work were written at different times, and
at different stages of his intellectual growth may, he hopes,
help to account for redundancies and repetitions, and other
blemishes of manner. In upholding the uses of his system he

---

[6] Cp. p. 1 with p. 42 of the tractate " De Sensu, Motu, et Idearum
Generatione " (in Dr. Parr's *Metaphysical Tracts of the Eighteenth
Century*).

[7] *Biogr. Lit.* p. 143.

presents a two-faced aspect; on the one hand urging its value in medicine, especially pathology and therapeutics, on the other hand showing how it leads to a true conception of logic and mental science, how it destroys logomachies, interprets ethical phenomena successfully, and through them leads the inquirer to religious investigations and truths [*De Sensu*, &c., pp. 38—40].

Hartley's suggestiveness, combined with thorough intellectual candour, (even though that candour induces him occasionally to lay bare to his readers sinuous processes of reasoning, and intricate methods of arriving at results, which it would have been better to have concealed), has gained him ten disciples, where James Mill's superior philosophy, encumbered as it is by an ungainly style, has attracted one; and has even charmed philosophers the most opposed to him in the current and tendency of their beliefs.[8] Mill's manner of philosophizing was very different. His severe simplicity and contempt for philosophical gossip and flowers of rhetoric was one of the distinguishing marks of his school, and as such will be noticed presently. He would turn neither to the right hand nor to the left out of the high road leading direct to the object in view. His own account[9] of the salient features in a coherent, as opposed to a rambling, discourse seems in its most literal sense to have been always present to him. His personal character and intellectual habits were firmer and more earnest—but, it must be added, narrower—than those of Hartley.

The differences in point of matter between the two philosophers were not great. Such as they were, they arose partly from the peculiarities of the men, partly from the characteristics

---

[8] Such as Coleridge, who called his eldest son after the name of the philosopher, as a mark of the interest and admiration with which he was then studying him. See *Biogr. Lit.* p. 86.

[9] See Mill's chapter on the Will (end of vol. ii. of *Analysis*).

of the times in which they severally lived. Mill was more bent
on the practical application of his views than Hartley, and
wrote more with the fervour of a man who expected his creeds
to be turned into deeds, and who attached an educational or
social value to every opinion which he expressed. Mill composed with the rigour and simplicity of a schoolmaster of the
world ; Hartley with the ingenuous babbling of a pupil of the
world. Consequently the former at once discarded vibrations ;
for, provided that people can be brought to perceive the uses of
association in education, it does not matter what physical
theory is put behind it as the cause of the cause. Nor on the
other hand will he follow his theory out into the nebulous region
of theopathy and theology ; for if men can be induced to con-
struct a morality on better associations, they will not be long
in constructing a better religion. Like Hartley, Mill deplores
the degenerate state of existing methods and principles, and,
like him, groans at the

> " Jarring and inexplicable frame
> Of this wrong world :"

but whereas Hartley contents himself with merely prophesy-
ing a " culbute générale " of most of the nations of christendom, Mill sets to work vehemently at schemes of reformation
in law, politics, and education. Hartley's literary atmosphere
was science and divinity, Mill's was the " philosophical radicalism " of the Benthamite reformers. If to the former, as
Professor Clifford said, must be given the credit of having
first seriously handled the problem of the chemistry of the
human mind, to the latter must be accorded that of having
first thoroughly examined its mechanical forces and the possibility of utilizing them for social and educational purposes.
But there are few specific theories broached by Hartley which
Mill has very much improved, though he has put several of

his predecessor's tenets into a more philosophical shape, besides adding some fresh elements of his own to the general system. His chief merit—as J. S. Mill observes [Preface to the *Analysis*, pp. xvii, xviii]—was a vigorous exercise of the qualities (somewhat lacking in Hartley) " which facilitate the access of recondite thoughts to minds to which they are new:" when, however, the critic goes on to say that the *Analysis* " attains an elevation far beyond Hartley's " [work] " in the thoughts themselves," as well as in their arrangement and elucidation, we are disposed to think the praise excessive. The doctrine of Inseparable Association was certainly elaborated by Mill, but the principle had been clearly enunciated by Hartley, and both the principle and the name were mentioned, though not illustrated in any very great detail, by Gay, or whoever may have been the author of the *Enquiry into the Origin of the Human Appetites and Affections,*[1] notably in these words: " By association I mean that power or faculty by which the first appearance of two or more ideas frequently in the mind, is for the most part changed into a lasting, *and sometimes into an inseparable union.*" Mill's analysis of the active or ethical phenomena of the mind was more explicit and accurate than Hartley's; but, on the other hand, he did not apply the doctrine of association to muscular motion with the same success as Hartley, nor did he improve on the latter's law of the three stages in the development of motive power,—automatic, voluntary, and secondarily automatic. His analysis, however, of the Will was certainly more full and satisfactory than Hartley's; indeed Hartley had no specific treatment of Volition as such, though he had a long discussion on Necessity or Mechanism (as he preferred to call it) and Freewill,—a subject omitted somewhat unaccountably

[1] In the *Metaph. Tracts* above referred to, p. 68. Cp. Mill's *Analysis*, vol. i, p. 91.

by James Mill—wherein he carefully distinguished between the "philosophical" doctrine of Freewill which asserts that a man can will two different things when all the previous and contemporary circumstances, internal and external, are the same,—a doctrine transparently false,—and the "practical" or popular doctrine of Freewill, which asserts that a man has control over his own actions, and can exercise choice between two different courses open to him,—a doctrine transparently true. This latter important distinction (not noticed by Mill) has no doubt helped to put moderns on the right track, and to show how meaningless is the controversy between so-called Libertarians and Necessitarians.[2] Mill's examination of Belief is much more profound and elaborate than that of his predecessor, but unfortunately is also less correct, because it bases Belief on the mere juxtaposition of two ideas in the mind, without postulating that irreducible element of conviction which Hartley saw was essential to this process, as distinguished from mere Imagination. Professor Bain it will be seen goes back to Hartley on this point, and does not follow Mill: he also (with Hartley) attaches great importance to action as the best, if not the only, evidence of Belief. In his system of Classification, too, Mill, so far as he ignores what have been since called "Natural Kinds," and regards the process as resulting from nothing beyond a desire for economy in naming, distinctly retrogrades from Hartley. On the other hand, he makes advances on his forerunner's system, in his minute analyses of some of the abstract relative terms. But the

---

[2] It is beginning to be generally understood now that Liberty and Necessity are two disparate conceptions, and that to compare one with the other is like comparing an inch with a minute. The proper antithesis to Liberty (in the sense in which it is used by Libertarians in the controversy) is Bondage, not Necessity; to Necessity (in the sense in which it is used by Necessitarians) Chance, not Liberty.

differences in the matter of the two philosophers are also
partly to be explained from the history of the Association
Theory.

II. We have already noticed [Part II. ch. i.] the forerunners
of Hartley, namely, Aristotle, Hobbes, Locke, Gay, and his
contemporaries Abraham Tucker and Condillac. Coleridge
indeed [*Biogr. Lit.* ch. v.] proposes to add several names to
these. He denies the claim of Hobbes's " discursus mentalis "
to be an original solution of the difficulty : and says that these
philosophers had been anticipated by Descartes in his treatise
De Methodo, which appeared a year before the *Human Nature.*
Descartes constructed on association principles a theory of
human language and naming, much as Mill did after him.
But, like Hartley, he resorted to a physical hypothesis to
explain the intellectual operation, and for that purpose brought
in " nervous fluids " and material configurations of the brain,
instead of, like Aristotle and Mill, resting content with the latter
as ultimate and irreducible. In his physical doctrines he headed
the class of " humoral pathologists" (as Coleridge calls them), as
opposed to the other physicists headed by Hartley, who resorted
to vibrations and an oscillating æther,[3] or to the more modern
sect who appeal to " chemical composition by electric affinity."
Nor is it certain (according to Coleridge) that there was much
originality in Hume's Essay on Association, the idea of which
treatise he is suspected of having borrowed from St. Thomas
Aquinas's Commentary on the *Parva Naturalia* of Aristotle.[4]

---

[3] These two rival theories are clearly described by Gay in the *Enquiry*
above mentioned [p. 60]. The nerves in the former case are regarded
says Gay, as bundles of threads or fibres, along which a tremor passes
during sensation ; in the latter case, they are considered as tubular, and
filled with a subtle fluid, or animal spirits. On Vibrations, see further
Ribot [*Contemp. Engl. Psych., Eng. Transl.*] p. 282, sqq.

[4] A copy of this work, once in Hume's possession, was found to have

Moreover, the functions of Association had been set out long
before even Hobbes by the non-scholastic Aristotelians Me-
lanchthon, Ammerbach, and Ludovicus Vives. The upshot of
Coleridge's account of these pre-Hartleian gropings is that they
were all based on the teaching of the " gran maestro di coloro
che sanno : " and that, moreover, Aristotle was often nearer to
the truth than those of his successors who sought to improve
upon him, in that, while clearly setting down in the *De Animâ*
five distinct principles of association,[5] he yet guarded himself
against going beyond what the facts warranted, and sternly
rejected physical hypotheses.

Such then was the intellectual ancestry of Hartley. Between the commencement of Hartley's and the close of James
Mill's life, we find in the same way of thinking Priestley
and the elder Darwin, and other disciples of Hartley, and, in
France, Condillac. From the last-named, however, Mill (according to his son) did not derive nearly so much aid as from
Hartley, compared with whose painstaking suggestons Condillac's generalizations seemed barren and void.   [J. S. Mill's
Autob. p. 68].

Tucker with his " translation," and Brown with his hints
as to "relative suggestion," which were their respective names
for association, (though the latter seems to have rather struck
out a line of his own to some degree), were the next to follow.
Belsham developed the moral side of Hartley's theory, and
Alison (*On Taste*) the æsthetic. Helvetius, Rousseau, Cabanis,
Darwin, and Bentham in their different ways paid attention to
the educational aspect of Associationism ; Bentham and

been read and carefully annotated by him, when subsequently lent to a
friend by Sir James Mackintosh, into whose hands it eventually came.

[5] Namely (1) connexion in time, whether simultaneous or successive,
(2) vicinity in space, (3) necessary connexion, such as that of cause and
effect, (4) similarity, (5) contrast.

Austin to the legal. The improvements in science which took place in the interval which separated the two men are also very remarkable, as well as the influence of Bentham and his followers in other and more practical directions, some account of which, as having largely helped to determine the line adopted by James Mill in philosophy as contrasted with that of Hartley, would seem to be necessary here.

James Mill expresses himself, in the *Fragment on Mackintosh*, very indignant at the supposition of there being in existence any Benthamite school at that time. Still there is no doubt,—indeed, it has been recorded by J. S. Mill in the *Autobiography*,—that there existed a body of men distinguished by certain common characteristics, aiming at certain common objects, and united together by a bond of strong moral and intellectual sympathy: the most prominent names among them being those of Bentham and James Mill. These common characteristics were a deep-rooted love of clearness and simplicity in writing and conversation, a tendency to mathematical precision, an utter contempt for sentiment in ethics, and for the graces of style and art in composition, an ardour and even bitterness in controversy, an abhorrence of everything which seemed like mystery, or presumed to defy the analytical processes in which they manifested such an unbounded belief. The common objects resulted from the common creed. Believing that men were formed by circumstances, these philosophers attached the highest value to education and legislation. Believing that the greatest good of the greatest number was the proper end of action and thought, they were always busy propagandists of their tenets. Believing that theory was all-powerful, that no hard and fast line could be drawn between the theoretically sound and the practically feasible, and that every simple and intelligible system only required energy and determination to convert it at once into a body of maxims and motives, they set to work in all directions with undaunted applications of their brand-new doctrines to the crude material of fact. And it is in these applications that Associationism and Utilitarianism have achieved their highest triumphs. It is difficult to overrate the importance of the effects which the former doctrine has had in the region of education (however incomplete an explanation we may deem it of the entire operations of the mind), or of the latter in legislation (under Bentham's and Austin's auspices), however unsatisfactory an account we may think *this* again of duty and the entire moral life in all its relations. Though we may believe that the mind is something far too subtle in its workings to be explained on the Æolian harp principle as the sport of circumstance, and the conscience not simple enough to be accounted for on the hypothesis of metaphorical pulleys and weights and levers; yet these chemical and mechanical laws (true in themselves, and only false when offered as interpreting more than they can) are of the utmost use in the practical fields to which they have been applied, since for these purposes it does no harm, and produces no error in our calculations, to regard men as building their habits of thought solely on association, or as led to act solely by a consideration of their own interests. In Legislation and in Education, as in Political Economy (as has been before noticed), we are at liberty to isolate special characteristics and tendencies of human nature from those ordinarily acting in conjunction, and intertwined, with them. But the result of this isolation, when put forward as a full and complete theoretical justification of morality, is not allowable; and this is the mistake which the school of Bentham and James Mill, as also some of their successors, though to a far less degree, have made. The theories in question are it is true palpable and plausible to ordinary intellects: most theories containing one principle are. "Here is something we can understand, couched in

plain language," is the Philistine's encomium : but though
plain language deserves all praise where it is possible, the
plainness and popularity of the doctrines conveyed, when we
consider the complexity of the phenomena analyzed, make
rather against than for their truth.[6] The simplicity affected by
their professors is of itself calculated to excite suspicion in the
minds of the reflective. Is everything, one asks, really so
simple as this? Are we to believe that we can only move
people to act rightly from motives of self-interest (however
refined that self-interest may be) ? Is it true that one man or
body of men in the possession of political power will constantly
endeavour to rob all the other citizens for their own advantage,
unless restrained by checks and police? Do we account for
the mazes of a creative imagination, when we have talked of
trains and sequences of ideas, and dispelled (to our own satisfaction) all "mystery" on the subject? This tendency to
simplification, and devotion to theory, characteristic of the
Bentham school was shared in ample measure by James Mill.
J. S. Mill [Preface to the *Analysis*, pp. xix, xx,] notices this
feature, accompanied " with a certain impatience of detail" in
his father's philosophizing. The latter was so anxious to seize
upon some commanding and comprehensive law under which all
the phenomena might be subsumed,—to attain some "specular
mount" from which a flood of light might be thrown on the
widest possible extent of material,—that minutiæ escaped
him. Correction and modification were not his strong points.
He longed to jump at once to the "Summa Axiomata," without
either verifying them afterwards by a reference to intermediate
laws, or previously passing through the intermediate laws to
them. He takes a simple and obvious principle, Association.

---

[6] As Malebranche says [*De Inquirendâ Veritate*, lib. iii. p. 194] : " the
assent and approbation of the vulgar on a difficult subject is a sure
argument of the falsity of the opinion to which the assent is given."

and fits it off-hand to every imaginable case. He will recognize no conception, no faculty, as ultimate. All must be
reduced to this principle. Hartley indeed was not quite so
exacting in his assertion of the authority of this law; but then
his idol was an idol of the theatre, as well as of the tribe, in
the shape of the all-sufficient vibrations. We find, consequently, that the efforts of Mill's successors in the way of
improving the general theory were directed almost entirely to
rigidly limiting its extensive application both by its founder
and its " second founder," and to the recognition of more and
more ultimate faculties and metaphysical conceptions. In this
way Professor Bain has recognized an unanalyzable element in
Belief and in Muscular Resistance [*Anal.* ii. 31], and similarly
J. S. Mill holds Memory and Expectation to involve Belief, and
Belief to be ultimate, as also [see his work on Hamilton] the
conception of the Self. All these James Mill considers to be
cases of Association; and, by his extreme anxiety to maintain
this view, he is sometimes driven into curious straits, as, for
instance, where he is forced to explain Belief by the Self (or
Personal Identity), and the Self by Belief. Resemblance,
Difference (as a case of Resemblance) Quality, Causality,
which James Mill equally holds to be instances of Association, J. S. Mill regards as either elementary, or at all
events involving something beyond Association : and to
the ultimate elements of Resemblance and Contrast, Professor
Bain adds Contiguity [*Anal.* ii. 120]. Indeed the latest
professors of the doctrine agree as to the unanalyzable
nature of nearly all the leading metaphysical conceptions
and distinctions, which James Mill believed quite capable
of analysis, excepting only the distinction between Sensations and Ideas, which even he was compelled to postulate
as ultimate.

We may notice a few more instances of the manner in which

James Mill's successors split up supposed identities, and modified the application of that Law of Parcimony—(" causes and existences are not to be multiplied more than is neces-sary")—to which he gave such undiscriminating allegiance. Nothing is more characteristic of James Mill's philosophy than the denial of the distinction between having a feeling and attending to or being conscious of it. This distinction however is restored on sufficient grounds by J. S. Mill and Professor Bain, as also the distinction between having two feelings and being conscious of their difference (also ignored by James Mill) : for, though the law of Relativity (in Professor Bain's sense) undoubtedly holds good ; that is, we only know feelings from their relations to their opposites, and, as Hobbes says, " to have the same sensation continuously, is to have no sensation at all ; " yet the exercise of the discriminative function on any particular occasion is not the same thing as the having sequent sensations, but is an element superadded to it, and separable from it in thought. Again in treating of sensations, Mill is so absorbed with the idea of the importance and efficacy of his universal solvent, that to make way for it, he even sets aside, or relegates to an inferior place, direct physical agencies, as, for example, in his account of the morbid trains of thought attendant on a diseased digestion, or of the sensations accompanying nervous bodily contortions, which are in reality concomitant effects of one and the same external cause,—or, again, of the painful emotions excited directly by the sight of another's suffering, and leading to acts of compas-sion,—all of which mental phenomena he ascribes to associa-tion alone. In these instances also his successors have set him right, and have declined to follow his excessive tendency to simplification. Abstraction, Ratiocination, and the Syllogizing process which James Mill dismisses in a very summary fashion as verbal merely, as well as Consciousness [*Anal.* i. 227 sqq.]

and Reflection (*Anal.* ii. ch. xv.) are also recognized by J. S. Mill and Professor Bain as more intricate in their nature and working than to be comprehended within the four corners of the law of Association. To the Will, which James Mill describes as a state of mind dependent upon contemporary and previous internal states and external circumstances, Professo Bain, though holding it to be merely "a collective term all the impulses to motion or action," yet gives a far independent and important place in his moral theory. J. Mill's analysis of Classification as based on Associ tion, referrible to a desire of economy, is insufficient to expla il any but the most elementary groupings, and leaves out of acco scientific classification altogether, as well as " Natural Kinds," and the Law of Relativity (to which we have alluded above) or knowledge by apprehension of doubles, which, and not any such desire as Mill suggests, led to the construction of relative terms to express the related feelings. Other instances of the gaps in James Mill's system will be noticed presently. Meanwhile we have chosen such of them only as exemplify the dominant impulse towards simplification of phenomena, to the undue disregarding of qualifications, which vitiated so many theories of the Benthamite school.

The peculiarities of this body of thinkers have been noticed, both by a vehement adversary, who afterwards saw cause to moderate his antipathy, [Lord Macaulay, in his review of James Mill's *Essay on Government,—Edinb. Rev.*, No. 97], and by one who was at first a member of the sect, but afterwards became a more qualified admirer [J. S. Mill, in his *Autobiography*]. The adherents of Bentham were men possessing a few ideas clearly conceived, which they were thoroughly bent on carrying out into practice. These ideas were admirable in themselves, and when not put forward to explain "all time and all existence." In a restricted sense, for instance, the doctrine of Association was accepted by Sir James Mackintosh,[7] though its extensive use by Mill found in him an uncompromising adversary.[8] Mansel [*Metaphysics*, pp. 233—248] treats it in the same respectful manner, and with the same limitations; while Sir W. Hamilton[9] devoted considerable attention to it, and was led by his examination of its principles, as expounded by its various teachers, to evolve his three laws of Repetition, Redintegration, and Preference, and to add some important elements and corrections to the original form of the theory. All these men were opponents of the doctrine only when pushed beyond its proper bounds into regions where it had no title, and could do no good. But it was to propagate their views on Association and Utility in *every* possible direction, and apply them to *every* field of thought and action, that the school of Bentham was (consciously or unconsciously) formed and took shape.

Some processes of human intelligence, however, resisted their analytical approaches to the last. No Benthamite could ever make much of the Imagination. They practically confessed themselves beaten, by conspiring to ignore it. Anything calculated to stimulate the fancy was disapproved. James Mill condemned the drama, and did not think much of Shakespeare. He has in one of his Commonplace Books a dialogue written by himself on the subject of players and theatrical representations, very little to their advantage, and quotes with approval Johnson's disparaging remarks on Garrick. His first literary production was a squib on a theatre in the *True Briton* newspaper, March 12, 1803. Bentham thought poetry mere misrepresentation, though, it is true, he

---

[7] In a lecture referred to by Coleridge, *Biogr. Lit.* ch. v.

[8] Sect. vi. of the *Dissertation*.

[9] Vid. his note on the Association Theory, in his edition of Reid, p. 911 sqq.

was passionately devoted to Music, the one form of Art which seems to secure votaries, when others are neglected. They banished the cultivating influence of the Imagination from their mental atmosphere, or explained it on precise scientific principles, which only betrayed the awkwardness which never fails to characterize the application of method to a material to which it is inapplicable.[1] They gave emotion the name of sentimentality, with what effect on the younger members of their clique, the eloquent pages of J. S. Mill's *Autobiography* are the best evidence. Human nature cannot be maimed in this way without eventual detriment. One side of it cannot be stifled and suppressed without injury to the whole. J. S. Mill, indeed, confesses that it was nothing but this suppression of the emotional and imaginative impulses which made him for a time despair of the world and of himself. It was a grievous mistake in reformers such as were James Mill, Bentham, Austin, and others, if they wished to rear up other reformers to succeed themselves, to ignore the importance of

> " The shaping fantasy that apprehends
> More than cool reason ever comprehends,"—

for of such stuff are reformers, if not made, at all events kept to their work in spite of constant disillusion and defeat.

In addition to this dwarfing of the fancy, and exclusive attention to the reason in its discursive rather than in its constructive use, together with the necessarily accompanying ruggedness and asperity of style,[2] and a terminology bar-

---

[1] On the inapplicability of precise methods to such material as artistic emotion, see Ribot (*Contemp. Eng. Psych. (Eng. Tr.)*], p. 232, Mansel's *Metaphysics*, p. 392, Hamilton's *Lectures on Metaphysics*, Lect. xlvi., Jouffroy's *Cours d'Esthétique*.

[2] James Mill, Bentham, Austin, Grote, Professor Bain are all noticeable for the baldness of their style. On the other hand, no more beautiful

barous, as in Bentham's case, or slovenly, as in Mill's,³—in
addition to these men's intolerance, blindness and bitterness in
controversy,⁴ to their contempt for the elegancies, and (in James
Mill's case) even for the pleasures of life,⁵ and to their efforts
to banish "the mysterious" by means of analysis which

> "Viewing all objects unremittingly
> In disconnexion dead and spiritless,
> And still dividing, and dividing still
> Breaks down all grandeur;"

—in addition to all these characteristics of the school, we
have to notice the extraordinary devotion of these men to
new-born theories, and their profound conviction that a
syllogism could always be applied red-hot to existing social
conditions. James Mill particularly detested the popular
separation of Theory from Practice. He has in his Commonplace Books several pages of argument levelled against this
false distinction. To him everything true in theory was
right in practice. J. S. Mill relates [*Autob.* p. 32] a characteristic anecdote of his father's impatience at his using a mode
of expression which implied a sharp separation between these
two conceptions; and in the elder Mill's works⁶ we are con-

style in philosophical writing has ever been seen than that of J. S. Mill.
James Mill avows his contempt for manner in his *Fragm. on Mackintosh*
(p. 127),—"if the matter of a book of philosophy be good, the manner
is a thing of very inferior consequence." Cp. Hobbes, "true philosophy
rejects of set purpose nearly every kind of ornament."

³ "Active phenomena of mind,"—definition of Disposition, Affection,
Motive, Will, &c.

⁴ Witness James Mill's *Fragm. on Mackintosh*, and the dogmatic and
dictatorial style of Bentham and Austin in speaking of views opposed to
their own.

⁵ J. S. Mill's *Autobiography*, p. 48.

⁶ *Fr. on Mack.* pp. 285, 286. *Essay on Education*, p. 5. *Analysis*,
vol. ii. p. 402. J. S. Mill's *Autobiography*, pp. 23, 37, 106. See also

tinually coming across strong statements of the identity of the theoretically demonstrable and the practically advantageous, and of the dependence of art upon system.   He was sanguine as to the possibility of altering the world by means of such schemes as Bentham's Chrestomathic Day-school, new Penal Codes, and proper Representative methods of government. He made as little allowance for the working of emotion and imagination in real life, as he admitted their presence to disturb a calculation or a conclusion.   And, accordingly, he failed to see that the grossest fallacies may lurk behind the forms of the Schoolmen as well as within the flowers of rhetoric ; and that in endeavouring to apply a syllogism, supported by abstract propositions, to social phenomena, he was trying to catch water in a sieve.   It is by the study of the comparative history and growth of these phenomena, accompanied by observation of existing needs and possible remedies, not by the purely individualistic treatment of the human mind, that a path is laid for successful reform.   And it was these very pre-requisites which Mill ignored.[7]   While lavishing contempt on the man who "for the tricksy word Defies the matter" of reason, he himself was for a tricksy method defying the matter of fact.   It was the obvious insufficiency of the purely Deductive Method in Politics to grapple with its material, which suggested to J. S. Mill what he called the Inverse Deductive Method, which is a sort of compromise between the purely Deductive, and the purely Inductive advocated by Macaulay in his strictures on the former [*Edinb. Review*, No. 97, pp. 188, 189], and which consists in

one of James Mill's articles on Indian affairs in the *Edinburgh Review*, vol. xvi. p. 136.

[7] And Hartley also, whose method was equally individualistic.   See Leslie Stephen, *English Thought in the Eighteenth Century*, vol. ii. p. 69.

forming general laws from the observation and comparison of particulars, but afterwards verifying and testing them, by seeing whether or no they are deducible from the known elementary laws of human nature. [J. S. Mill's *Autob.* 209, 210]. James Mill's habit of deducing practical conclusions from a very few simple principles of human nature, with scarcely any suspicion of the complexity and intricacy of the phenomena to which he was applying them, led him not only to hold false views of those fields of human activity which he considered in this light, but also to discard altogether all examination of the spheres to which such a method was not immediately applicable, such as those of Metaphysics (in the proper sense of the word), Art, and Religion. By neglecting these, he and his brethren marred the completeness of their doctrines, and gave a hard and repulsive look to the Utility and the Pleasure which they proclaimed. There seemed to be in the creed of Bentham and James Mill an indifference both to the past and to the future of the human race,—both to history and to religion. They had a large conception of the spatial extent over which utilitarian considerations and motives were to operate,—James Mill is continually advocating the widening of the circle of sympathy from Family to Friends, from Friends to Country, and from Country to Mankind,— but they do not seem to have taken much account of Time, as do the Positivists and other priests of humanity at the present day. Religion was regarded by James Mill merely as a social force (as we see in several articles in his Commonplace Books), just like Aristocracy, or any political institution,[8] not as a permanent sentiment in human nature,—an irresistible

---

[8] James Mill was not, however, so cynical as Bentham in his treatment of religion. Bentham wished to use it in legislation, like a constitutional monarch, merely to confirm the decrees of Utilitarianism, to reign and not to govern.

stretching out of hands towards the infinite. So too of the
artistic impulse. In their entire system, the Associationist
School of the last generation, though not confining their view
to the Here, certainly appeared to confine it to the Now. But
it is from the latter, quite as much as from the former, that
the spirit of man is ever seeking to escape; and on this desire
it is that it constructs for itself Art, Poetry, Metaphysics,
and Religion.

Still we must recognize that in their steady application of
ideas to facts, James Mill and his circle were but following a
long-established English habit and tradition. English philosophy has always been uncomfortable in the æther of pure
abstractions, and has always instinctively run to illustration
and application. In one sense no nation is so philosophical as
the English, that is, in their way of illuminating small facts
by large theories; in another, no nation is so unphilosophical,
that is, in their inability to keep the head from becoming
dizzy amidst abstract ideas. To some nations, the Germans,
for instance, philosophy is indeed, in Bacon's metaphor, the
barren virgin consecrated to God; to us, she is a useful maid-
of-all-work. Unless our thinkers have in external facts their
bases of operation and places of refuge, and in practical application their convenient outlets, they are uneasy. We rarely
find men in England devoting themselves to philosophy, pure
and simple; though many devote themselves absolutely to
science. Those who take up philosophical pursuits in this
country do so in the intervals of business or pleasure, (much
as Plato describes men doing in his day,) and of this both
Hartley and James Mill are conspicuous instances. Philosophy thus gains in popularity and influence on life, though it
loses in thoroughness. Though we may call barometers and
agricultural journals "philosophical," and encourage that
"hairdressing on philosophical principles," which so scanda-

lized Hegel,[9] yet we keep free from those endless logomachies and hair-splittings upon which even that great philosopher expended so much time and lost labour. The school of Bentham and James Mill are certainly not to be blamed on account of the useful, and even noble, impulse which led them to apply their theories to existing facts : what they were to be blamed for is having applied those theories too systematically and persistently, and without letting facts themselves to a great extent guide them in the process of application. The sanguine hopes conceived by the masters, and raised in the minds of the disciples, were doomed to cruel disillusion.   Let any one who wishes to recognize the inevitable fate of all attempts at reformation with too simple a watchword, compare J. S. Mill's eloquent record of the enthusiasm with which he first read and studied Bentham, and of the confidence with which he felt that he had found in him "a creed, a doctrine, a philosophy ; in one among the best senses of the word, a religion," with the description of his own state, when his education, with its precocious and premature tendency to analysis, its cultivation of reason and neglect of imagination, had left him stranded " with a well-equipped ship and rudder, but no sail,"—when Association was found to enervate those creative forces of the mind which rule the world,—and when Pleasure and Self-Interest turned out merely the delusive mirage which is never any the nearer reality for pursuing it.   A more powerful, because informal and involuntary, indictment of all theories

---

[9] Werke, xiii. 72, vi. 13.

[1] Cp. the *Autobiography*, pp. 66, 67 with pp. 134—150. One of the most curious examples of the morbid fostering of the analytic tendency in J. S. Mill, is furnished by the story which he relates of himself (p. 145) to the effect that the casual thought that musical combinations might one day be exhausted, gave him for days the greatest pain, and tended to destroy his enjoyment of music.

with a single solvent for every difficulty, could scarcely have been written.

Several of the deficiencies noticeable in the writings of Hartley and James Mill have now been supplied, and many imperfections removed, by their successors. The somewhat meagre outlines of the theory of Association in its original shape have been, and are still being, slowly filled out. A goodly army of disciples have extended its influence in all directions, and (what is far more important) have brought to bear upon it the issues of a variety of scientific investigations which have been inaugurated since James Mill's time. The supplemental matter furnished by these disciples constitutes the "wings" (as Niebuhr used to call his pupils) of Associationism and Utilitarianism, which but for them would have long since sunk into oblivion.

The first pioneer was the younger Mill, who has recognized the fact that though the masters of a doctrine may formally declare that they mean their "utility" to include all the objects of human interest (as did James Mill), yet this alone will not suffice to move men to accept the doctrine, or to act upon its laws. It is (so far) barren and tautological, and the only means of giving it a definite colour and complexion, is the somewhat empirical one of observing the lives and practical principles of its advocates and professors. To find out what James Mill and his philosophical associates meant by man's interests, as they do not tell us (except in general terms) themselves, we must discover what they seem to mean by them in their mode of living and habits of thought. When we look at these, we find (as J. S. Mill did in time) that the interests and impulses of imagination and emotion are wofully neglected, that poetry, for instance, is defined to be "misrepresentation" merely [Bentham], or else tolerated as "more easy to remember than prose," and therefore having a certain educational value

[James Mill] ; that too much division and dissolution renders construction impossible in practice, and neglected in theory ;[2] and that associations formed artificially by the dispensation of praise and blame do not after all lead to very exalted action or conceptions of morality. Accordingly the younger Mill (at some cost of consistency perhaps) did away with this neutral idea of utility and morality, recognized the necessity of the constructive element in thought (more particularly in Classification and Abstraction), and of the cultivation, for purposes of education, of the imagination, emotions, and passive properties of the mind,[3] and finally put the absurd controversy between the advocates of Free-Will, and of Necessity, on its proper footing.[4] He perceived, moreover, that it would not be an unmixed good for men to be *drilled*, even into excellence, by educational methods and legislative devices, that the individual was of more importance than the type in moral life, and that there might be a despotism of systems and opinions quite as strong as those of persons and castes.[5] To precision in practical

[2] "Those who have studied the writings of the Association Psychologists must often have been unfavourably impressed by the almost total absence, in their analytical expositions, of the recognition of any active element as spontaneity in the mind itself." [J. S. Mill's *Dissert. and Discuss.*, vol. iii. p. 119, art. on Bain, who himself largely helped to restore the constructive functions of mind to their proper place; he recognizes (e. g.) constructive associations as one species of associations in general.]

[3] See *Autob.*, pp. 49—51, 15, 16, 110—113, 144, 151, where we may see James Mill's conception of poetry, art, and emotion vividly contrasted with the attitude of J. S. Mill when driven to Coleridge, Carlyle, and Wordsworth to seek satisfaction of those impulses which had been almost stifled in him by his education. Professor Bain gives Feeling or Emotion a large place in his theory, and thereby improves greatly on James Mill. See Ribot's *Contemp. Eng. Psych.* (Eng. Tr.), p. 246.

[4] *Autobiography*, p. 169. Cp. the chapter on Necessity in the *Logic*.

[5] See the *Essay on Liberty*, and the *Autob.*, pp. 255, 256.

R

schemes he also opposed himself, though he still adhered to his father's scholastic terminology and orderly exposition in philosophy.[6] In regard to religion, he saw in later life the justifiability and even necessity of indulging the distinctively human tendency and aspiration, of which religion is one among other expressions, and which his father, to all appearances, ignored [*Autob.* 46, 69]. In the explanation of intellectual phenomena, the most noticeable gaps in James Mill's system which were filled up by his son had reference to mathematical axioms and syllogistic reasoning, as to which Induction was substituted as a basis in the place of the elder philosopher's Verbal Identity [*Anal.* vol. i. pp. 180—192]. The theories moreover of Naming, Causation, Belief, Memory, and Imagination have been greatly improved both by J. S. Mill and Professor Bain, as we have already seen in the course of these pages. [See also an admirable article on Knowledge and Belief by David Greenleaf Thompson, *Mind*, vol. ii. pp. 309—335].

Another line has been taken up by such men as Mr. Herbert Spencer and George Henry Lewes, with the help of the results of Biology, the Darwinian theory of Evolution, and other scientific laws, such as the Correlation of Forces. On such

---

[6] *Autob.* p. 18. The elder Mill's precision and accuracy of reasoning was attributable in large measure to his study of Plato. It is curious on what differently constituted minds Plato has exerted a large influence. One class of men (of whom the elder Mill and Bacon are examples) he has attracted by his reasoning and classifying powers, another class of men (Coleridge, Shelley, Hegel, &c.) by his imaginative genius. James Mill in early life either wrote, or inspired, an article on the Platonic Dialogue. (See Bain's Life of James Mill, *Mind*, vol. i. p. 521.) The article in the 14th vol. of the *Edinburgh Review* (p. 187) on Taylor's translation of Plato, though not mentioned by Professor Bain in his list, certainly looks as if it had been written by Mill. He was fond of writing dialogues himself on the Platonic model. [See *Autob.* p. 64.] For the influence of Plato's *method* on him, see his son's *Autobiography*, p. 21.

principles, as applied to sensation physiologically, have been founded new versions of the doctrines of the Inconceivability of the Opposite, and of Space and Time relations, which were very imperfectly handled by Hartley and James Mill. Hartley's doctrine of Vibrations appears in a very much altered form in G. H. Lewes's " neural tremors " and groupings. Researches into the physical conditions of thought in other respects, and into the connexion of body and mind, have been undertaken with considerable success, by Erasmus Darwin, Cabanis, Dr. Carpenter, Dr. Maudsley, Professor Bain, Mr. Galton, &c., most of them belonging, like Hartley, to the medical profession. Psychology has been treated in Germany as a natural science by Lotze and Herbart, and, to a still further extent, by Helmholtz, Fechner, Maury, and Wundt,[7] who have introduced a special science of Physiological Psychology, the germs of which are to be found in Hartley's *Observations*. The growth of the faculties of children from infancy has been made a subject of special study by M. Taine and Dr. Darwin.[8] The phenomena of the infancy of collective human life, gathered from the history and comparison of the institutions and customs of savage tribes, have been examined, with the happiest results, by Mr. Tylor and Mr. Herbert Spencer; and so a theory of the Social Organism, founded on the doctrine of Hereditary Transmission, has been established, which was wholly beyond the ken of Hartley and James Mill, who disregarded the past, and failed to contem-

[7] As instances of the extraordinary extent to which mathematical forms are applied to every variety of material (in a way that would have delighted Hartley) we may refer to such ideas as that of a Hedonistic Calculus, Franklin's Moral Algebra (see Ribot, p. 247), the Golden Section of Æsthetics (see below), and a Spectrum of Pleasure and Pain, all of which have been lately introduced.

[8] See *Mind*, vol. ii. pp. 252 sqq., and 286 sqq. (two very interesting articles).

plate the human mind as growing and progressive.[9]　In politics too, the comparison of social data, customs, mythologies, &c., so wanting in the individualistic system of James Mill, and so earnestly advocated byMacaulay and J. S. Mill, has been undertaken by Mr. Herbert Spencer, Sir Henry Maine, Mr. Freeman, and the French and English Positivists.　In educational science, many have now developed James Mill's suggestions;[1] so that J. S. Mill could truly speak of education and its improvement as the subject of more, if not of profounder, study than at any former period in English history [*Autob.* p. 1], whereas James Mill was always complaining of the wretched systems of education in vogue during his time.　The crude theories of Government and Legislation to which we have already adverted, have now been enormously improved by the superior historical and comparative methods employed by Guizot, De Tocqueville, Sir Henry Maine, and others.[2] The philological speculations, derived by James Mill from Horne Tooke, have been superseded by those of Professor Max Muller,[3] and a large following, who have in this department rendered incalculable service to the theory of association.　In

---

[9] Cp. an article by R. Flint on Associationism and the Origin of Moral Ideas, in *Mind*, vol. i. p. 321 sqq., and Ribot, *Contemp. Eng. Psych.* (Eng. Tr.), pp. 25, 26.

[1] Professor Bain (in his *Education as a Science*), Sir William Hamilton (*Literature and Education*, 1852), Mr. Herbert Spencer, and Godwin, hold James Mill's views as to the absurdity of society avenging itself on the malefactor, and not on the causes which make him what he is. [See Leslie Stephen's *Hist. of Eng. Thought in the Eighteenth Cent.*, vol. ii. p. 267.]

[2] See the *Autobiography* of J. S. Mill, pp. 157—160, 201, 202, where the author notices with much acuteness the imperfections of his father's political theories.

[3] *Science of Language*, espec. vol. i. ch. 2, and an article on the Original Intention of Collective and Abstract Names, in *Mind*, vol. i. p. 345 sqq. Cp. Ribot, pp. 51, 52, and *Mind*, vol. i. p. 525.

fact the importance of philological laws, based on a careful collection of data, is now fully recognized in most systems of psychology, not necessarily Associationist, such, for instance, as those of Mr. Morell and M. Renan. The utter absence in the works of Hartley and James Mill of any satisfactory theory of the imaginative functions of the mind in relation to Art and Poetry has been remedied by the æsthetical treatises on association principles of their successors, Mr. James Sully (*Sensation and Intuition*, also three articles on Art and Psychology, in *Mind*, vol. i.), Mr. Grant Allen (*Physiological Æsthetics, Mind*, vol. ii. p. 38, and article on the Sublime, vol. iii. p. 324, &c.), and, in Germany, Fechner and Zeising (with his law of the Golden Section, and other curious applications of mathematics to the phenomena of Art). Lastly, the principles of Association have been used for the elucidation of history, by Grote, and in expounding the philosophy of history, by Buckle.

In view of all these improvements and amplifications of the system of Hartley and James Mill, what are we now to say of the doctrines of Associationism and Utilitarianism, whether as originated by the masters, or as developed by the disciples? What are the radical errors and defects in the theory as applied to explain Thought, Morality, the State, and Art, which not even the advances of biology and philology, and the allied forces of Evolution, Sociology, and Statistics, together with the latest methods of collecting and comparing phenomena, have been able to remove? On these wide questions the reader will pardon us for declining to enter. To do justice to either side, or to represent the case with anything approaching to fairness, would lead us far beyond our present limits. Our aim has been to determine the place which Hartley and James Mill respectively filled in the history of the Association theory, and of what is now called Utilitarianism; their relation to one another; and the different veins of thought which the later of the two philosophers left to be worked by his successors. What may be the value of the theory of Association as a whole, and when taken at its best, we leave the reader to determine, 'after having placed before him some of the materials for a decision.

BIBLIOGRAPHICAL APPENDIX.

I. Authorities for the Lives.

The life of David Hartley is recounted in the edition of his works by his son (de q. vid. inf.), in the preface to the second volume. Some additional particulars are furnished by the article on Hartley in the *Biographical Dictionary* (edited by Chambers), and also in Rose's *Biographical Dictionary*, vol. viii. Compare Watson's *History of Halifax*, and the *Monthly Review*, vols. liii., liv., lvi.

The life of James Mill is chronicled in detail by Professor Bain in three articles contributed to the periodical called *Mind* (vol. i. pp. 97—116, 509—531, vol. ii. pp. 59—55). The style and tone of these articles are, however, somewhat dry and unsympathetic. The character and influence of the man is best depicted in the earlier part of J. S. Mill's *Autobiography* (pp. 1—205). The article on him in the *Encyclopædia Britannica* by Andrew Bisset, assisted by J. S. Mill and David Barclay, and that in the *Penny Encyclopædia* (vol. xv.), may also be consulted. Dr. Bowring's *Life of Bentham*, which contains references—though not always accurate—to that philosopher's friendship with, and influence upon, James Mill, may be looked at with advantage.

II. Their Philosophical Writings.

David Hartley :

1. *Conjecturæ Quædam de Sensu, Motu, et Idearum Generatione*, a short Latin treatise (no date) printed in Dr. Parr's *Metaphysical Tracts of the Eighteenth Century*, London, 1837. Contains the same views as the larger work, only much more succinctly expressed.

2. *Observations on Man, his Frame, Duty, and Expectations*, 2 vols. 1749.

3. The same, in three vols. With notes and Essays by Dr. Pistorius, Rector of Poseritz, in the island of Rügen. Life by Hartley's son, &c. 1791 and 1801.

4. Hartley's *Theory of the Human Mind on the Principle of the Association of Ideas, with Essays relating to the subject of it.* By Joseph Priestley, 1775. (This edition has the advantage of omitting the vibration theory, and the theological speculations. Otherwise it is the same as the above. Some of the Essays by Priestley, especially Essay II., are illustrative and useful).

James Mill :

1. *Analysis of the Phenomena of the Human Mind.* 1829.

2. The same, edited by J. S. Mill, with notes by Grote, Professor Bain, and Andrew Findlater. 1869. [By far the better edition of the two in which to study the author, as the reader is furnished with the latest developments of the theory, as he proceeds.]

3. The *Fragment on Mackintosh.* 1st edition (anonymous) 1835. 2nd edition 1870.

4. *Essays on Government, Jurisprudence, the Liberty of the Press, Prisons and Prison Discipline, Colonies, the Law of Nations, and Education.* Reprinted from the Supplement to the *Encyclopædia Britannica.* London, 1828.

5. The Essays in the *Edinburgh* and other Reviews referred to above in the Life of James Mill (Part I. of this work).

III. Elucidatory Works.

For Hartley :

1. Gay's *Dissertation on the Fundamental Principle of Virtue,* prefixed to Edmund Law's Translation of Archbishop King's *Essay on the Origin of Evil.* 1732.

2. The Treatise called *An Enquiry into the Human Appetites and Affections, showing how each arises from Association* (1747, 1753). in Dr. Parr's *Metaphysical Tracts* (referred to above). This is an anonymous production; the name of the author being unknown even to Dr. Parr. E. Tagart [1855, a writer on Locke] attributes it to Gay. The style and thought in it are certainly very similar to that

in the above *Dissertation* by Gay. It is a piece of very cogent and lucid reasoning, and is well worth reading.

3. Condillac's *Origine des Connaisances Humaines.* This may advantageously be read with Hartley.

4. Belsham (W.), *Essays, Moral and Philosophical*, 2 vols., 1799.

5. Belsham (Rev. T.) *Elements of Logic and Mental Philosophy.* 1802. This book James Mill reviewed [see his *Life*]. 4 and 5 are developments of Hartley's ethical and psychological theory.

6. Antony Collins' *Enquiry concerning Human Liberty*, 1790 [Collins holds the same views on the mechanical nature of Volition as Hartley, though he ignores both Vibrations and Association].

7. The introductory *Essays* of Dr. Priestley (above referred to).

8. Erasmus Darwin's *Zoonomia, or the Laws of Organic Life*, 1794. (A very interesting development of Hartley's system of vibrations, associationist principles, and medical theories and illustrations.)

9. Leslie Stephen's *English Thought in the Eighteenth Century.*

10. Sir James Mackintosh's *Dissertation on the Progress of Ethical Philosophy, chiefly during the 17th and 18th Centuries*, 1830. Section on Hartley.

11. Coleridge's *Biographia Literaria.* Chapters v., vi., vii.

For James Mill :

1. Preface, by John Stuart Mill, to the *Analysis.*

2. *Edinburgh Review*, No. 97 (March, 1829). Review of the *Essay on Government*, by Macaulay.

3. J. S. Mill's *Autobiography*, 1873 (pp. 1—205).

For both Hartley and James Mill :

1. Ribot's *Contemporary English Psychology* [English Translation 1873]. Gives a succinct history of the Associationist doctrines from Hartley to Professor Bain. Very little criticism ; exposition clear.

2. Flint's criticism of *Associationism and the Origin of Moral Ideas*, in the first volume of *Mind.* [The volumes of *Mind*, as far as that production has gone hitherto, will be found replete with matter from the Associationist's point of view].

3. Alison *On the Nature and Principles of Taste*, 1790 (the doctrines of which work were adopted by James Mill in the æsthetical part of his system).

4. Mansel's *Metaphysics* [pp. 233—248, and passim].

5. Uberweg's *History of Philosophy*, vol. ii. (translated from the 4th

German edition by G. S. Morris, 1874). Especially the Appendix on late English Philosophy, by Dr. Noah Porter.

6. G. H. Lewes's *History of Philosophy*, vol. ii. (2nd edition). This should be referred to, because the history is written from the point of view of Association, supported and enriched by the latest results of Positivism and the Sciences.

7. Sir William Hamilton's elaborate note on the genesis and growth of Associationism in · his edition of Reid's *Essay on the Intellectual Powers*, pp. 911 sqq.

8. Sidgwick's *Methods of Ethics* (the part relating to Utilitarianism).

9. Besides the above, if the reader wishes to follow out the Association theory in its numerous recent ramifications, or trace it back to its sources, he should consult the principal works of the authors mentioned in Part III., a list of which will be given in any good history of philosophy, such as that by Uberweg.

THE END.

GILBERT AND RIVINGTON, PRINTERS, ST. JOHN'S SQUARE, LONDON.